Break Out

An Orlando Storm Novel

Marissa James

For Benjamin
I couldn't have done this without you in my corner always supporting me.

Synopsis

Sun, sand, and a fake relationship with your best friend. What could go wrong?

Brody Thompson is the perfect fake boyfriend. He's been my best friend since high school. The one person I can always count on. Having him by my side in Key West at my youngest sister's wedding will keep my mother at bay. Or so I hope.

Falling for each other was not part of the plan. It was supposed to be fake. Until it wasn't.

The only problem? He plays hockey for the Orlando Storm. And I just got to my dream job, in Hawaii. So our fun will have to end when our week in paradise ends even if it means breaking both of our hearts.

Content Warning: Mentions of difficult family relationships.
Tropes: Sports (Hockey), Friends to Lovers, Fake Dating.
Intended for audiences 18+. Contains open door spice.

Chapter One

Aubrey

Five.

Four.

The small crowd around me shouts the countdown to the New Year as one voice, echoing across the backyard and the lake.

It's an intimate party but they're still loud. I guess that's what happens when you party with a professional hockey team.

Brody and I have been friends since high school, but this is the first time I've gone to a team event with him. I was shocked when he asked me if I wanted to go to their New Year's Eve masquerade party. I've met a few of his teammates over the years—the guys he's played with his whole career—but that's been it.

Now I can't help but wonder why that is. Is Brody ashamed of me? Is that why he's never introduced me to the rest of his team?

I saw the surprise on his teammates' faces when he introduced me. Can't say I blame them. They probably didn't even know I existed before tonight.

Sighing, I turn and make eye contact with the guy standing next to me who I'm sure is one of Brody's teammates. Which one, I can't tell, thanks to these masks.

When did he walk up?

Have I been that lost in thought that I didn't hear him approach?

I smile although I'm not sure he can see it, given how dark it is. He takes a step closer, and I nod to him before turning to scan the backyard. I don't want the guy to think I'm rude but I'm running out of time to find Brody.

Three.

I peek over at the guy again and squint, trying to figure out who he is. I can't see much because he's still standing in the shadows of the trees, hidden from the small amount of light the twinkle lights strung around the backyard give off. Not that it matters. I don't know most of Brody's teammates well enough to be able to tell them apart in the daylight, how will I be able to tell in the dark?

Where the fuck is Brody?

I glance over my shoulder, trying to find my best friend who is wearing a red mask that matches mine, but I don't see him.

My heart sinks. A tiny part of me had hoped that this was going to be the year that he finally kissed me on New Year's Eve.

That I'd finally find out what his lips taste like.

I thought this was why he invited me to the party.

Two.

I turn my attention back to the guy standing next to me. I'm not superstitious. Not exactly. But I still think it's bad luck not to get a kiss at midnight. Even if that kiss won't be from Brody.

One.

I don't know which one of us makes the first move, but the noise fades away as my lips connect with the mysterious hockey player's. What starts off as a chaste kiss quickly deepens when his tongue darts out and swipes across my lips. I open for him with a groan that he swallows. His hand on my back where my dress dips down sends goosebumps across my skin. His other hand grips my hip. My hands fist his shirt, pulling him closer as I get lost in the kiss.

Fuck, I wish I knew who this was.

Shit.

Shit.

I'm kissing one of Brody's teammates. I'm kissing one of my best friend's coworkers. I push away and thankfully he lets me go.

I stumble back, my heels sinking into the grass.

I can't do this.

I raise a hand to my lips. But hot damn. That was arguably the best kiss of my life. My gaze flits from masked partygoer to masked partygoer, expecting to see Brody's brooding face lurking around a corner.

But I don't.

My mystery kisser is standing there staring at me, and for once I'm thankful for this mask, because he doesn't know who I am, and I don't know who he is.

I plan to keep it that way.

I don't want to know who he is.

No, I'd much rather let this kiss be an anonymous New Year's kiss. Yeah, that's what it'll be. He opens his mouth to say something I assume but I don't hang around to find out. With a shake of my head, I turn and hightail it toward the house and away from the rest of the party.

Get it together.

I'm not usually that brazen, that daring, kissing a guy I don't know. Blame it on the alcohol. Although I only had two drinks tonight. Fine, blame it on the fact that I'm lonely and can't remember the last time I kissed a guy.

Groaning, I tear off my mask, searching for Brody. My chest is tight as I turn around and search the backyard for my best friend, but he's nowhere to be found.

What if the guy I kissed tells Brody?

I can imagine how that conversation would go. The logical part of my brain tries to reason that there's no way he'd know it was me. I mean, I was wearing a mask. It was dark in the backyard.

Ugh, where is Brody?

Maybe he found someone to kiss at midnight and now he's preoccupied. I pull out my phone from my clutch and send him a text.

Me: I'm going to get an Uber back to my hotel.

His response is instantaneous.

Brody: Ubers don't come into the complex. I'll be right there.

I throw up my hand in frustration and open the sliding glass door, stepping into the living room. Now what do I do? Wait for Brody? I'm still reeling from that kiss. What if I blurt out that I kissed one of his teammates? Or what if he knows that I kissed someone?

Before I can decide, Hannah–the wife of Brody's teammate and one of his closest friends, Cole–walks toward me.

"Aubrey, you okay?" she asks, glancing around, probably looking for Brody.

I take a deep breath, trying to pull myself together. "Tired and ready for bed."

She studies me for a second before she hooks her thumb over her shoulder. "Cole and I are leaving if you need a ride. Or are you waiting for Brody?"

"I think he's staying," I say, the lie slipping out of my mouth. "If it's not too much trouble. Or drop me at the front gate and I'll get an Uber."

"Nonsense. We'll drive you."

"Hey Aubrey. Ready Han?" Cole asks, walking up and wrapping his arm around his wife's waist.

"Yeah. I told Aubrey we'd give her a ride. Where are you staying?" Hannah asks, leaning into Cole. He nods and I follow them to the front door.

"The Marriott on Eaglewood Drive." As much as Brody protests and tells me I can stay with him, I always stay in a hotel. I like my space. I like not having to worry about waking him up. And tonight, I'm even more grateful I don't have to go back to his condo and see him after I kissed a random stranger.

I should wait and say good night to him, but I can't. Part of me is disappointed that he's not the one I got to kiss at midnight.

Is that why I'm fleeing?

I shake my head and climb into the backseat of Cole's SUV. This is turning into one hell of a New Year. I hope it isn't an indication of what this year is going to bring. I take my phone out and send him a text before shoving it back into my clutch.

Me: Cole and Hannah are giving me a ride to the hotel.

Cole and Hannah drop me at the entrance to the hotel, pulling away once I'm safely inside. The lobby is silent and empty except for the woman at the front desk, who wishes me a Happy New Year. On the elevator I check my phone and see that my message to Brody is still on delivered.

Guess he's still busy with whatever kept him away from me at midnight.

Chapter Two

Brody

May

The chiming of my phone startles me awake. I sit up, scrubbing a hand down my face, trying to orient myself.

My couch. I take a deep breath. I'm on my couch.

Netflix is mocking me with its "Are you still enjoying this show" message. How many episodes of Seinfeld did I sleep through? My back cracks as I grab my phone. I'm too old to fall asleep on the couch like this. I unlock it and see I've been re-added to the group chat that some of my teammates and, dare I say it—although I'll never tell them this—friends started at the end of the season. I know they mean well, they're worried about me, but I want to be left alone to wallow in my anger and frustration. The season didn't end well for any of us but most especially for me.

I blame Caleb, my closest friend and Captain of the Storm, for the onslaught of messages. It was his idea that I befriend Hunter Rhodes, another forward and my linemate last season. Little did I know that it would mean I would become a de facto part of Hunter's friend group that consists of Weston Reynolds, one of our defensemen, and Holt Abbott, the backup goalie. The group that is the source of all the text messages I'm getting.

Wes: Anyone up for a beach day?
Holt: Depends. When were you thinking?

Wes: Saturday in three weeks.
Hunter: Madison and I are in.
Hunter: Unless it's a guys' only beach day.
Wes: The more the merrier. Caleb? Cole? Brody?

With a groan, I exit out of the chat and drop my phone on the sofa without answering. Something I've been doing a lot lately.

I keep expecting one of them or, heaven forbid, all of them to show up at my door. I was a no-show at the end-of-season team events, and I know it's only a matter of time before someone comes knocking.

Any other year I would have gone to Caleb's end-of-the-year party. I would have jumped at the chance to hang out with my teammates, eat good food, drink some beer, swim in his pool, and maybe even take his boat out on the lake. All those things usually sound like a good time.

But not this year.

This year I skipped it.

Therein lies the reason why I keep getting re-added to this group chat. It's why Caleb keeps texting me. Why Cole, another teammate and friend, has been calling me more often than usual. Although he's not as insistent as the others because he's got a newborn.

I couldn't bring myself to go to the party after I was the reason we got eliminated from the playoffs. The reason our season ended the way it did. I know the other guys said they didn't blame me. But the thing is, I blame myself. I've watched the game tape so many times I can see the play in my head when I close my eyes.

Me getting a pass from Hunter.

Being in the circle near the net. The place I like to shoot from. The place I never miss from.

Shooting.

And missing.

A shot I've made hundreds of times—maybe even a thousand—in my fifteen-year career.

Pings off the goal post as the buzzer sounds ending the game.

I even had a clear shooting lane.

And I missed it.

I missed the shot that would have tied the game, and given us a chance in overtime to win. Yes, we could still have lost, but I blame myself for not giving us the opportunity to try. I'm one of the alternate captains for fuck's sake, it's my job to be one of the leaders of the team and I failed.

Everyone was counting on me to make the shot.

And I didn't.

My phone dings multiple times. Don't these guys have better things to do than text each other all day? I grab it from where it's wedged in the cushions. I should probably respond so they don't show up at my door.

Me: I'll pass on the beach. I have plans that day.

It's a lie, but maybe they'll stop pestering me. I half think about booking myself a vacation on some remote island. Then at least I'll have a plausible excuse not to have dinner or drinks with them. But that seems pathetic. Alone on vacation watching couples and families having a good time. Drowning in drinks and sunshine. Although—I rub a hand down my face scratching at the couple of days old beard that's started to grow in since I've been too lazy to shave—it does sound intriguing. My phone lights up with more messages.

Holt: He's alive.

Wes: Brod, we miss you.

I tip my head back against the couch cushions, staring at the ceiling. Why?

The only person who I don't mind using that nickname is Aubrey, but of course Wes being, well, Wes, he decided to adopt it too. I want to text back and correct him, but that would mean getting sucked into their conversation, and that's the last thing I want to do right now. So I ignore it. My phone dings again before I can put it down, this time with a message from Hunter in a separate text thread.

Hunter: You okay, Brody? If you want to talk, let me know.

I like Hunter, he's a good guy and a great hockey player. He'll make a great Captain one day. His game grew so much this past season, and I'm sad that we won't get to play together again. Hockey is a big part of my life, and I fear it's about to end since the Storm haven't called to offer me a new contract. Not that I'm surprised given the way the season ended for me. The missed shot in the playoff game was the last in a string of bad games for me that started somewhere around the new year and got worse as the season progressed.

Before I can respond to Hunter, another message comes through. This one shocks me the most because I've barely heard from her in months.

Aubrey: Hey. Miss you. I'll be in your neck of the woods over the weekend. Do you want to have dinner? Or drinks? Both?

I haven't seen her since Caleb's New Year's Eve party where I did something rash. Except she didn't want me. She doesn't want me. She made that clear when she ran away from me after we kissed at midnight. Acted like it didn't happen. And I was too shocked and embarrassed to call her out on it.

New Year's Eve changed our relationship. It's the elephant in the room that neither of us wants to address for whatever reason. The humiliation of her rejection is still stinging.

Regardless, she's the one person I will always make time for, no matter the state of our relationship. Or, in this case, the one person I'll put real pants on for and venture out of my condo to see. I'm curious why she's here. Her job and life are in Gainesville, which is part of the reason why we don't see each other that often. Although now that it's the off-season I have all the time in the world to do what I want, and maybe that means visiting her. Figuring out how to fix our broken friendship. I stash that idea away for later and respond to her message.

Me: Hey. Sure. Either or both are fine. What are you doing in town?

Aubrey: Final dress fittings for Clara's wedding.

That's right. I remember Aubrey telling me that her youngest sister, Clara, is getting married in Key West in June. I got the impression that she wasn't thrilled about it. I guess I wouldn't be either if I had a mother like Aubrey's. I have a feeling being the oldest and last unmarried Fairchild sister is stressing her out. Not that Aubrey is dating anyone and chomping at the bit to get married—it's more that her mother is pressuring her to settle down.

Unless something's changed.

Maybe that's why she's avoided me since New Year's. And it has nothing to do with what went down between us when the clock struck midnight.

The thought of Aubrey being with another guy sends a chill down my spine, and my fists ball up. I take a deep breath, willing myself to calm down. *She's your friend*, I remind myself. She made it perfectly clear that's all she wants to be.

But I want her for myself. I've been in love with Aubrey Fairchild since practically the day I met her in sophomore year of high school when she was my algebra tutor. Except I've never been good enough for her, not then and certainly not now when I'm staring the end of my career in the face. If only I could figure out how to convince my heart it's time to get over her.

But I don't know how.

I don't know if I'll ever know how.

Chapter Three

Aubrey

I set the phone down and rub my temple. Another text message from my mother about Clara's wedding. As if I don't have enough to worry about, now she's asking me, no, telling me that I better have a date. It's bad enough that I have to spend the week with them in Key West, and now she expects me to bring someone.

I groan, dropping my head into my hands.

Where am I going to find a date? And not just a regular one-evening wedding date. Oh no, this person must be willing to travel to the wedding and spend a week with me. I mean, at least it's Key West and it's the summer. There could be worse places to be stuck for a week with family. But still.

"You okay?" Summer's voice pulls me out of my thoughts.

"Fine." I frown and shake my head. "Well, no, not really."

"Clara's wedding?" she asks, stepping into my office and taking a seat in the chair across from my desk.

I tilt my head and watch my friend grab a Hershey's Kiss from the jar on my desk and peel off the wrapper.

We've been friends since my first day on the job, when she plowed into my office and announced that we were going to be the best of friends since we're the only two women in the astronomy department.

We're complete opposites.

She's outgoing and loud. I'm quiet and reserved. Her bright red hair and green eyes are a stark contrast to my brown hair and blue eyes.

She's always wearing a wild, loud outfit that only she can pull off. Today, it's a blue and green plaid skirt, which I'm pretty sure is actually a kilt, black stilettos, and a black, oversized button-down.

I, on the other hand, am wearing my *work uniform. A.K.A.* a pair of black pants, a light blue button-down, and black flats. My hair is piled into a messy bun on the top of my head.

"Yeah." I rub my temple again, feeling the beginning of a stress headache. Closing my eyes, I stretch my neck, hoping to relieve some of the tension that's taken up permanent residence.

"Want to talk about it?"

I open my eyes to see Summer leaning forward in her chair, watching me. I shrug. I've told her some of the details of my relationship with my family, specifically my mother. She knows how much she's been pressuring me to get married, settle down.

It's not that I don't want to find love.

Be in a relationship.

Even get married.

Because I do.

I'm just not willing to sacrifice something for it. At least not yet. Maybe never. Because that's what happens when you fall in love—you make sacrifices. And you end up turning into someone you're not. I've seen it firsthand everywhere I turn.

My middle sister, Brielle, was going to go to law school when she got pregnant with her daughter, Anabelle. My youngest sister, Clara, sacrificed too. She was going abroad for a year to study fashion so she could open a clothing boutique when she met Chet, her fiancé, and decided against it.

Even Thad, my brother, sacrificed. Although he didn't have a choice. His marriage to his wife, June, was a business arrangement to merge two companies. When they first started dating and got married, I thought that perhaps they'd fall in love and end up happy. For a while it seemed like they were well on their way.

At the wedding they couldn't take their eyes off each other and seemed to be in love. It didn't last very long. Shortly after their first child was born, two years later, something happened between them.

June stopped going to family events. Thad refuses to talk about what happened.

It's gotten worse over the years. Apparently, June even has her own wing in their house. June and the kids aren't even coming to the wedding. But they're stuck with each other, they have an ironclad prenuptial agreement, so whoever files for divorce loses everything.

Apparently, a business deal was more important than their children's happiness to my father and June's father.

My mother sacrificed too, and maybe that's why all my siblings have as well. She was an up-and-coming actress in New York City when she met my father. She was waitressing at a restaurant he had a dinner meeting at. Apparently, it was love at first sight and they spent the weeks he was in the city together. When he went back to Florida, they tried to do the long-distance thing for a few months, but eventually she gave up her career to be with him.

Maybe it was the right choice in the beginning, but I remember hearing them fight late at night, when I was supposed to be asleep. She'd yell at him about how she gave up everything for him and he was hardly around. His response was that it was because he was trying to build a business so she could have the life she'd always dreamed of.

Everyone in my family had to make a sacrifice for their partner, for what was expected of them. But I refuse. I refuse to give up my career to get married. I've worked too hard and for too long to get where I am today to give it up. I went to Brown, damn it, I have a PhD in Astronomy.

So I guess I'll be the spinster Fairchild.

The fun single aunt.

But I don't say any of that. Instead, I huff out a breath and say, "It is what it is. But on a more exciting note, I got *the job*."

Summer's mouth falls open. "You did!"

"Yep!" I say, popping the *p*. "I heard back from them this morning."

"Holy shit, Aubs. I'm proud of you," Summer says, leaning forward to prop her hands on my desk, a huge grin on her face. "Why aren't you more excited?"

"It feels surreal. It hasn't sunk in. Plus, maybe I shouldn't take it." I chew on my bottom lip. "I'd have to give up my job here."

"Yeah, but the deputy director position is your dream. Of course you should take it. Why wouldn't you take it?"

"It's only for a year. I'd lose my tenure. What happens if it doesn't work out?"

Summer stares at me for a moment before saying, with a shake of her head, "you figure it out if it doesn't work out. But the Eclipse Observatory is *the* place for infrared research. You've been saying for years you want to go visit and get in some lab time. Now you'll be there for a year. At least. I'm sad my bestie is moving to Hawaii though. But you need to go. Otherwise you'll regret it."

"I'll think about it."

"Aubrey," Summer scolds. "Don't think. Accept it. We should go out this weekend and celebrate," she says, snagging another Hershey's Kiss.

"I can't. I've got to go to Orlando. Unfortunately."

"Bummer. Okay, next weekend we'll celebrate. Gives me more time to plan. Are you seeing Brody?" Summer asks, wiggling her eyebrows and shimmying her shoulders.

I laugh. How did she know?

"Yeah. We're having dinner tomorrow night."

"Are you going to finally tell him about New Year's Eve?" she asks, taking another chocolate from the jar.

"There's nothing to tell."

"Aubrey. You came back and told me you had the best kiss of your life," Summer says, pinning me with a look that says she won't let me get out of this conversation.

I lean back, crossing my arms. "Yeah, but I don't know who with."

"That's why you should ask him about it. Maybe he can help you figure out who it was. Or better yet." She raises a finger to the sky like a light bulb went off in her head. "Set up a kissing booth and invite all his single teammates. You kiss them all and find out who your mystery guy is."

I roll my eyes. Not only is that a ridiculous idea, but I can picture Brody's face if I ask him to help me kiss all of his single teammates. Steam would be billowing out of his ears and his face would turn beat red. Brody is a lot of things, including being overprotective of me and our friendship.

"I can't ask him that," I hiss. "Plus, you just convinced me to move to Hawaii. It won't matter if I do find out. I won't be here."

Summer laughs. "Fine, but I still think you should ask. Okay, I'd love to stay and chat, babe, but I've got work to do. Come say bye before you leave." She hops to her feet, rapping her knuckles on my desk before spinning on her heel and leaving my office.

I turn back to my computer to try to get some work done. But my thoughts keep drifting to that kiss on New Year's Eve. Not that I'm looking for anything serious, but it would be fun to know who my mysterious kisser was.

The rest of the day passes in a whirlwind of paperwork, emails, and meetings. Before I know it, it's time to head home and get ready to leave for Orlando.

The entire drive to my townhouse I contemplate what Summer said—that I should talk to Brody about what happened on New Year's Eve. But no matter how I frame the conversation in my head, I'm convinced the outcome would be him being pissed off that someone touched me, kissed me. Not that he has any claim over me—we're *only* friends. Something he made clear years ago. Plus, if I tell him, I'm sure he'll use it as a reason not to invite me to another team event. No, there's got to be another way to find out who I kissed.

Either that or forget the whole thing and move on with my life.

Yeah, that's probably the more logical thing to do.

Chapter Four

Brody

I steer my Range Rover into a parking spot outside the Vietnamese restaurant that Aubrey and I agreed to meet at. It's one of my favorite spots in town and one I visit frequently. The food is good, the staff is friendly, and I never get recognized. I'm just another customer, a frequent customer that the staff knows by name, but I'm not treated differently because I'm a professional hockey player.

Heck, I don't even know if they know who I am. Which I'm grateful for. It's nice to be a *normal* person every once in a while instead of a professional hockey player that everyone wants a piece of.

I hop out of my SUV and walk toward the restaurant, scanning the parking lot for Aubrey's car. I grin when I spot her red Civic with its Orlando Storm bumper sticker parked a few spots over. Probably the first time I've smiled in weeks. If anything can put me in a good mood, it's seeing her. Pushing the door open, I blink, letting my eyes adjust to the dimly lit interior.

"Hi, Mr. Thompson. Dr. Fairchild is already seated." The hostess greets me and beckons me to follow her.

"Hey, Brody," Aubrey says when we arrive at the table. She stands and I pull her into my arms, loving the way she fits against me. I've missed her. I've missed this.

"Hi, Aubrey." I reluctantly let her go, helping her back into her seat before taking my own.

"I ordered us drinks. Figured you'd want a beer with dinner now that the season is over." Aubrey's expression sobers. "I'm sorry about the loss."

"Thanks," I say, picking up the menu. There's nothing that can be said to change how the season ended.

"There's always next year."

"If there is a next year," I murmur, staring at the menu. I'm not sure why I'm studying it so intently because I always get the same thing—beef pho with summer rolls to start. We're both creatures of habit and always order the same meals. The hostess still gives us menus and time to look over them, but if I had to guess, the cook is already preparing our dinners.

"What?" Aubrey puts her hand on my arm, and I glance up, meeting her blue eyes. "What do you mean? Of course there's going to be next year."

I stare down at her hand on my arm, it feels like it's burning a hole into my skin. I'm not sure why. We hug and occasionally touch, but this feels different, like she's branding me. I take a deep breath. "My contract is up with the Storm. They need to sign me to a new one. I don't know if they're going to."

"Oh" is all she says as she removes her hand. The conversation comes to a pause as the waitress brings us our drinks and takes our orders.

"So," I say, changing the subject. "How are things with you? What's new?"

She takes a sip of her wine peering at me over the rim of her glass, I'm sure she's debating whether to call me out on the subject change. After a few seconds she says, "I got a job offer yesterday."

"That's awesome. I didn't know you were applying for jobs." Why is this the first I'm hearing about this? And why isn't she more excited about it?

"It's for a deputy director job—" She frowns. *Odd.* "In Hawaii."

Hawaii? She's moving almost five thousand miles away. Shit. I'm happy for her, but we definitely won't be visiting each other as often as we do now. She won't be a couple of hours away. I know we went almost five months without seeing each other, but that's the longest we've ever gone, and it was torture.

Will she come back to visit?

The time difference will make phone calls nearly impossible. At least we can text.

But I don't say any of that. She has enough people who guilt trip her for not doing what they want, and she doesn't need to think I'm disappointed or hurt by her decision. Not that I could ever be. I'm just sad.

Sad that my best friend is moving thousands of miles away.

"That's awesome. I've never been there but I hear it's beautiful," I say, picking up my beer.

"I haven't decided if I'm taking the job."

I take a deep breath. "Of course you are. It sounds like a once-in-a-lifetime experience."

"It is. It's just that . . ." She fiddles with her fork and napkin.

"Just that, what, Aubrey? What aren't you telling me?" I ask, leaning closer to her, fighting the urge to put my hand over hers to stop her fidgeting, or tilt her chin up so she's looking at me.

"It could be a risky career move. I'm only guaranteed a one-year contract. I have to reapply every year for the position. I'll be giving up my tenure track for a job that could only last a year." She finally glances up at me. Everything she isn't saying is written on her face—she's scared and nervous about this role but also really wants to take it.

"How long was the current director there for?"

"Ten years. During the interview, he told me he decided to retire this year and that's why the job was open," she says, taking another sip of her wine.

Before I can say anything, her phone buzzes from her purse multiple times. With a sigh, she pulls it out, then grimaces as she reads the messages. With an aggravated huff, she shoves it back into her purse, grabs her glass, and gulps down her wine.

"What's going on?" I lean over the table, closer to her, and place my hand on her arm. She's trembling.

Fuck.

Who was that?

Anger bristles inside of me. What did they say to upset her?

"It's nothing. I'm fine," she says, waving me off. But she's not fine. I know her, and I know something's wrong, so I press her again.

"You don't seem fine." I gesture to our waitress that Aubrey needs another glass of wine. She appears at our table with the bottle and fills the glass.

"What's going on?" I repeat the question.

She shakes her head and rubs her face with her hands. "My mother. She's disappointed in me. In my choices."

I rear back, my mouth falling open. How anyone could think Aubrey's a disappointment is beyond me. She's got a PhD, and even if she didn't, she's anything but a disappointment. She's kind. Considerate. Thoughtful. She must read the expression on my face because she lets out a small laugh.

"For fuck's sake. She hasn't changed, has she?" I grind out. I take a deep breath, willing myself to calm down. I'm not angry at her, of course not. I'm pissed that her mom says these things to her. "Why, Aubrey?"

The waitress arrives with our food. After checking to make sure we have everything we need, she disappears.

"Aubrey," I prompt when we're alone again.

She picks up one of her spring rolls, lifting it to her mouth to take a bite. I wait patiently for her to finish chewing, knowing she probably needs the time to get her thoughts together.

"My sister's wedding is in a month," she finally says.

I nod.

"It's all I've been hearing about since Clara got engaged. How my youngest sister is getting married and I'm single. Alone. Basically a spinster. Now my mother is insisting that I have a date for the wedding. It won't look good if her oldest daughter is unattached at the wedding of her youngest daughter. She sent me pictures of potential dates that she's picked out for me."

I growl. Aubrey raises her eyebrows at me, but I don't miss the way her eyes are glassy, and not from alcohol. From the shit her mother is slugging her way. I hate seeing her like this. I hate her mother even more for saying that to her. For fuck's sake? Can't she see how wonderful of a person Aubrey is? Having a spouse isn't going to change her.

"I'll do it." The words are out of my mouth before I can think twice about them.

Chapter Five

Aubrey

I stare at him for a couple of seconds, my mouth moving but no sound coming out. I had to have heard him wrong, right? I finally recover enough to ask, "Seriously, Brody? I can't ask you to do that."

"You didn't. I volunteered," he says, shoving a hand through his brown hair that's fallen into his eyes. He probably needs a haircut, although I like it when his hair's a little longer and unkempt. I haven't seen it this length since high school. Not that it's that long, it's just a lot longer than he usually has it.

"It's not just the wedding."

"Well, I assumed there was a rehearsal dinner and a couple of nights in Key West." He shrugs like his volunteering to go as my date is no big deal. "Not like I'm doing anything these days. Plus, you need me."

"Brody." My eyes go wide. "It's a *week* with my family, his family, plus a whole bunch of other people. There are events and excursions planned. A week, Brod." I wave my hand around.

"Oh," he says, before picking up his spoon and taking a bite of his soup.

"Yeah, that's what I thought." I go back to my food. It was sweet of him to volunteer to go with me, but I knew the minute I mentioned it was a week-long event and not two or three days, he'd back out. I don't blame him. My family is a lot to handle. Add in my sister's friends and her fiancé's friends, and that's even more people. I'm sure the last thing he wants to do is spend his downtime with a bunch of people he doesn't know.

We eat in silence for a few minutes before he surprises me by saying, "It's fine, Aubrey. The offer still stands. Text me the when and where. I'll be there."

"What?" I peek up at him. "I can't ask you to do that."

"You didn't ask me. I offered."

"Yeah but . . ." I say, at a loss for words.

"But what? Do you not want me to go as your date?" he asks, studying me.

"I do. I just . . ."

Of course I want him to go as my date. I'd much rather go with someone I know and actually like spending time with. But this feels like it's crossing a line for us. I don't know why though—we've spent time together before. He's gone to work events with me as my plus-one, and it wasn't a big deal.

Maybe because this requires us to share a hotel room, be in a small space together for an extended amount of time, because it's not like we could get separate hotel rooms.

No. Knowing my mother, she'll insist I share a hotel room with my date. Heck, I wouldn't have put it past her to have me share a hotel room with whatever man she arranged to be my date, either.

"What's the problem then?" Brody asks, then takes a bite of his food.

"Nothing. Yes, I'd like you to go with me as my date. If you don't mind being stuck with me for a week. Or you could always come down on Friday morning and be there for the weekend. That works too."

He frowns. "And leave you alone with your family for the other days? Nope. I'll be there the whole time."

"If you're sure." I don't know why I'm still arguing with him. Why I don't accept his offer. It's way better than the alternative. Having my mother set me up with someone I don't know.

"I told you I was sure."

"Okay. I'll pick you up," I say, accepting his offer before he can change his mind.

"No way am I sitting in your Civic for eight hours," Brody says with a shake of his head.

"Fine." I let out an exasperated sigh and throw up my hands in mock surrender. "We can take your SUV."

"Nope, we are not driving for eight hours. We'll fly."

"That's ridiculous. Last-minute tickets are going to be expensive," I protest, glaring at him.

He gives me a look that says *remember who you're talking to and how much money I have*. "Leave it to me. Don't you worry about it."

"Brod, that's too much."

"Aubrey, let me do this. Please." The last word is whispered.

"Fine." I huff. He winks at me before going back to his dinner. "So, how's Brantley? And Mel?" I ask, changing the subject to ask about his brother and sister-in-law.

"They're good. They're leaving next week to go on a cruise to Alaska. All Wyatt's talked about every time I've spoken to them is how he's going to get to see really big whales."

I grin at the mention of Brody's ten-year-old nephew, Wyatt. "You should have gone with them."

"Could you see me"—he lets out a bark of laughter—"on a cruise ship for fourteen days? I'd go crazy."

"Nah, you'd have a good time. Plus when was the last time you saw your brother? And your nephew?"

"When we played in Seattle, in February, they came to the game. Went to lunch with them."

"You should think about going to visit them. Spend more time with them. I'm sure Wyatt would love that. Now that you have time."

"I'll think about it." Brody frowns, and something akin to anger or sadness crosses his features. What's that about?

"You okay, Brod?" I ask, watching him closely, trying to figure out what's going on. "Everything okay with Brantley?"

"Yeah." He scrunches his forehead. "Why do you ask?"

I study him for a minute, trying to figure out how to approach the subject without having him shut down on me. Something's going on that he's not telling me about. Don't ask me how I know, I just do. Call it many years of friendship and knowing the many faces of Brody. There's something going on. Maybe not with his family but with something else.

I take a deep breath and say, "You made a weird face when I suggested you go to visit them because you have time. Now that it's the off-season," I amend.

He runs a hand through his hair. "I don't know. Still upset that our season ended the way it did, I guess."

"Okay," I say, although I'm not entirely satisfied with that answer.

He changes the subject, and I let him even though I think there's something he's not telling me. But I won't push him, the same way he doesn't push me to talk about things when I'm not ready. That's probably why we became such good friends in the first place—because we let each other be and don't try to change the other person.

"You ready?" Brody asks twenty minutes later when we've finished eating and he's paid the bill.

"Yeah, I guess." Leaving dinner means I'm one step closer to seeing my mother and I'm dreading it.

"Want me to come with you?" Brody asks as we walk out the door, as if he read my mind. He probably did. He's good at reading people, it's why he's so good on the ice. He's got a sixth sense about things and not just when it comes to playing hockey.

"Nah," I say with a shake of my head.

"Are you sure?"

"Yes, but thanks, Brod. For everything," I say glancing over at him and meeting his gaze. Hoping he can see the sincerity in what I'm telling him.

"You know I'd do anything for you, Aubrey," he says quietly, and the sentiment goes straight to my heart.

We reach my car and I unlock the door, then turn to face him. His brows are pinched together, and he appears to be deep in thought, like there's something else he wants to say. But he shakes his head and, instead, pulls me in for a hug. I breathe in his comforting scent of pine and cedarwood and relax into his arms, not questioning why he felt the need to give me a second hug tonight.

We hug—just not normally this much.

Far too soon, he's letting me go, and I reluctantly climb into my car. Brody steps back, his hands in his pockets, and watches as I start my car and back out of my spot. Finally, with a wave he heads to his SUV.

Hopefully tomorrow goes as well as dinner tonight did.

Here's to hoping.

But if I know my mother and Clara, something is going to go wrong.

If only I knew how wrong it would go.

"I'm on my way, Mother." She hangs up without even a goodbye, and I shake my head, turning up the radio and concentrating on the road.

Today is going to be so much fun. Yes, that's sarcasm. She felt the need to call me as I was driving to meet everyone to make sure I was on time. I hate that she feels the need to remind me a million times what time the appointment is and to not be late.

Like I could forget.

I pull into the parking lot of the bridal boutique, Refined Silk, put my car in park, and take a deep breath. My middle sister, Brielle's, van is parked a few spots over, and I let out a sigh of relief. At least I won't have to face Mother and Clara alone. I take a few deep breaths before getting out of my car.

"Hey, Aubs."

I turn toward the voice and see Bri getting out of her van. "Hey, Bri. How are you?"

When I get close enough to her, she puts out her arms, and I step into her embrace. We've always been close, especially growing up and being two years apart.

"I'm good, big sis. How are you?"

"Fine. Ask me in a couple of hours and that answer might change."

She laughs and raises her eyebrows at me before linking her arm through mine and steering us toward the shop. "I got your back, sis."

"She already called me on my way over here to make sure I wasn't going to be late," I say, rolling my eyes.

Bri shakes her head, pulling the door open. We're greeted by a sales lady who leads us to the back of the shop.

"Hello girls," Mother says, coming over to greet us. She gives us both the once-over and must like what she sees because she doesn't comment, giving us each a peck on the cheek instead.

"Your sister is trying on her dress. Come sit." She waves us over to where the rest of Clara's bridal party are already seated on a large couch, sipping from champagne flutes.

A few minutes later, my sister comes out of the fitting room wearing her dress, a white lace strapless mermaid style—I think that's what I remember her calling it—dress. Our mother hurries to her feet, shaking her head and clicking her tongue. Whirling around, she snaps her fingers for the sales lady, who scurries over. I can't hear the words that are exchanged, at least my mother has the decorum to keep her voice down, but there's a lot of head shaking and pointing. From where I sit, the dress is pretty and seems to fit Clara well, but apparently my mother disagrees. Finally, my sister goes back into the fitting room to take it off. I guess that's as much of it as we're going to see.

"So, Aubrey," My mother says, sitting down on the couch next to me. "I found you the perfect date for the wedding. He's a neurosurgeon—"

"Mother," I interrupt her, "I'm perfectly capable of finding my own date. Or, you know, going alone. Is that such a big deal?"

She looks me up and down. "Go alone?" Her voice pitches higher at the end. "Absolutely, positively not. I told you I'd find you a date, and I did. His name is James. Nice boy."

"Mother." I groan, trying not to roll my eyes. "I have a date."

"Aubrey Elizabeth, if you're lying to me," she says, all but glaring at me.

I glance over at Bri, silently asking her to jump in and save me. Or at least back me up. But she only widens her eyes at me. Guess I'm on my own. Before I can answer, Clara steps out dressed in regular clothing, and the bridesmaids scurry to the fitting room.

"What are we discussing?" Clara asks, taking a seat on the couch.

"Your sister's date to the wedding."

"Oh lovely," Clara says, leaning around Mother. "I think you'll like James. He's friends with Chet."

Of course he is.

Chet, her perfect lawyer fiancé. Chet who plays golf at the country club every Saturday morning with his equally perfect friends. I take a deep breath, counting slowly back from ten in my head. "I'm sure he's perfectly nice. But I have a date."

"Oh don't be silly, Aubs. When have you had time to find a date? We know all you do is work. Can't be good for your social life." Clara shakes her head.

Every day she's a little bit more like our mother. I don't know how Bri or I escaped that curse, but I thank my lucky stars I have at least one sister on my side.

"I'm in a relationship with someone actually," I blurt out.

Shit. Shit. *Shit.*

Why did I say that?

"Oh really?" Mother turns back to me.

"Yes," I say, the lie tumbling out of my mouth. "We've been doing the long-distance thing because he lives here. We wanted to see how things went before we told anyone."

Shit, what the hell am I saying?

Guess this is happening. There's no going back now.

"Oh." She tuts. "Who is he?" She shakes her head at me like I'm a child that she's caught in a lie. "Aubrey Elizabeth, you'd better not be making this up."

"It's Brody, Mother. You remember Brody Thompson?" Bri bristles behind me and jabs me in the back with her finger, but I ignore it. I say a silent prayer that Brody doesn't kill me.

"Brody, as in the kid who played hockey and never went to college? The sophomore *you* tutored your freshman year?" I can hear the disgust dripping off her tongue. She's got certain standards for her children's partners. They must have college degrees and come from well-to-do families. Well, what she considers well-to-do.

"Yes," I say, ignoring the barb. "He plays *professional* hockey for the Orlando Storm. You know, the National Hockey League team here in town."

"How lovely."

I sigh hearing the sarcasm in her voice. Clara has been silently staring at me, her eyes wide, mouth open. Before I can say anything else, the bridesmaids step out from the fitting room and Mother is on her feet to inspect them.

Clara leans over and whispers to me, "I know you're lying about you and Brody being together, but I'll keep my mouth shut. For now. I can't wait to see how this plays out." With that, she hops to her feet and goes over to her bridesmaids.

What have I gotten myself into?

Why couldn't I keep my mouth shut?

"Are you serious?" Bri whispers.

I don't have time to answer as we're summoned to the back to try on our dresses. When I'm in my fitting room, I pull out my phone and send a quick message to Brody.

Me: We have a problem.

Chapter Six

Brody

I pause the treadmill and take a sip of water while reading Aubrey's text message.

Aubrey: We have a problem.

I'm not sure if my heart is racing from the sprints I was doing or because of Aubrey's text message. I type out a quick response.

Me: Are you alright? Do you need me to come to you?

I get off the treadmill, pacing around the room. Should I get in my car and head toward her? Just in case? *You don't even know where she is.* I'm kicking myself for not getting the name of the store she was going to.

Aubrey: I'm fine. But can I come over when I'm done here? In about an hour?

I heave out a breath and type a response.

Me: Yeah.
Aubrey: See you then.

I push off the wall of my home gym, grab my headphones from the treadmill, and walk down the hall to my bedroom. There's enough time to shower and have a protein smoothie before she gets here.

As I'm finishing the last of my smoothie a little over an hour later, there's a knock at my door. I set my empty glass down on the kitchen counter and hurry over to the door, glad I don't have to wait any longer to find out what happened this morning at her dress fitting. My mouth drops open at the sight in front of me. Aubrey's wringing her hands and shifting back and forth. I don't say a word, simply open the door wider for her to walk past me. I follow her into the living room where she begins pacing.

"Aubrey," I say, walking up to her and gently putting my hands on her shoulders so she's forced to stop. "What happened?"

She huffs out a breath, looking everywhere except at me. Chewing on her bottom lip, she finally meets my eyes. "I told my mother we were dating. In a relationship. She wouldn't stop trying to set me up with a date for the wedding. Some neurosurgeon named James. She didn't believe me when I said I had my own date."

I chuckle. That's what's got her in a tizzy? "So you told her I was your boyfriend?"

"It's not funny," she says, smacking me on the chest. Groaning, she pulls away and throws herself on the couch, then pulls one of the small throw pillows onto her lap and hugs it to her chest. "What are we going to do?"

I shrug and take a seat next to her. "I can be your fake boyfriend if you need me to."

"Are you sure? This is more than you going as my date to a wedding. Which would have been bad enough if . . ." She trails off, clutching the pillow tighter.

"If what, Aubrey?" I prompt.

"If the news got out. Or someone snapped a picture and it got on the internet. You and I both know the rumors would fly," she finally says with a resigned sign.

"I couldn't care less about the rumors, Aubrey. Let them speculate all they want. Although I'm sure the press has got better things to do than speculate about who a random hockey player is dating."

She chuckles. "You're not some random hockey player, Brody. You're, well . . . you."

Now it's my turn to laugh. "If you say so. I think you're making this into a bigger deal than it is. I already said I'd go with you as your date. What difference does it really make if I'm your date or your fake boyfriend? Right?"

"Yeah." She blows out a breath. After a few minutes of silence she says, "I feel like this *fake relationship* should benefit both of us. So what can I do for you? Any team event coming up you need a date for?"

"Besides a week in Key West with my best friend?" I ask, contemplating the question. *What do I want?* A light bulb goes off in my head. "The guys have been bugging me to go out with them. I didn't go to Caleb's end-of-the-season party and that's made it worse. If I tell them it's because you and I have been spending time together, that we're dating, they'll back off."

"Aren't you worried about what they'll say?" The side of her mouth quirks up. "That they won't believe you."

"Honestly? They'll be thrilled." I close my eyes, shaking my head imagining the guys' reactions to the news. I'm sure Wes will go on about soul mates and romantic gestures. "Maybe they'll stop nagging me about everything."

"Fine, but we need rules," she says, tucking her feet up under her as she gets more comfortable on the couch.

My eyes pop open. I guess we're doing this.

"Rules, Aubrey? Really?" I raise an eyebrow at her. I don't know why we need to have rules. We've known each other for almost twenty years, but if that makes her feel better, I'll go along with it.

"Yes, Brody. Rules."

"Okay, but I think this calls for a drink first. Want some wine?" I ask, getting to my feet. I don't normally drink in the middle of the afternoon, but if there's any occasion to do so, it's discussing the rules for fake dating your best friend.

"Yeah, okay, Brod." A grin springs across her face that makes her blue eyes sparkle. I nod and head to the kitchen. It only takes me a couple of minutes to pour her a glass of her favorite wine and open a bottle of beer for myself.

"Here you go." I hand her the glass of riesling and take a swig of my beer before sitting down next to her. "Okay. What are the rules?"

She takes a big sip of her wine, like she needs some courage to say whatever it is she wants to say. She swallows. "First, we sleep in our own beds. My mother said she was canceling the second room since I'm bringing my boyfriend. I'll call the hotel and make sure we're getting a room with two beds."

"Fine. Okay." Sleeping in separate beds is probably a good idea. I'd hate to wake up accidentally touching her in a way that makes her uncomfortable.

"Second, no kissing."

I shake my head. "Aubrey, if we're going to sell this, there will need to be kissing. We're supposed to be in a relationship. People will expect us to kiss. Be affectionate with each other."

She stares at me for a few beats, chewing her bottom lip. I watch her, fighting the urge to reach over and pull her lip from between her teeth. *Settle down.*

"Fine. Fine," she concedes. I smirk at her. "Kissing is allowed. But only on the cheek and only when we absolutely have to. And no catching feelings." She narrows her eyes at me, gesturing between us. "That would complicate things when we end our fake relationship."

"Okay." *I'll take whatever she's willing to give. I'd be lying if I said I haven't thought about kissing her again.* I drain the last of my beer to keep myself from saying anything else.

She surprises me when she says, "Do you have any rules?"

I study her for a few beats before saying, "No dating other people. It has to seem real to everyone. The last thing either of us needs is this coming out as fake."

"Of course. We should decide on our end date now. It'll make things easier."

"However long you need me to be your fake boyfriend for, I'm in."

She finishes her wine and sets the glass on the coffee table next to my beer bottle. "A week or two after my sister's wedding? I haven't told anyone but you and Summer I got the job, so I'll wait until after the wedding to tell them. We can say we decided we were better off as friends because your job is here, and mine is in Hawaii."

"If that's what you want, Aubrey. I'll go along with whatever you want." And that's the truth. I'd agree to anything for her.

"Anything else you want, Brody? Out of this arrangement? I feel like you're getting the short end of the stick."

I rake a hand through my hair. What do I want out of this fake relationship besides being able to tell the guys I'm dating someone? An idea forms in my head. A way to spend more time with her outside of the wedding week.

"Well, when you put it that way. The guys have planned a beach day in a few weeks. They keep pestering me to come. Go with me?"

She stares at me for a few seconds, and I worry that I pushed too far. Asked her to do something she's not comfortable with.

Finally, she says, "Sure, okay. Sounds good. Let me know when, and I'll be here. Anything else?"

"I don't think so. Want another drink?" I ask, standing up. I need a moment to breathe before I ask her for something like another kiss.

"Sure." She hands me her empty wine glass.

"Thank you." she says when I walk back into the living room a few minutes later. I'm not entirely sure if she's thanking me for the drink or for agreeing to a fake relationship.

"You're welcome. Are we good?"

She takes a deep breath and fiddles with the pillow that's back in her lap. "I think so."

"Good." I tip my head toward the TV. "Want to order takeout and watch a movie?"

"Okay."

"What do you feel like?" I ask, grabbing my phone from the coffee table.

"Sushi?"

"You don't even have to ask." I pull up the menu for my favorite place. Once our delivery order is placed, we settle on a movie.

For the first time since I got the Storm eliminated from the Stanley Cup playoffs, I feel like I can breathe.

Like I can relax.

And it's all because of the woman sitting next to me.

My best friend.

Who just became my fake girlfriend.

And I couldn't be happier.

Chapter Seven

Aubrey

A few weeks later, I'm back on the road to Orlando, this time to spend the weekend at Brody's. The first real test of our fake relationship. Tomorrow, we're going to the beach with his teammates. I haven't slept well the past few nights because every night I lay in bed until the wee hours of the morning, my mind racing with all the what-ifs surrounding this weekend.

The thing is, I've met his teammates. They're nice. It's not them I'm worried about. It's me.

Will I give up our ruse?

Will everyone see right through us?

It's probably good we're doing this test run first. If we can't even sell our relationship to Brody's friends, his teammates, how the hell are we going to sell it to my family? But if it does become a problem, that's something future Aubrey will have to deal with.

For now, I'll focus on the task ahead—getting to Orlando in one piece and making it through tomorrow. Brody decided I should stay with him this weekend to make it appear that we are dating. His argument was that it would be suspicious if someone saw the girlfriend of Brody Thompson, forward for the Storm, staying at a hotel. I reluctantly agreed.

That's where I'm headed now.

If I ever get there.

I groan at the hardly moving traffic. Finally, after another fifteen minutes of barely going twenty miles an hour, the highway opens back up.

"There was no reason for that," I grumble, stepping on the accelerator and bringing my Civic back up to the speed limit.

Thankfully the rest of the trip goes smoothly, and before I know it, I'm pulling into the parking garage for Brody's building. The doorman knows me, so I wave and head to the elevators. I use my key to let myself in, and yell toward Brody's room that I'm here. He shouts back something, but the shower muffles his voice.

I drop my bags in the entrance way and slip my shoes off before I pad into the kitchen. I stress ate my emergency stash of gummy bears on the drive over here, and now I'm craving something sweet.

I pull open the cabinets one by one. I've been here numerous times and should have known to stop somewhere for some more sweet snacks. Guess I'm running over to Publix unless I'm happy eating an apple or a banana for my sweet fix. Newsflash, I'm not. I make my way to the walk-in pantry and pull the door open, but what meets my eye shocks me.

"What are you doing?" Brody's voice comes from behind me.

I whirl around, my eyes going wide at the sight of my best friend shirtless in a pair of athletic shorts, a towel in his hand. I can't help but stare at him, my gaze flirting over the tattoo of the Stanley Cup on his right pec, the years he's won the Cup around it, and across his chest to two crossed hockey sticks with his number above them and a puck below them.

I love tattoos, on other people. I'm a wimp when it comes to pain, and needles, no way. Plus, it's a lifelong commitment, and I'm afraid I'd change my mind or hate whatever I picked.

My eyes have a mind of their own as they travel down, taking in his six-pack abs and the neatly trimmed hair leading to his . . . I clear my throat, stopping that train of thought, and force my gaze back up to his.

What has gotten into me?

I've seen him shirtless many times over the years when we've gone out on his boat. Maybe it's that I haven't had sex in a while, over a year, that makes me notice how good he looks. I take a deep breath, willing my lady parts to calm down and remember that he's off limits, focusing instead on what I found in his pantry.

"What's this?" I ask, holding the bag of gummy bears up.

He gives me a half shrug, his face turning a light shade of pink. I turn back to the pantry and step further in to examine the rest of the snacks and wine bottles he's got stored here. There are three bottles of my favorite riesling by Château Saint Michelle, quite a few bags of gummy bears, a couple of dark chocolate bars, and even a bag of the mixed nuts I like. None of which I've ever seen him eat or drink. So I know it's all for me.

"Brody, what'd you do?" I peek over my shoulder to where he's leaning against the doorframe.

"I know how much you like them," he says, like it's no big deal.

This man.

I shouldn't be surprised that he stocked his pantry for me. That's the kind of guy he is. Sweet. Caring. And fucking gorgeous. I take another deep breath, trying to calm my racing heart. Not sure if I'm more turned on by his proximity or that he bought all my favorite treats.

"That was sweet of you," I say, grabbing a bottle of wine off the shelf.

"The one from the other week is still in there," Brody says, inclining his head toward the fridge.

"Right." I hold up the bag of gummy bears. "You think of everything."

"Wanted to keep my fake girlfriend well fed," he says, and his lips quirk up into a grin. "How was the drive?" He steps back so I can walk out of the pantry but not far enough away that I don't get a whiff of his body wash—cedar and pine.

Shit, he smells good.

Seeing him standing in front of me shirtless, fresh from the shower, his tattoos and muscles on display, is torture. When we met in high school, I had a crush on him, but unfortunately he didn't feel the same way. Lucky for me, we ended up as the best of friends and while it wasn't what I initially wanted I've at least gotten to be part of his life.

It takes all my strength to turn away from him and walk over to the fridge. Maybe if I stop looking at him and focus on something else that'll help.

"Who's coming tomorrow?" I ask as I grab a wine glass from the cabinet and pour myself some wine.

"Hunter and Madison, Holt, Wes, and Cole said they might come depending how Nate is in the morning."

I nod, trying to remember the faces that go along with the names. I know Hunter and his girlfriend, Madison. Holt and Wes I draw blanks on. I think one is a goalie. But the other one I can't remember. Cole has played with Brody for years, and I've hung out with his wife, Hannah, on several occasions when I've gone to watch Brody play. They just had a baby—Nate—who I can't wait to meet.

"Sounds like a good group. No Caleb and Jenna?" I ask, turning around. I hand him the bottle of beer I opened for him as I lean against the counter.

Brody takes a drink before saying, "Caleb wasn't sure if they'd make it. And Holt said something about his little sister being in town, so I guess she might come."

I'd never hung out with that many of his teammates until I went to the New Year's Eve party with him. The one where I kissed one of them. I take a sip of my wine, pushing that memory away.

"How about we go sit down," Brody says.

I follow him out of the kitchen, snagging the bag of gummy bears off the counter, and make myself comfortable on his couch while he hangs up his towel.

A few minutes later, he comes sauntering into the living room, having pulled on a shirt. I'm a little disappointed that he's no longer shirtless but also glad that his muscular stomach and tattoos won't be on display, tempting me to touch him. I give myself a mental shake. What the hell am I thinking? *He might be your* fake *boyfriend but he's still your* real *best friend, Aubrey. Don't do anything you'll regret once this fake relationship is over.*

"Want to watch Frasier?" Brody asks, dropping down onto the couch next to me and picking up the remote from the coffee table.

"You don't even have to ask," I answer, getting comfortable as he navigates to the show.

"You think they're going to buy it? Us?" I ask, fixing the strap of my white bathing suit cover up. I lean back in the passenger seat of Brody's SUV as he navigates it through downtown traffic toward the highway.

He glances over at me for a second before focusing back on the road. "Yeah, I do, sugar."

"Sugar?" I ask, wrinkling my nose even though he can't see me.

"You don't like it?" He chuckles, reaching up to adjust the bill of his Storm hat.

"Not particularly."

"Okay, darlin," he drawls, with a fake Southern accent.

"That's not any better." I groan, shaking my head. "And where did that accent come from?"

"You don't like nicknames?" he asks, glancing at me again.

"Not the cheesy ones."

"They're not cheesy." He laughs. "They're terms of endearment. We're in a relationship, so you need a nickname."

"Nope." I cross my arms. "I do not need a nickname."

"Whatever you say, pumpkin," he teases.

"Brody, that's the worst one yet."

I haven't seen this playful side of Brody in a long time. Heck, I thought he'd forgotten how to be anything but serious.

"Well, I'm going to keep trying until we find one you like, sweets." He shakes his head. "Nope, definitely not that one. That's what Hunter calls Madison."

I laugh, reaching over and turning the radio up. We cruise down the highway, making good time since there's not a lot of traffic even though it's midmorning on a Saturday. An hour later, we're pulling into the parking lot at Sunset Park in Daytona.

"Hey, guys." Hunter greets us as we climb out of the SUV, Madison trailing behind him.

"Hey, Aubs." Madison smiles, pulling me into a hug.

"Hi, Mads." I've met them once, at the party, but Madison and I bonded instantly. Have you ever met someone and felt like you've known them forever? That's how I felt when I met Madison.

"Wes, Holt, Kitty, and Hadley are here already. They've got a spot on the beach. Cole said they're on their way. Haven't heard from Caleb," Hunter says when we're done greeting each other.

"Hadley? Kitty?" Brody asks.

"Hadley is Holt's little sister. She's here visiting him. And Kitty, well, she's . . .   " Hunter glances at Madison, who shrugs her shoulders. He blows out a breath and says, "I think she's Holt's girlfriend. Or ex-girlfriend turned hook up."

"Oh. That's . . . interesting," I say, glancing over at Brody who is shaking his head as he moves around to the back of the SUV and starts to take out our stuff. I grab my bag and the cooler I packed.

"Hadley seems nice," Madison says. "Holt said she's a photographer. Kitty is, well . . . You'll see," she says, blowing out a breath and shrugging before following Hunter back to his truck to get their stuff.

I help Brody unload our chairs and the umbrella I insisted we bring.

"Ready, sweet cheeks?" Brody asks, turning to me, his arms full of beach chairs.

I heft the cooler over one arm and grab the beach umbrella. "Yep. Let's do the thing."

"No comment on the nickname?"

"Brody!" I grumble.

"Fine. Fine. Not that one. After you, my dear."

With a smile, I stroll toward the beach, inhaling the saltwater and fresh air. The waves crashing and the murmur of people enjoying a sunny day is the perfect greeting as I walk down the boardwalk.

"They're over there. To your right," Brody says from behind me as I pause to take off my flip flops. It doesn't take us long to get to where the rest of the group has set up chairs and umbrellas.

"Was surprised you said you were coming today. Especially with . . . everything," Holt or Wes—I don't remember who is who—says to

Brody as we're setting up our chairs. I glance at Brody in time to see him shooting a glare at his teammate.

Huh? What am I missing?

Hunter and Madison arrive at that moment with their beach gear, and introductions are made. I get the distinct impression that Hadley doesn't like Kitty, whose real name is Kat, from the way she rolls her eyes every time Kat speaks. Once all the chairs and umbrellas are set up, everyone starts putting sunscreen on or grabbing drinks from the coolers.

"Can you put sunscreen on my back, please, Brod?" I ask, pulling off my cover up to reveal my black and silver bikini. It's one of my favorites, with stars and constellations all over it.

He sucks in a breath behind me, and I turn to see him staring at me.

Chapter Eight

Brody

"Can you put sunscreen on my back, please, Brod?"

I suck in a breath because Aubrey's bikini, while modest and covering everything, doesn't leave much to the imagination. I've seen her in a bathing suit before, so why does this feel different?

She peeks at me over her shoulder and holds out a bottle of sunscreen. I shake myself out of my stupor to slather it on my hands and rub it on her back, loving the silky feel of her skin. Is the rest of her body as soft?

I bet it is.

And now I'm picturing her spread out, naked on my bed, her gorgeous brown hair fanned out on my pillow, her blue eyes watching me, waiting for me to explore her body. To find out what she tastes like. How wet she is. My cock stirs to attention at the vision I've conjured up. I take a deep breath, forcing myself to think about something else.

This is a fake relationship. There will be none of that. Besides, she doesn't want me like that. She made it clear on New Year's Eve. I force myself to focus on my task and not on how smooth her back feels, like a freshly surfaced ice rink.

"All done, sweetheart," I say, reluctantly pulling my hands away from her body.

"Thanks," she says. She spins around and takes the bottle of sunscreen. "Want me to do you?"

I pull off my shirt, and she gestures for me to turn around. My eyes close and I try not to squirm as she rubs my back. I want to groan as her soft hands slide over my skin, but I don't. Instead, I open my eyes and focus on the waves rolling in and out along the shore.

"You're really tight, Brod. Everything okay?"

"Fine. Fine," I mumble.

Am I okay?

I don't know anymore.

I'm the reason we didn't make it to the next round of the playoffs. My career might be over...and then what happens? It's something I've been mulling over for the past few weeks, since Aubrey and I started this fake relationship, really. Something about agreeing to be her fake boyfriend made me start to think about what's next.

I'm only thirty-five. I have a long life ahead of me. Except I have no idea what I want to do with it or who I want to spend it with. While I could never work a day in my life again—the perks of investing most of my salary and living modestly—I don't know if that's what I want to do.

I never thought I wanted a family, or to put down roots. That's why I only bought a condo instead of a big house with a backyard. But watching Cole and Caleb both have their first child this past season has made me question everything I thought I wanted.

Having a backseat view of Hunter meeting and falling in love with Madison. The way they love each other, help each other through the difficult times, support each other. It makes me wonder if maybe I do want that.

Maybe I want the roots.

The family.

I feel Aubrey's eyes on me and peel my gaze from the ocean to look at her over my shoulder. She's studying me. I wait for her to call me on my bullshit, but she doesn't. Instead, she gives me a smile and proceeds to put sunscreen on the rest of her body. I heave out a breath and do the same.

A few minutes later Cole and Hannah arrive with their son, Nate. Soon after, Caleb and Jenna walk over to us with their daughter, Bailey.

"Hey, buddy. Glad to see you here." Caleb claps me on the back before he takes the seat next to me that Aubrey vacated to go in the ocean with Madison and Hadley.

"Hey. How's everything going?" I ask, glancing over to Jenna and Hannah chatting in the shade with the babies.

Cole grabs a chair and takes a seat on the other side of me. I have to admit it's a nice day to be at the beach with friends.

"So, you and Aubrey, eh?" Cole asks, wagging his eyebrows at me and taking a sip from his water bottle.

"Can't believe you kept that from us all season," Caleb says.

"It hasn't been all season." I feel bad lying to my teammates. I do. But it's better than them worrying about me. They have families that need their attention, not me.

"I didn't believe it at first," Cole says, scratching his head. "But I'm happy for you."

"Didn't believe what?" Wes asks, flopping down on the sand in front of us.

Hunter and Holt walk up behind him. *Great.* Party's all here. Let the interrogation begin. Although, frankly, I've been expecting it since I casually mentioned that Aubrey and I were together in the group chat.

"Brody and Aubrey," Cole says.

"Why's that?" Hunter asks, his gaze turned toward the ocean, and I know he's watching Madison and the girls in the surf like I am.

It's a relatively calm day with not a lot of waves, but that doesn't stop me from keeping an eye on them. Aubrey is a strong swimmer, she was on the swim team in high school, but I still worry about her. I heard her educating the other ladies on what to do if they get caught in a rip current, which made me smile. Always watching out for everyone else.

"When did you finally get your head out of your ass and ask her out?" Wes asks as I take a sip of water and nearly choke on it.

Shit. Aubrey and I didn't come up with a story of how we got together.

"During the All-Star break," I finally say. I make a mental note to tell Aubrey the first chance I can in case they ask her.

"You owe me fifty bucks, Wes," Holt says, turning to Wes.

"What the fuck?" I ask, glancing between the guys.

"I had nothing to do with it," Hunter says, putting his hands in the air. Caleb and Cole both shake their heads.

Again, what the fuck?

They bet on me? Or, better yet, on me and Aubrey getting together.

Wes chuckles. "It was clear on New Year's Eve that you two were inevitable. It was just a question of how long it would take you to realize it." He grabs a can of beer out of the cooler. "Anyone else want one?" he asks, holding it up. Everyone except Caleb and Cole put their hands out, and cans are passed around.

"How long's your sister here for?" I ask Holt, changing the subject.

"A couple of weeks. She mentioned having a few photography gigs next month back home."

I see Wes perk up out of the corner of my eye and glance out at women in the water. Is something going on there? I make a mental note to ask Hunter if he knows.

Wait, who am I, and why do I care who my teammates are interested in?

"And Kat?" I ask the question no one else seems to want to ask. "What's the deal with her?"

Hunter sucks in a breath next to me.

"What's this, an interrogation?" Holt mutters. "Kat's my girlfriend from high school. Ex-girlfriend. We split up when she went to university and I went to play juniors. She got transferred to Orlando recently, so we reconnected. We're seeing where things are going."

"Don't think Hadley likes her that much," Wes mumbles.

Holt either doesn't hear that comment, or chooses to ignore it because he asks Hunter what his summer plans are. The conversation shifts, and I reluctantly tell the guys about going to Key West with Aubrey for her sister's wedding.

"That's a big step, meeting the family," Caleb says.

"I already know them. Remember, we've been friends since high school."

"True. True," Caleb concedes.

"I'm going to go in the water," Hunter says, getting to his feet and dropping his empty beer can in the trash bag we have tied to one of the umbrellas.

"Sounds like a good plan to me," Wes says, standing.

Holt and I are both out of our chairs before Wes can make his way down the beach. Cole gets up to go check on Hannah and Nate. I follow the guys into the ocean where we make a beeline for our women.

"Hey," I say when I reach Aubrey, Madison, and Hadley who were standing in waist-high water, not far from shore talking. The rest of the guys come up behind me and greet the women. I frown, glancing around wondering where Kat is. I finally spot her off on her own, floating on her back a few feet away. Holt wades over to her.

"Hi. What were you all talking about up there?" Aubrey asks, gesturing toward our abandoned chairs.

"Guy stuff," I answer with a wink.

She throws back her head and laughs. I take the opportunity to grab her around the waist and pull her toward me, then pick her up so I can toss her into the ocean.

"No, don't," she says, swatting at me. "Put me down."

With Aubrey in my arms, I walk further into the water until it comes halfway up my chest. Not so deep that she can't stand but deep enough that I can actually swim around and not look like a fool.

"Brody," she whines. "I don't want to lose my hat or sunglasses."

"I'll buy you new ones if you do," I say, lifting her up higher as if I'm going to throw her in. But at the last minute, I take pity on her and lower her down so we're face to face.

She wraps her legs around me, and I'm very aware of how close she is. Her breasts pressed against my chest. My bathing suit and hers, the only fabric between us. My cock starts to grow hard, and I shift under the water, adjusting myself. I glance over at the rest of the group, but they're standing with their backs to us. Wes is pointing at something.

"What are you doing?" Aubrey whispers in my ear, looping her arms around my neck.

"Holding you. We're supposed to be a couple. If you were really mine, I wouldn't let you out of my sight." And I'm trying not to think about how I could slip my fingers under her bathing suit bottoms and into her pussy. *Get a hold of yourself, Brody. This is fake. There will be no pussy touching.*

"Okay," Aubrey says, leaning back in my arms so she can peer up at me. Except now her breasts are in my face, and it's all I can do not to think about what they look like, what they taste like. My cock grows harder. What the fuck is wrong with me?

I clear my throat. "What's going on with Kat?" I ask, lowering my voice.

"Oh, you mean *Kitty*. I'm not sure. She barely said two words to us and went off by herself. Doesn't help that Hadley was glaring at her the whole time."

I shake my head. "Why'd she come if she doesn't want to be here?"

"Your guess is as good as mine."

We fall silent, each lost in our own thoughts for a few minutes.

"I wonder what they're looking at." I say breaking the silence, gesturing toward where the rest of the group is huddling a few feet away before walking closer.

"We saw dolphins," Hadley says, pointing into the distance, as we come to stand next to her.

"You better hope it was dolphins and not a shark, sis," Holt says from where he and Kat have joined us. After that comment Hadley and Madison decide it's time to get out of the water.

"What do you want to do?" I ask Aubrey, who's still in my arms, as everyone else heads to the shore.

"This is nice. Relaxing. I'm fine staying in if you are." She unhooks her legs from around me, and I reluctantly let her go. We swim around for a while, chatting about random things, and I have to agree with her that it is relaxing.

"Seems like they're having a good time." I gesture toward the guys on the sand who have started a game of football.

"I'm glad we came."

"Me too."

"Do you think they're buying it?" she asks.

"I think so." I turn to my friends. It's still weird to me to call the whole group of guys friends, but they are. Some more than others. As much as I didn't anticipate it, Hunter, Wes, and Holt weaseled their way into my life.

"Looks like Caleb and Jenna are getting ready to head out. We should say goodbye," I say, watching everyone hug. Caleb has their beach bag flung over his shoulder.

"Sounds good. I'm getting hungry anyway." Aubrey begins to paddle toward the shore.

I follow behind her. I'm not usually a beach guy, but today with her was the most fun I've had in a long time. So much so that I don't mind the sand that has already taken up residence in places where sand shouldn't be, nor do I mind all the salt water that I accidentally drank.

Chapter Nine

Aubrey & Brody

Monday

Brody: I'm assuming I'll need a suit for the wedding. What color is your dress so I can get a tie to match?

Aubrey: Happy Monday to you too. It's pale pink, but you probably don't need a suit. Let me ask Bri what Devon is wearing. He's not in the wedding, either.

Brody: Okay.

Tuesday

Aubrey: Sorry, yesterday got away from me. Here's what Devon's wearing. *photo attachment.* The outfit was approved by Clara and Mother so something similar would probably be fine.

Brody: Okay, sounds good. Thanks.

Aubrey: You okay?

Brody: Yeah. Why?

Aubrey: You sound off.

Brody: Aubrey, it's a text message. How do I sound off?

Aubrey: *Shrugging emoji* You just do.

Brody: I'm fine.

Aubrey: If you say so.

Thursday

    Brody: Caleb invited us to his party for the fourth.

    Aubrey: Sounds fun.

    Brody: I'll tell him no.

    Aubrey: Why would you do that?

    Brody: Because it's after our end date.

    Aubrey: So? We can still go together.

    Brody: If you're sure. It might be weird.

    Aubrey: Why would it be weird?

    Brody: Because the guys will want all the details. Wes will try to get us back together.

Friday

    Aubrey: Sorry. I got busy. It's up to you. I can go with you if you want.

    Brody: I'll tell him maybe. It's still quite a ways away.

Monday

    Brody: You're flying from Orlando to Key West with me, right?

    Aubrey: No. Saturday is Summer's birthday, and I promised her I'd go out for dinner and drinks.

    Brody: Okay. I'll find you a flight from Gainesville.

Tuesday

    Aubrey: Why did I get an email with first class airline tickets?

Brody: Because first class is way more comfortable. The seats are bigger. More legroom.

 Aubrey: First class?! That's too much.

 Brody: Aubrey, it's no big deal. Let me do this.

 Aubrey: Fine. *eye roll emoji*

 Brody: Wow. I'm shocked you didn't argue more.

 Aubrey: I'm too tired to argue. Plus it's your money not mine.

 Aubrey: Thank you, Brody.

 Brody: You're welcome.

Wednesday

 Brody: Any last-minute things I should know? Got the itinerary. Quite a schedule.

 Aubrey: Tell me about it. Are you still sure you want to do this? You can back out if it's too much. I'll tell everyone you got sick and couldn't come.

 Brody: I told you I'd be there for you, and I will.

Thursday

 Aubrey: Thanks.

Sunday

 Aubrey: I cannot wait until this wedding is over.

 Brody: Anything I can do to help?

 Aubrey: No, but thanks.

Chapter Ten

Aubrey

I fall into seat 3B on my flight to Key West. I barely made it in time to go through security, use the bathroom, and find the gate before it was time to board. I misjudged what it would be like driving through downtown Gainesville on a Monday morning to get to the airport and got stuck in bumper-to-bumper traffic. If it hadn't been Summer's birthday on Saturday and we had plans to go out for dinner and drinks, I would have opted to spend the weekend in Orlando and fly out with Brody.

Thankfully, there was no line at security, so I was able to get through relatively fast. I'm not sure what I would have done if I'd missed my flight. Probably get in my car and drive to Key West, like I'd originally planned. Thankfully, I didn't have to cross that bridge.

As much as I protested when Brody bought me first class tickets, I'm secretly thrilled about it because the seats are so much nicer and wider than economy and there are only two seats per row.

I push my carry-on bag under the seat in front of me and buckle myself in. The aisle seat is still empty, and I wonder if anyone's going to sit there. How much luckier could I get? First class and no one else in my row? A flight attendant comes down the aisle asking if anyone would like a complimentary beverage while the rest of the plane boards. I opt for a glass of wine. When in Rome and all that jazz. Brody has definitely spoiled me. I don't know how I'm going to go back to flying economy after this.

This is already far better than driving for eight hours. Even if I have a connection in Charlotte. Yes, that's right, I go from Gainesville to Charlotte to Key West.

How does that make sense?

I take a sip of my wine. Here's to hoping the next week is smooth sailing. I'm ready for this wedding to be over and done with. All the late-night FaceTimes and constant text messages from my mother or sister have taken a toll on me. Not that I expect to relax much on this trip because of all the preplanned group activities. Which means I'll be spending all my time with Clara and her friends. And my mother.

"Hello," a deep voice to my right says. I turn and smile at the guy in jeans and a red polo sitting down next to me. He grins back at me, running a hand through his curly blond hair.

"Hi," I say, taking a sip of my wine. I reach into the seat back pocket and grab my phone so I can set it to Airplane Mode. I unlock it and see I have a message from Brody.

Brody: See you soon. Meet you at baggage claim. A car's going to pick us up.

I type a quick response telling him I've boarded my first flight and turn my phone to Airplane Mode before returning it to the seat back pocket.

"Work or vacation?" the guy asks.

I sigh quietly. I hope he doesn't plan to talk to me the whole time because I was hoping to read a book. I love to read but between my job and this wedding, I haven't had time to.

"My sister's wedding. What about you?"

"Vacation." He blows out a breath. "A much-needed vacation."

I'm saved from having to think of a reply by the pilot coming over the loudspeaker to tell us that they're closing the doors and we're first in line to take off. A flight attendant steps into the aisle and gives the safety demo as we taxi down the runway.

Within twenty minutes we're airborne. I pull out the book I packed for the trip. I'm excited to dive into the new fantasy novel by my favorite author. I don't even get through the first chapter before my seatmate is talking to me again.

"You a fan?" the guy asks, and at first, I think he's asking about my book until I notice he's eyeing my Storm shirt.

"You could say that," I answer, going back to my book and hoping he gets the hint that I don't want to talk.

"Me too. Horrible way their season ended with Thompson missing that goal."

The hairs on the back of my neck stand up, and I glance up at him. "Come again?"

I know the team lost in the first round in a heated series, but Brody didn't tell me the details. I didn't get to watch any of the games except the first one. The first round of the playoffs fell right at the end of the semester when I was spending all day and night dealing with office hours, final papers, and exams. Now, the comments from his teammates at the beach make a little more sense.

Shit.

Why didn't he say anything?

But also, how did I miss that?

Because I've been a bad friend. I avoided him for months after the kiss with his teammate.

"Yeah, it was game five, and the Storm were down by one with seconds to go of the game. Thompson got the puck. Had a clear shot of the net. He missed. Bounced off the post," the guy says with a grimace.

Before I can respond the flight attendants come around with drinks and snacks. Shortly after my seatmate falls asleep, and I'm left to read in peace. Unfortunately, that's where my luck runs out. The Charlotte airport is busy, and we sit on the tarmac for thirty minutes waiting for a gate. By the time the plane's doors open, my hour-long layover has turned into a few minutes. Thank goodness the flight attendants came around and made sure those with connecting flights got off first.

I make my way out to the concourse and sprint toward the gate for my flight, which appears to be almost done boarding. I let out a breath when I'm buckled into my seat. At least I made it. And this time, I do get lucky, and the seat next to me remains empty. I hope that my luck holds out and somehow my luggage makes it too.

Although I highly doubt it.

My stomach rolls at the thought of my luggage being lost. I'm sure there are places in Key West to get clothes. The issue is there are quite a few events that I need more than a pair of shorts and a T-shirt for. I take a few deep breaths. There's nothing I can do right now. At least I packed a change of clothes and my necessary toiletries in my carry-on. I shove my bag under the seat in front of me, after pulling out my book, and buckle my seatbelt.

The flight attendant goes over the emergency procedures, and before I know it, we're in the air headed toward Key West. Leaning back in my seat, I close my eyes, and I don't open them until the pilot announces our arrival into EYW, the Key West airport. I stare longingly at my book—so much for reading on the flight—but apparently, I needed the sleep. I grab my phone and switch it off Airplane Mode.

Brody: Landed.

I type a quick response telling him that I landed too but there's a chance my luggage didn't make it since my flight was delayed into Charlotte. I don't have time to see if he responds as everyone around me begins getting to their feet.

Once out in the terminal, I stop to use the bathroom and refill my water bottle before following the signs to the luggage carousels.

I spot Brody leaning against the wall, a suitcase at his feet and a leather duffel bag slung over his shoulder. I take him in as I approach—his Miami Marlins hat pulled low, black shorts that show off his muscular legs paired with a hunter-green T-shirt. Black sneakers on his feet.

My best friend is hot.

I've always known that, but lately I've been noticing it even more. Like I used to when we were in high school or when he first started playing hockey. Maybe it's because we're fake dating and I've been spending more time with him. Or maybe it's because this wedding is a reminder that I haven't been in a relationship for way too long. I shove all those thoughts down as I thread my way through the crowds toward him.

Here's to hoping that after this week we're still friends.

Chapter Eleven

Brody

The sweat is pouring down my back, and I haven't even stepped outside yet. I don't know if it's from the heat or because there are so many people around. I'm starting to regret agreeing to this arrangement until I see the beautiful woman coming toward me. And I remember why I agreed to this.

She's dressed in a simple pair of denim shorts and a faded Orlando Storm shirt, her brown hair thrown into a messy bun. Her gaze darts around before landing on me. Her lips tip up into a grin when we make eye contact, and I can't help but smile too.

"Hey," Aubrey says as she stops in front of me.

I push off the wall and pull her into a hug. I'm not sure why I feel the need to hug her, but I do, and I don't regret the decision. She's stiff at first, but after a couple of seconds, she relaxes into me and hugs me back.

"Hey," I whisper into her hair.

"I don't think my luggage made it," she says with a frown as she moves out of my arms. "My flight from Gainesville sat on the tarmac in Charlotte for so long I barely made it. I doubt my luggage did. And now I don't know what I'm going to do for clothes. It's not like I can wear this all week." Her voice pitches up at the end, panic seeping in.

"Want to wait and see just in case?" I ask, gesturing toward the carousel that shows her flight number on the board above it.

"Yeah, okay."

Eventually, luggage from the flight starts appearing, but as predicted, hers doesn't show up. She fills out a missing baggage form, and the employee tells her they'll be in contact when they locate it but that it's likely still in Charlotte.

"You okay?" I ask once that's taken care of, even though I know she's not based on how much she was biting her lip and fiddling with her hair the entire time.

Aubrey readjusts her bun for the umpteenth time. "No, Brody. What happens if they don't find my luggage?"

"We'll figure it out. I'm sure there's places to buy clothes here," I say, laying a hand on her arm and turning her to face me.

"It's not just needing clothes. It's needing clothes my mother would approve of," she says, her eyes watering. "I'd never hear the end of it." She shakes her head, reaching up to swipe away the unshed tears.

"Hey. It's okay." I pull her into me and wrap my arms around her. "We'll figure it out. I promise. Let's go outside and find our car. Check in and have some dinner. If you don't hear from the airline by the morning, we'll go shopping."

Aubrey nods against my chest. I hold her for a few seconds longer before reluctantly letting her go. She gives me a small grin as she readjusts her bag on her shoulder. I grab my bags, and we head outside to the car I hired.

"Mr. Thompson. It's a pleasure, sir," the driver says when I greet him and confirm we're at the correct car. "Al, at your service. Can I help you with your bags?" he asks, but he's already lifting my suitcase into the trunk. Once everything is loaded, Aubrey and I climb into the backseat of the sedan and buckle our seatbelts.

"It was a terrible loss," Al says, glancing at me in the rearview mirror as we head toward the hotel.

I pull on the bill of my cap and try to smile. Of course I got a driver who is a hockey fan. What are the chances?

"You'll bounce back," he continues, focusing back on the road. "I've been a fan for a very long time. I have faith that the Storm will win the Cup this upcoming season. Don't listen to those naysayer commentators. You've still got many years ahead of you."

I chuckle. At least he's a loyal fan. I feel Aubrey's eyes on me, but I don't look at her. "Thanks, Al. I appreciate fans like you who stick with us through the highs and lows."

"Of course. I'm no fair-weather fan."

"You okay?" Aubrey whispers, leaning closer to me.

"Fine," I mumble, turning to stare out the window.

The rest of the short drive passes quickly with Al pointing out different places we should check out while we're in Key West. After I pose for a selfie and sign the Storm hat he pulled out of his glove box, he shakes my hand, and we go inside the hotel.

"Does that ever get old?" Aubrey asks as we make our way to the check-in counter where she greets the clerk and gives him her driver's license. I'm not sure how to answer her question, so I shrug when she turns to look at me.

I appreciate the fans because that's who we play for, but it does get old. Sometimes I wish I could go back to the days when I was a no name rookie instead of one of the top scorers in the league who *everyone* recognizes. What I wouldn't give to just be normal Brody Thompson for one day instead of Brody Thompson, top five in points in the league last season *and* the guy who lost his team the chance at the Cup.

Aubrey studies me, perhaps waiting for me to answer her question, but we're interrupted by the clerk who says, "I've got your reservation. Two adults for six nights. You're with the Fairchild/Daniels wedding."

"Yes, that's correct."

"Good news, you got upgraded to a suite," he says, studying his computer screen.

"Oh?"

"We have you in a one-bedroom king bed suite," he says, reading from his screen as he keys our keycards.

"There's been a mistake. We should have a room with two queen beds. Do you have any regular rooms with *two* beds?" Aubrey asks, frowning at the clerk.

He glances between us but doesn't say anything. Instead, he clicks some keys on his computer. "I'm sorry Dr. Fairchild, that's the only room we have available. There's also a note with your reservation that this was done at the request of the"—he mumbles something under his breath before continuing—"the bride."

"Clara." Aubrey huffs under her breath. "Okay, thank you."

The clerk gives us our keys and directs us to the elevators that we need to take to get to our suite.

When we're on the elevator, Aubrey turns to me. "What are we going to do?"

"It's fine. We'll figure it out." I lean against the wall, watching the numbers light up as we slowly ascend.

We finally arrive on the sixth floor, and the door opens. I gesture for Aubrey to go first and follow her down the hall.

At the door she pulls out the keycard and taps it on the lock. With a click the door unlocks and we walk in. Just inside the doorway is a small kitchen area. I'm impressed that we have a full-sized fridge, a two-burner stovetop, a microwave, and even a dishwasher. Not that we'll have need for any of them, but I suppose it's nice in case we end up with leftovers we need to reheat. We walk through the kitchen and into a small sitting room with your typical stiff looking hotel couch, two side chairs, a coffee table and a TV on a table on the far wall.

Aubrey sets her bag on the couch and walks into the bedroom.

"Maybe the couch is a pullout," she says when I step in behind her.

I highly doubt it, but I don't say that. Instead, my gaze sweeps around the decently sized bedroom. There's another TV in here, mounted on the wall across from the bed. A nightstand on each side of the bed and a dresser against the wall near the doorway. Off to the right are two doors—one is probably the closet and the other I assume is the bathroom.

"Aubrey, we can share. We're adults. We've been friends for how many years? It's not like we're strangers. It'll be fine."

"Brody," she protests. "I'm going to see if the couch is a pullout bed." She steps around me and walks out the door.

I run a hand through my hair. Why is she so stubborn? We've been friends since high school. Surely we can share a bed for a week.

Walking out into the living room I find her sitting on the couch with her head in her hands, all the cushions on the ground.

"You okay?" I ask, dropping down next to her.

"No," she mumbles through her hands. "It's not a pullout."

"Come on." I place my hand on her arm. "Let's get something to eat and then we'll figure out the sleeping situation. I'll sleep on the couch if you really don't want to share the bed. It'll be fine, I promise."

Her lips quirk up. "You'll sleep on the couch? I don't think you'll fit."

"We'll figure it out," I repeat, standing up. "Let's go eat, there's a restaurant downstairs. Unless you want to shower first."

"Food first, please," she says, and at that moment, her stomach lets out a rumble. I bite my lip to stifle a laugh and walk toward the door. Aubrey continues, "It's not like I have any clean clothes to change into." I come to a halt and turn back to her.

"Say that again?" I ask, my eyebrows raised.

"It's not like I have any clean clothes to change into. I mean, I have a change of . . ." She pauses, her face turning pink, before she continues. "Undergarments and a shirt and shorts for tomorrow. But otherwise, I'm out of clothes."

Her statement has me picturing her underwear and bra and wondering what she wears. If she wears thongs or simple cotton ones. If her bras are lacey or not. Why am I picturing Aubrey in her underwear? It's not like I'll ever get to see them. We might be dating, but it's fake. So, it doesn't matter what she wears because I won't get to see them. And I have no business thinking about them.

I clear my throat, running a hand through my hair. "Oh-kay, well, let's go eat." I turn back to the door, willing the conversation to change so I don't have to be tortured by thoughts I definitely should not be thinking.

"I might need to borrow a shirt to sleep in," Aubrey continues, coming up behind me.

My eyes widen as I picture her in one of my shirts and nothing else. My dick stirs at that image, and I hold back a groan. I shift from one foot to the other, subtly adjusting myself, willing my dick to calm down. "I'm sure I have something you can borrow."

I open the door and walk out, forcing myself to think about plays from last season instead of the conversation we just had. Maybe it is a good idea for me to sleep on the couch. Or the floor. Anywhere but in the same bed as Aubrey. Because this is starting to feel like a slippery slope. The last thing I want to do is ruin our friendship by doing something she doesn't want. Like accidentally grabbing a boob in my sleep. And now I'm thinking about Aubrey's boobs and what they feel like.

Shit.

Fuck.

Must stop.

I take a few deep breaths, pushing all the thoughts I shouldn't be having out of my head.

We make our way to the elevator and back to the lobby where we follow the signs to the restaurant. The hostess seats us at one of the high-top tables in the corner of the bar. I'm surprised at how empty it is for being six thirty. I suppose most people choose to eat out downtown, or have already eaten.

The waitress approaches our table a few minutes after we've been seated. "Hello. I'll be your waitress tonight. What can I get you two to drink?" she asks. Her eyes widen when I meet her gaze. "Holy shit." She clamps a hand over her mouth, glancing around. I bite back a laugh. "I'm sorry," she mumbles, removing her hand. "You look like my favorite hockey player—Brody Thompson. He plays for the Orlando Storm. I'm sure you get that a lot."

I debate telling her I am who she thinks I am but decide against it. I don't really feel like hearing about our loss again or how we'll do much better next year.

"Thank you. I'll have a glass of water, and a rocks pour of your best bourbon, please." I'm going to need it to get through tonight's discussion of who's sleeping where and Aubrey walking around our hotel room in one of my shirts. The waitress nods and turns to Aubrey.

"I'll have a glass of water and a riesling."

"I'll put that right in for you and let you look over the menu," the waitress says.

"Why'd you do that? Not tell her you are who she thought you were," Aubrey asks once we're alone.

I glance up at her and shrug before going back to the menu. "Because for once I'd like to have a nice quiet dinner with my girlfriend without someone asking me for my autograph or a photo. I want to be just another customer . . ." Instead of Brody Thompson, the guy who cost the Storm their chance in the playoffs.

"There's no one around. You don't have to call me that."

I nod toward the other patrons in the bar area. "I don't know all the people in your sister's wedding. Maybe one of them is here. Don't want the wrong person to hear something and it gets back to Clara, or worse, your mom. We wouldn't want that, would we, *girlfriend?*" I stare at her until she rolls her eyes at me and, with a shake of her head, goes back to her menu.

If I'm being honest with myself, I like calling her my girlfriend. I haven't had the desire to call anyone that in years, but suddenly, saying the word, even if it started out in jest, makes me feel something. Something I probably shouldn't be feeling for my best friend.

The waitress comes back with our drinks and takes our dinner order before disappearing into the back again. We chat about life, and Aubrey tells me about some research she's doing since she isn't teaching this semester. I only understand about half of what she's talking about but from what I do understand, it sounds impressive.

When the check comes, I insist on paying even though Aubrey tells me to charge it to the room. I grab an extra cocktail napkin and scribble my name and my number—ninety—on it and leave it for the waitress along with a generous tip. As I stare at the napkin, I realize this could be one of the last times I sign my number. I rub a hand over my chest, trying to ease the ache that's taken up residence there.

"You okay?" Aubrey asks, putting her hand on my shoulder.

"Fine. Fine." I push out of my chair and follow her out of the restaurant. We barely make it to the lobby before we're greeted by her sister pushing a baby carriage.

"Aubs," Brielle says. "Hey, Brody." She smiles at me.

"Hi, Brielle."

"Hey, Bri." Aubrey hugs her sister and peeks into the carriage to say hi to her niece before turning and hugging Brielle's husband.

He glances over at me, and I see the moment he registers who I am. Shit, this is going to be a long week if all the wedding guests are like this. So much for flying under the radar.

"Oh," Aubrey says, stepping back to my side. "Devon, this is Brody, my boyfriend."

I put out my hand to shake Devon's hand, and he stares at it for a beat before taking it. "Shit. I'm a huge fan. I never thought I'd get to meet *the* Brody Thompson. Nice to meet you."

"Nice to meet you, too."

"Wait, you're a hockey fan?" Aubrey asks Devon. "How have I never known that before?"

He shrugs.

"You'll have to get them tickets to a game, Brod," Aubrey says, nudging me with her shoulder. I smile weakly and nod. I'm sure that even if I'm not playing for the Storm next season, Caleb or Cole would be happy to get me tickets.

"Oh, not me. Just him," Brielle says, holding up her hands and shaking her head. "I don't know the first thing about hockey."

We all laugh. The baby starts fussing, and Brielle reaches down to soothe her.

"It's past Anabelle's bedtime, so we should go. We'll see you in the morning," Brielle says.

She pulls Aubrey into a hug and says something quietly to her. I can't make it out, but I have a feeling it has something to do with me because she glances my way a couple of times. They finally head toward the elevators on the north end of the hotel, and we make our way in the opposite direction.

Aubrey yawns as we get on the elevator.

"Ready for bed?" I ask, even though it's only a little after eight.

"Yeah."

"What'd your sister say to you?"

She looks over at me, crossing her arms. "She said we need to make it more believable that we're dating."

I rear back. "What? You told her?"

"No, of course not." The elevator doors open, and we step off on our floor. "She's right, you know. We weren't really acting like we're dating. If Bri noticed in the five minutes we spent with her, everyone else will for sure pick up on it." She pulls out her room key and opens the door to our suite.

"Sorry," I mumble, stepping into the room and closing the door behind me.

"It's not your fault." She spins around to face me, and now we're standing so close. Close enough for me to see the small scar above her right eyebrow that she got in high school when she fell off her bike. Faded now, but I know where to look for it.

She says it's not my fault, but that doesn't stop me from blaming myself. Add it to the list of other things I've screwed up recently.

One thing I refuse to mess up is our friendship, which is why I take a deep breath and step around her, needing to put distance between us.

Chapter Twelve

Aubrey

Bri's words echo in my head. *"I find it hard to believe you and Brody are finally dating because that would mean you took your head out of the sky and admitted you have feelings for him. But if that's the story you're going with, you're going to have to work a little harder to make it look believable. Because if Mom gets a whiff that this isn't real, you'll never hear the end of it."*

I hate that she's right. I guess I assumed that since Brody's teammates and their partners took us at our word, everyone else would. Add it to the list of things I'm stressing about.

It's fine.

It's fine.

Everything is fine.

No. It's not. But it needs to be.

"You okay?" Brody's voice pulls me from my thoughts.

"Yeah. Tired. It's been a long day. I think I'm going to go shower." It's not the complete truth, but it's also not a total lie. I am tired. It has been a long day.

Taking a deep breath, I pick up my carry-on bag from the couch and bring it into the bedroom. During dinner, I'd forgotten about my no suitcase predicament, but now I'm reminded of it as I pull out the one shirt and pair of shorts I have with me and hang them in the closet. I'm going to be so screwed if my suitcase doesn't show up.

"Here," Brody says as he hands me a pair of black athletic shorts and a well-worn Storm shirt over my shoulder.

"Thanks," I say, spinning to face him. "I hope my luggage comes tomorrow because I don't know what I'll do if it doesn't. I can't exactly wear shorts and a T-shirt to every event this week. Mother will kill me. I could ask Bri if I can borrow something, but we're not exactly the same size. There's got to be a store nearby or on one of the other islands where I can find some outfits, and I could—"

"Aubrey," Brody says. "We'll figure it out. Don't worry about it tonight. There's nothing we can do right now."

I take a deep breath, hugging the clothes he handed me to my chest. "Okay. I'm gonna go shower now."

Fifteen minutes later I feel like a new person. What is it about a shower after a day of travel that makes you feel like that? Dressed in Brody's shirt and shorts that I had to fold a bunch of times so they didn't fall down, that I absolutely did not spend a few seconds sniffing because they smell like him, I walk out to find him on the couch watching television.

"Your turn."

Brody glances over at me, and I swear I see something in his expression akin to lust. But that's not possible. Is it?

We've been friends since high school, since Brody made it perfectly clear to me that that's all he wanted from me. Besides, his focus has always been on hockey, on his career, and mine was on getting my PhD and is now on my career. Plus, I'm moving to Hawaii, so the point is moot.

There can't be an us.

A tiny voice in the back of my head pipes up and says that maybe the reason I've never been happy with any other guy is because they weren't Brody. I give myself a mental shake. This is not the time or the place to be thinking about that. I need to focus on one thing and one thing only—surviving this week and making my fake relationship with Brody believable. Okay, so that's two things. And, okay, a third thing, not ruin our friendship.

"Okay." He stands and hands me the remote before picking up his suitcase and going into the bedroom.

I pull up the guide and flip through what's on, smiling when I come across Seinfeld. Finally, something is going right for me on this trip. Settling back into the couch, I focus my attention on the television and try not to think about the fact that Brody is in the next room. Showering. Naked. Groaning, I close my eyes, trying to shut out the image, but that only makes it clearer.

Brody naked.

Brody hovering over me, naked in bed.

I groan again. What the hell is wrong with me? Lusting after my best friend.

"You okay?"

"Shit." I jump, opening my eyes to see him standing next to me, his brown hair still wet, dressed in a different faded Orlando Storm shirt—how many Storm shirts does he have?—and a pair of gray sweatpants. There's a crooked grin on his face like he somehow read my mind and knows what I was thinking about.

"Fine. Fine," I mumble, turning my focus back to the television.

The couch dips next to me as he sits down. "Oh, I love this episode."

I turn my attention from the screen to the man sitting next to me. "You do?" I raise an eyebrow.

"Yeah. I binged the entire series over the All-Star break."

Well, color me shocked.

"This is one of my favorite episodes," I say.

We watch in silence for a while. When the credits come on, I hand the remote over to Brody and stand. "I'm exhausted. I'm going to head to bed."

I make my way into the bathroom and brush my teeth. When I come out, he's sitting on the end of the bed. I climb in and curl up under the covers, while he takes his turn.

"I'm going to call down to the front desk and see if they can send up an extra blanket," he says a few minutes later.

I open my eyes. He's standing at the foot of the bed, a pillow in his hands. He's changed into a pair of gray athletic shorts much like the ones he gave me that are now discarded on the other side of the bed. I contemplated keeping them on to sleep in but decided against it. I figured I'll be under the covers the whole night, so it's not like he'll see my underwear. That and his shirt is practically a dress on me.

I sigh. I can't make him sleep on the couch. I just can't. Between it not being comfortable and it being too short for him, he'll be miserable.

He's here pretending to be my fake boyfriend to help me out. He's sacrificing his precious time off for me. The least I can do is let him sleep in the bed. Besides, it's king-size. There's plenty of room for both of us to have our own space and not be on top of each other.

"Come on." I reach over and pull back the edge of the comforter, nodding toward the side closest to him.

"Aubrey." Brody stares at me, not moving.

"Brody, get in. There's plenty of room, and like you said, we're adults. We can share a bed."

He stares at me, running a hand through his hair, and for a minute I think he's going to argue and insist on sleeping on the couch. But he doesn't. He sets his pillow down and climbs into bed, letting out a moan as he sinks into the mattress. I'd be lying if I said the sound of him moaning didn't send a shiver down my spine.

"Man, this bed is comfortable. That or I'm old and really exhausted from all the travel."

"It sure is. If you're old, then that makes me old too."

Brody laughs, a deep rumble that goes right to my core. What the fuck is wrong with me? I take a deep breath, which is a big mistake because now my senses are flooded with the smell of pine and cedar. I close my eyes and roll over so my back is to Brody's side of the bed.

He shifts around a little before he whispers, "Good night, Aubrey."

Chapter Thirteen

Brody

My eyes snap open, and I'm slightly confused to feel a leg over mine and a hand on my arm until I remember that I'm in Key West.

With Aubrey.

Pretending to be her fake boyfriend. And we're sharing a bed. Because someone—her mom most likely, regardless of what the clerk said—decided to upgrade us to a suite with one bed. The clock shows it's a little after six. I groan silently, wishing I'd been able to sleep in longer.

I watch her sleep for a minute, wishing I could lean over and kiss her awake. Last night was only the first night and the lines are already beginning to blur. I take a deep breath and gently extract myself. Aubrey sighs in her sleep and rolls closer. I say a silent prayer that she doesn't wake up. Just because I'm awake this early doesn't mean she needs to be too.

When it's clear that she's still sound asleep, I get out of bed and dress in gym clothes. I remember seeing signs for a fitness center when we were checking in. A run sounds like just what I need, a distraction from my thoughts about my best friend. Thoughts I have no business thinking.

Dressed, I make my way quietly out of the room and head for the elevators. The lobby is quiet, and the fitness center is empty. It's about the size of our suite, maybe smaller. A treadmill sits in front of the one small window, a stationary bike next to it in the corner, and the other wall is taken up by some random machines, stands of free weights, and a bench. I take a few minutes to stretch before hopping on the treadmill, shoving my headphones in, and starting my favorite playlist. A few miles should help to burn off some of this weird energy I woke up with.

An hour and a half later, I'm stepping off the elevator on our floor. It wasn't the best workout, but at least it was something. After a five-mile run, I used the free weights to do an upper body workout and finished up with more stretching. I even located a foam roller and spent some time foam rolling my legs. Anything to keep me occupied and away from where Aubrey is sleeping so I don't do something rash. She's made it perfectly clear that she only wants to be friends. Using my key card, I let myself back into the room.

"Hey," Aubrey greets me with a smile, her legs tucked up under her on the couch, wearing my shirt—that she looks so fucking good in—a cup of coffee in her hands.

"Morning."

"There's coffee over there," she says, pointing at the room service cart against the wall near the kitchen. "I got some breakfast too. I know we're having brunch with everyone but it's not until eleven. I don't know about you, but I'll be starving by then."

"Good idea. I'm going to go shower first." I hook a thumb toward the bathroom.

"Okay." Aubrey takes a sip from her coffee mug.

Ten minutes later, I'm showered and dressed in a pair of gray sweatpants and a faded Marlins shirt. As I'm hanging up my towel, I hear Aubrey's voice in the other room. At first, I think she's talking to me but then I realize she must be on the phone.

"Okay. Thank you," she says, hanging up as I make my way out of the bedroom. Suddenly starving, I walk over to the room service cart to pour myself a cup of coffee and check out the food options.

"That was the front desk. The airline found my bag and dropped it off a few hours ago. It's downstairs. Someone is bringing it up," Aubrey pipes up.

"That's great." I say serving myself a couple of hard-boiled eggs and some mixed fruit.

"I wasn't sure what you wanted," she says as I walk over to her with my plate and coffee. "And I wasn't sure when you'd be back."

"This is great, Aubrey." I take a seat next to her. "Did you sleep okay?"

"Yeah, I did. Your phone went off a couple of times while you were in the shower."

"Thanks. Probably the guys," I say, taking a sip of coffee and letting out a contented sigh as the first drop of caffeine hits my blood stream.

"How are we going to convince my family we're actually dating?"

Well, alrighty then. I knew this conversation would come up, but I didn't expect it to be right now. I take a bite of melon, chewing and swallowing before answering. "What do you think we should do?"

Aubrey takes a deep breath but doesn't say anything. I can see the wheels turning in her head, going over and over whatever she's working up the courage to say. She's chewing on her bottom lip and, fuck me, I want to reach over and pluck it from between her teeth, be the one to chew on it.

What the hell is wrong with me? *She wouldn't appreciate you doing that*, I remind myself. *You kissed her on New Year's Eve, and she ran. Clearly, you're not who she wants.*

I watch her studying the pattern on the couch like it'll solve all her problems, giving her another moment to collect her thoughts before she speaks. If there's one thing I've learned over the years, it's to not rush her. So I wait, silently eating my breakfast.

She rolls her shoulders and looks up at me. "We should hold hands."

That's it? We hug all the time, so why was it so hard for her to suggest we hold hands? "Okay. What else?"

"I don't know." She blows out a breath, her shoulders sagging. "No one's going to believe us. I'm never going to hear the end of it from my mother . . ."

"Hey. Hey," I say, setting my plate down and reaching for her hand. "What's really going on?"

"It's been nonstop from my mother since Clara got engaged about how I'm still not married and I'm the oldest. That's all she seems to care about—us getting married and having kids. I have a PhD for fuck's sake, but the only three letters she cares about is Mrs."

"I'm sorry," I whisper, tugging her closer to me and wrapping my arms around her.

Before I can say anything else, there's a knock at the door. Aubrey pulls out of my arms and goes over to answer. A minute later she comes back into view, pulling her suitcase behind her.

"I should go hang my clothes up," she mumbles, refusing to meet my eyes. "Everything is probably super wrinkled now. Thank goodness I packed my steamer."

I stay silent watching her. I know what she's doing, she's avoiding the conversation. I hate that she does this. But for now, I'll let her. Because if I push too hard, she'll shut down on me. I nod and finish my breakfast in silence, turning over in my head what she told me about her mom. It's nothing new. Why does it bother her so much now? Maybe because she's about to watch her *baby* sister get married?

I set the empty plate on the coffee table and go in search of my phone. I unlock it and see there are quite a few text messages in the group chat.

Holt: B, you alive?

Wes: He's probably busy with Aubrey. Getting busy. *winking emoji*

Caleb: Don't be crude.

Wes: Just pointing out the obvious.

I shake my head at their ridiculousness, a smirk playing on my lips. I type out a quick response.

Me: Yes, I'm alive. We have brunch in a few hours. Ask me later if I'm still alive.

Wes: Good luck, Brod.

Hunter: I'm sure it'll be fine.

Caleb: Have fun.

Before I can respond, Aubrey calls me from the other room. "Brod, can you come in here?"

I find her in the bathroom with a steamer in her hand, multiple outfits and jumpsuit things hanging from the shower rod. Yep, Aubrey is stressed. This is what stressed Aubrey does—organizes or cleans. Or in this case, steams all her clothes.

"Do you need me to steam anything for you?" she asks, waving the steamer in the air.

I run a hand through my hair, mentally going through my clothes. "I don't think so. But thanks." What can I do to make her feel better, maybe not about what her mother has said to her, but about our fake relationship?

She unplugs the steamer and sets it on the counter. "I was thinking," she says, spinning back around to face me.

"I think we should practice kissing." The words are out of my mouth before I can stop them. I might regret saying this, given what happened the last time we kissed, but I can't help myself.

Chapter Fourteen

Aubrey

"I think we should practice kissing."

My mouth falls open, and my brain short circuits at his words. "Wh-what?" I finally sputter, searching his face for hints that he's joking or just saying something to get a reaction out of me. But there's none. Because of course there isn't. Brody doesn't say anything he doesn't mean.

"I think we should practice kissing," he repeats, crossing his arms and leaning against the doorframe of the bathroom.

I blink at him a couple of times, sucking in deep breaths. His signature scent floods my senses.

"Why?" I rasp out.

"We're going to have to kiss at some point in front of your family. If it's awkward, they'll know something is up. Maybe not all of them, but some of them will. Brielle already saw through us yesterday. If you want this fake relationship to be believable, we need to practice."

I consider his explanation for a moment. He's got a valid point. One I can't argue with. Not that I want to at this point. The last thing I need is for Clara or, heaven forbid, my mother to figure out the truth. I'd never hear the end of it.

"Fine. But not in here."

Brody pushes off the doorframe and walks out into the bedroom. "Where do you prefer?"

My palms start sweating as I follow him.

Am I really about to finally kiss my best friend?

He sits on the edge of the bed and gestures for me to come closer. I walk over but stand just out of reach, shifting from foot to foot. I feel like I'm standing on the edge of a cliff. One from which I can't see what's below me. Will I hit the ground? Hit water?

"Aubrey. How do you expect me to kiss you if you're that far away?" Brody asks softly as he stands up, reaches over and pulls me closer.

"I'm going to kiss you now. Is that okay?" he whispers, staring down at me, his hands gripping my waist.

I suck in a deep breath.

This is fine.

It's only a kiss.

It's fine.

Everything is fine.

I nod because it's all I can manage.

He leans down and ghosts his lips over mine. A barely there kiss. His lips on mine feel divine. He goes to pull away, but I tug him closer, kissing him harder. Might as well go all in. He kisses me back, and déjà vu washes over me.

"It was you!" I push against his chest, pulling back, and he lets me go. I stumble back a step, staring at him, my chest heaving as realization sinks in. The mystery man I kissed on New Year's wasn't a mystery man at all.

It was him.

It was Brody.

All this time. How did I not realize? Better yet, why didn't he say something?

He tried, the tiny voice in the back of my head reminds me, *but you ran*.

"What was me?" Brody raises his eyebrows, watching me from the edge of the bed, his lips swollen from our kiss.

"New Year's Eve," I whisper.

His mouth opens and closes a couple of times, but no words come out. Finally, he seems to snap out of it and says, "of course it was me.

You—you didn't know?" He crinkles his forehead, a look I can't place washing over his face.

"No. It was dark. All I could make out was the mask. It wasn't yours. How was I supposed to know?" I stare at him, my gaze dancing back and forth over his face.

Brody throws his hands in the air and begins pacing. "I tried to say something, but you ran away. All this time I thought you didn't want me."

I rear back. "Didn't want you? You're the one who didn't want me in high school. I flat out told you I liked you, and you told me we were better off as friends. That hockey kept you too busy to date."

What the hell? Am I in the twilight zone? Is he for real? He wants me? Now? After all these years? After telling me he didn't see me as anything except a friend?

"Aubs," Brody growls, stopping his pacing and stepping closer to me.

I shiver. This is the first time he's called me by my nickname. I don't know why, in all the years we've known each other, he's always insisted on calling me by my full name, but now. Today. He's using my nickname, and it does something to me.

"It would never have worked out then, you had your whole future ahead of you with college and all your dreams. And what did I have? Hockey. I wasn't good enough for you. But I've spent the past I don't know how many years wanting you," he continues. "Trying to be good enough to be worthy of you."

"Why did you never say anything?" I ask, stepping back even more. I can't think with him this close. My back hits the dresser.

I'm so confused.

I've daydreamed about the guy I kissed on New Year's Eve, about kissing him again, more times than I'd like to admit. But I never thought I'd be able to. And yet, here we are.

"What was I supposed to say? You were off at college, then in grad school. Then you were pursuing your career. Doing amazing things. What do I have to offer you? I'm *just* a dumb hockey player." His voice hitches at the last statement as he steps closer to me.

"You're not *just* a dumb hockey player," I say, squaring my shoulders and meeting his eyes. "I've never thought of you that way. You know that's not how I see you. What do you mean you aren't worthy of me?"

Brody's shoulders drop and he stares at the floor. "Your parents thought of me that way. Your mother still thinks of me that way."

My breath catches in my chest, and I can't believe the words I'm hearing. "What do you mean?"

He peels his gaze from the carpet, taking a deep breath before saying, "I heard your parents talking about me. About us. One night when I was over at your house. We were outside looking at the stars, and I went inside. I don't remember what for, but I overheard them in the living room talking about how I wasn't good enough for you. And then trying to figure out how to keep me away from you so I didn't ruin you."

"Ruin me?" I furrow my brows at him, anger building up at my parents. How could they? First of all, how could they talk about a high schooler like that, but second, how could they think that Brody wasn't good enough for me. If anything, I'm not good enough for him.

"I don't know. That's when I started making a big deal about how we were only friends. Threw myself even more into hockey. I hoped that maybe your parents would believe me and I could at least stay in your life as your friend."

My heart breaks hearing him tell me these things. Knowing that we missed out because of my parents and their need for . . . who the hell knows. Control? A good image? Whatever it was, it wasn't worth it.

"I got my bachelor's degree last year," Brody says, so quietly I almost don't hear him.

My jaw hits the floor. "You what?"

"I've been taking classes during the off-season. It took me forever, but I finally finished my business degree last summer," he admits, his face turning pink. Is he embarrassed?

"That's amazing, Brody. Why didn't you tell me?"

He stares at me blinking rapidly before saying, "I don't know." He pauses glancing around the room. "I thought maybe if I had a college degree, your parents would approve of me." He hesitates for a second before adding, "And I could prove to my father that I'm not a total idiot."

"I'm proud of you, Brod." I lay my hand on his arm, not sure what I'm doing but knowing that I need to touch him. "But I hope you didn't get your degree to prove a point. Or because you thought it would make you worthy of me."

He sighs, staring down at my hand. "It might have started out that way, but the further I got into it, the more I realized that I was doing it for me. That I enjoyed the classes. Even if it never made me worthy of you."

"Fuck that," I spit out. "I don't give a shit what my mother or anyone else thinks about whether you're worthy of me. That's such bullshit."

Brody looks up at me, his mouth falling open. I don't think he's ever heard me curse that much in all our years as friends, especially about my family. I suck in a deep breath, locking eyes with him, hoping that he can read the sincerity in my face and that he really hears what I'm about to say.

"Brody, you were always good enough for me. I have never cared that you didn't go to college. Heck, it wouldn't have mattered to me if you didn't make it to the NHL. But I'm so fucking proud of you. I hope you know that. You didn't have to get your degree. Hell, you'll never have to work a day in your life when you retire so there's no reason to. But you did. I can't even imagine how much dedication that took." I shake my head.

His lips quirk up in a grin, but he doesn't make a move toward me.

"Brody," I rasp out. I want to kiss him again. Taste his lips.

"Aubrey?" He steps closer, boxing me in, one hand gripping my hip and the other propped against the top of the dresser. He leans in, and I close my eyes, breathing him in. "I'm going to kiss you again. And not because we need to practice kissing. Okay?" He ghosts his lips along my jaw, and I all but whimper. He pulls back, and I open my eyes, staring up at my best friend, who's watching me like he wants to devour me.

"Okay?" he repeats, his gaze raking over my face, looking for what, I'm not sure.

"Yes. Please. Brod."

That's all it takes for him to crash his lips down on mine. I let out a whimper as his tongue darts out, seeking entrance. I open, letting him in. We get lost in each other for who knows how long until a knocking begins on the door. With a groan, Brody pulls back.

"Aubrey Elizabeth. Open up. You'd better not still be asleep." My mother's voice comes from the hallway. I roll my eyes.

Brody steps back, and I answer the door, even though I really don't want to. No, I want to keep kissing my best friend. But I can't. Because she'll keep knocking, and I won't hear the end of it if I ignore her.

My mother, Beatrice Rose Fairchild, stands on the other side of the door. Her short brown bob is neatly curled and pinned back. Not a hair out of place. Her knee-length navy-blue dress is free of wrinkles and paired with nude heels. The pearls around her neck match the barely there studs in her ears. She's the picture of a compliant housewife, if this was the nineteen seventies. Except I know better—she's not timid, nor is she a housewife.

No, she runs the family's business, the biggest conglomerate of commercial real estate developers in Florida—heck, I think at this point it's the biggest in the Southeast—although technically, my brother, Thad, is the CEO having taken over the role when my father died. But we all know that she's the true boss. She's cutthroat in and out of the boardroom. I don't remember her always being this way. I remember a time when she was loving and caring. Or so I thought. Now, I don't know what to think, given what Brody told me about my parents. Growing up I always believed they had mine and my siblings best interests at heart, but now I wonder if it was all about image for them.

"Yes, Mother," I say to her, trying to keep the annoyance out of my voice that she felt the need to show up at my hotel door.

"Aubrey. You're not dressed yet." Her eyes sweep down the length of my body before she sighs and glances at her watch tapping a perfectly manicured fingernail on it. "Brunch starts in thirty minutes. It's a good thing I came by to check on you."

"Thirty minutes is plenty of time for me to get dressed," I protest, crossing my arms.

"And do your hair? And put on makeup? Good grief, Aubrey, you have no sense of time management." She huffs with a shake of her hair and a hand on her pearl necklace.

"Did you need something, Mother?"

"To make sure you weren't going to be late. It's important you get there on time. And look presentable. Chet's family will be there. Since you didn't come to the engagement party, you haven't met them yet. You need to make a good first impression." I refrain from rolling my eyes at her, barely. She brushes a hand down her dress, smoothing out the nonexistent wrinkles. "I hope you brought something appropriate. This is not a shorts and T-shirt event." She grimaces like wearing shorts and a T-shirt would be a personal affront to her.

"I did, Mother. Now if you'll excuse me, I have to get dressed."

I move to close the door but not before she has time to say, "Do your hair and makeup. Don't be late, Aubrey. And make sure your *boyfriend* is also presentable."

I don't dignify her with a response, closing the door and collapsing back against it instead. I meet Brody's gaze from across the room, noting the look of disgust on his face, his crossed arms, and his furrowed brows.

He takes two steps toward me. "Is she always like this? I thought she was bad when we were in high school, but that was ten times worse." He visibly blanches.

I clench my jaw nodding.

"For fuck's sake. Is she serious? She really thinks you're going to be late? You've never been late in your life." He studies me intently.

"I was late once. Once." I hold up a finger, emphasizing my point. "And that was because there was an accident on the highway that caused a traffic jam. I left in plenty of time, but I still got to dinner late. That was three years ago. Now she's convinced I'm going to be late if she doesn't remind me or call me to make sure I'm managing my time well."

"What was with the whole 'make sure you wear something appropriate' comment?" he grinds out, his eyes blazing with anger.

"Settle down, tiger." I pat his chest. He growls and pulls me into him, then kisses me softly. I melt into him for a moment before remembering exactly who it is that I'm kissing. "Brody." I pull back. "What are we doing?"

"Practicing kissing."

I laugh, shaking my head at him. It's not a lie, but that was more than us practicing kissing. "Okay. Let's practice more later. We should get ready before we really are late."

Brody nods and steps away from me. It doesn't escape my notice that he adjusts himself as he walks away, and a thrill runs through me that I have that effect on him. Who would have thought? I shake my head and push the thoughts away like I told him we needed to.

Twenty-five minutes later, he pokes his head into the bathroom, where I'm fixing my hair, and catches my eye in the mirror. "Am I dressed okay?" he asks, tugging on the collar of his shirt.

I turn around and take him in. He's wearing a light-blue short-sleeve button-down shirt, a pair of khaki shorts that cling to his thighs, and brown shoes. His hair is messy like he's shoved his hand through it a hundred times, which he probably has. But I like it that way.

"Yes." My voice comes out breathy, and I hope he doesn't notice. "It's fine."

"You're beautiful," he says, and I don't miss the heated look he gives me, his eyes sweeping down my body.

My cheeks heat at his blatant perusal and compliment. I glance down at the sleeveless lavender sundress I chose for brunch. It's super lightweight, a must for the islands, and lands just above my knees. Not my usual style, but I knew it would be Mother approved.

"Thanks. It's new. I got it for this trip. Along with a couple of others," I ramble, waving my hand at the closet. "You look nice yourself. If I didn't say that earlier."

"Thank you. You ready?" Brody asks, shoving his hands in his shorts pockets and watching me from the doorway.

I take one last look at myself in the mirror, satisfied with my hair half pinned up, the minimal makeup I applied, and my dress, and shut off the light.

"Let's go," I say, walking toward the door. He follows behind me, and it's not until we're on the elevator that he speaks.

"I'll be right there with you the entire time."

"Huh?" I ask, glancing up at him.

"You're nervous. You've fixed your hair three times already. That's what you do when you're nervous." He gestures toward my hair.

I blink at him a couple of times, my hands frozen on my hair clip. I didn't even realize I was doing it. I let go of the clip and stare down at the floor, wishing I had something to do with my hands. If only this dress had pockets.

As if he can hear my thoughts, Brody reaches for me and intertwines our fingers. I take a deep breath as the doors open and we step out into the lobby. We follow the signs toward the ballrooms, where brunch is taking place. If I remember correctly, all of Chet's family will be here, plus most of the wedding party, and a small portion of the guests.

We step into the ballroom where there are a bunch of tables set up in the middle covered in light pink tablecloths, each with a bouquet of roses as centerpieces. The chairs are covered in white slipcovers. Yes, that's a thing—I learned about it during this whole wedding process.

Three long tables at the opposite side of the room are covered in food trays, and there's a crowd of people serving themselves. Easels are set up around the edges of the room displaying poster-sized pictures from Clara and Chet's engagement photo shoot. Thankfully, we're not the last family members to arrive. I haven't seen Bri and her family here yet. Although I'm sure my mother would give her a pass for being late because she has a baby.

"Come on. Let's get food." Brody gestures toward the buffet.

"Oh no. Not yet," I say with a shake of my head.

"Why not? There are people eating." He points to a group of people seated in the middle of the room.

"They're not family," I mumble, recognizing some of the guests as Clara's friends and their husbands. "Mother expects the family to eat last. Be the perfect hosts."

Brody scoffs at me. "Seriously?"

Before I can answer, one of the waiters carrying a tray of champagne walks over to us, and I grab a glass, gulping it down quickly before setting it on one of the tables. Can't have my mother seeing me with a glass of champagne. Brody asks about coffee. The waiter points to a drink station in the corner.

"Ah, there you are, Aubrey Elizabeth. You're late," Mother says, coming over to me with my stepfather, Arthur, trailing behind her. Brody stiffens next to me. I shake my head a tiny bit and hope he sees.

"Mother."

"Aubrey, girl," Arthur says, stepping around my mother and putting his arms out. I drop Brody's hand and step into his embrace.

I don't know how Arthur puts up with my mother because he is the total opposite of her. Where she's cold and calculated, he's warm and loving. The only thing they have in common is the business. Arthur was one of my father's business partners and the CFO, a role he still has today. Bri thinks they're only married on paper and don't actually spend any time together. They didn't get married until I was in grad school, a year after my father died, and since I avoid family get-togethers as much as possible I haven't been around them much to form an opinion.

Stepping out of Arthur's embrace, I turn to Brody. "Brody, this is my stepfather, Arthur. Arthur, this is—"

Arthur interrupts me, letting out a bark of laughter. "Brody Thompson? Forward for the Orlando Storm. It's a pleasure to meet you, son. Big fan."

Chapter Fifteen

Brody

"Yes, sir," I say, shaking Arthur's hand.

He grins back at me. "Well, I'll be," he exclaims, glancing between me and Aubrey. "You've been holding out on me, Aubrey girl."

Aubrey chuckles, her cheeks turning pink. "Sorry, Arthur. I didn't realize you were a fan."

Arthur shakes his head at his stepdaughter before turning to me. "You'll have to indulge an old man and tell me what it's really like to play in the NHL."

I nod my head, doing my best to hide my shock. Arthur is not the kind of man I expected to see Aubrey's mother, Beatrice, with. Neither Beatrice nor her late husband—Thad Senior—ever asked me about hockey or took an interest in my friendship with their daughter. Arthur's friendliness is refreshing and makes me think that maybe this brunch won't be so bad, not if I have someone to talk to while Aubrey is busy.

Beatrice steps around us. "I need to borrow my daughter. Help yourself to the buffet, Brody. Come on, Aubrey Elizabeth, we need to make the rounds since you got here after everyone else arrived." She claps her hands before turning around, setting off toward the tables of people eating.

Aubrey visibly blanches, her shoulders dropping. I touch her arm, silently asking if she's okay, and she gives me a small smile. I wish I knew why Beatrice treats Aubrey the way she does. I don't remember it being this bad when we were in high school. Beatrice was always a bit of an ice queen, but I thought that was because she didn't approve of our friendship.

Aubrey never really talks about her family except for the odd random comment about one of her sisters, and maybe this is why. I never stopped to think about it because it's not like I have the best relationship with my family either, well, aside from my older brother, Brantley.

"Come on. Let's go get some food," Arthur says, pulling my attention back to the present. "I don't know about you, but I'm starving." He pats his stomach and chuckles before gesturing for me to follow him.

"You okay if I go with him?" I whisper, leaning closer to Aubrey.

"Yes. I'm being summoned anyway." She gestures toward her mom, who has stopped in the middle of the ballroom and is watching us.

"Uh-oh, someone's in trouble," I mumble. "I'll save you a seat." I brush my lips across her cheek and turn to hurry after Arthur, who has already made it to the buffet.

We fill our plates, and Arthur guides me to the closest table and introduces me to everyone. "That's Chet—Clara's fiancé—and you know Thad and Devon, I assume." Arthur points at each of them in turn, and they all look up from their food and nod. "This is Brody Thompson, Aubrey's boyfriend."

Devon greets me with a smile before turning his attention back to his daughter, who is sitting in her stroller next to him. Thad offers a simple hello before going back to his phone. Chet makes an odd face but doesn't say anything.

"Hi," I greet them before glancing around for Aubrey. She's standing with her mom and sisters in the corner talking to a woman who I'm guessing is the wedding planner. I wonder if I should make a plate of food and bring it to her. Fuck her mother's whole they get to eat last.

I glance over at Thad scrolling on his phone with an empty plate in front of him. Why isn't he over there with his sisters? He's a Fairchild too. Isn't he a host? Or does her mom only delegate the role of "hosting" to the women in the family? Whatever the reason, it fucking drives me nuts.

"So, what do you do?" Chet asks, breaking the awkward silence that has prevailed over the table since we sat down. "Are you a scientist like Aubrey?" he asks before turning his attention back to his plate.

I take a bite of waffle, chewing and swallowing before answering. "Nah. Not smart enough. I play hockey. For the Storm."

I lift my head in time to catch his reaction. His fork stops midway between his plate and his mouth, and he lifts his head, meeting my gaze, his brows furrowed. "Like the Orlando Storm? The NHL team?"

"Yep," I say, putting another bite of waffle in my mouth.

"And Mrs. Fairchild is okay with you, a hockey player, dating her oldest daughter?" he asks after a few seconds of silence.

What the hell?

That's when I notice that everyone is watching the conversation in rapt silence except Thad, who hasn't looked up from his phone.

Arthur clears his throat and meets my gaze before saying, "I'm not sure what you're implying, Chet, but that borders on being rude. Aubrey is a grown woman. She can date who she chooses. I could say the same to you. Mrs. Fairchild is okay with you marrying her youngest daughter? You're *only* a lawyer."

I mask my laugh with a cough before going back to my brunch.

"Well . . ." Chet says.

"I think that's enough," Thad pipes up. "Not that it needs to be explained, but Brody and Aubrey have known each other since high school. If there's any relationship we should be questioning, it's yours and Clara's. You haven't been together a year and you're already getting married. Hmmm." He punctuates the last part of his statement by setting his phone on the table and glaring at Chet.

Well, shit.

Chet lets out a huff but thankfully lets it drop and goes back to his food. Thad nods at me and goes back to his phone. I sigh and continue to eat, occasionally answering questions Arthur asks me about hockey. He at least seems genuinely interested. Thad even joins the conversation at one point.

I've finished my plate and am considering a second when Aubrey sinks into the chair next to me.

"You okay?" I whisper, putting a hand on her thigh.

"I'll survive," she says, blowing out a breath. "But Mother told me a bunch of Clara's friends are going shopping downtown and some of the guys are going to play golf. I told her we'd pass. I hope that's okay with you." Her shoulders sag, and she studies my face.

"Of course." I'm not a big fan of golf. A lot of the guys on the team love it, though, and anytime we have a day off while we're traveling, they'll find a course. Occasionally, I'll go with them, but it's not my favorite thing to do.

"Want me to make you a plate?" I ask because Aubrey looks exhausted. Whatever happened while she was with her mother really took it out of her.

"That would be great."

"I'll be right back."

I make my way to the buffet and grab two plates. On one plate I add a fresh waffle and a scoop of berries, then pour some syrup over top. On the second plate I add some eggs, bacon, and melon. I walk back to the table and set the plates in front of Aubrey.

"I've gotta go get utensils," I say before leaning down to kiss her on the forehead. That's the second time I've kissed her here, and I try to tell myself it's because we're with her family and we want to make it believable, but there's a part of me that knows that isn't true. I push the thought out of my head, going back to the buffet, making myself a second plate, and grabbing utensils.

"How did you know? Thank you," Aubrey says with a grin as she takes the fork I hand her as I sit back down with my own food.

She pulls the plate with the waffle closer. I bite my lip to keep from laughing. If there's a waffle that's the first thing she's going to eat. No matter what the other food options are.

"I've always wanted to go snorkeling off the reef here," she says a few minutes later, pushing her empty plates away.

"That sounds fun. I'm sure we could do that this afternoon. Anything else you'd like to do? Or see?"

"You're not coming shopping with us?" Clara asks, interrupting our conversation, her eyes trained on Aubrey. When did she show up?

"No, I'm going to pass."

Clara pouts. "I was hoping we were going to get to spend the day together. Now both of my sisters are abandoning me."

"Clara, we're going to be together all day on Thursday when we go to the spa," Aubrey says.

Clara crosses her arms. "Fine,"

Good grief. She reminds me of a petulant child who got told no in the toy store. I don't know how Aubrey puts up with Clara and her mother.

Maybe that's why she moved to Gainesville.

Aubrey shakes her head at her sister and turns her attention back to me. I raise my eyebrows at her, silently asking her if everything's okay—feels like I'm doing that a lot today—and she gives me the slightest of nods. I lean back in my chair and slip my arm around her, pulling her closer to my side.

"I'm ready to go whenever you are," I whisper in her ear. She shivers and it doesn't escape my notice.

"We should probably hang around for a little while longer," she whispers back.

I nod although I hate that answer. If it was my family and they treated me the way her mom and sister treat her, I wouldn't have even come to the wedding. She has a lot more patience than I do.

Finally, after what feels like forever but is really only an hour, the ballroom starts clearing out, and Aubrey finally stands and beckons me to follow her.

We say our goodbyes, and with my hand on her lower back, I guide her toward the elevators. I've found myself touching her more and more as the day has gone on.

It's fine, right?

We're supposed to be in a relationship, so this is what a boyfriend would do, right?

I have no clue because it's not something that's been on my radar in a long time. The last girlfriend I had was in high school. The only relationship I've been in for a long time has been with hockey.

Aubrey leans against the wall of the elevator, closing her eyes, and it takes everything in me not to wrap my arm around her and pull her against me. I tuck my hands in my pockets instead.

"If you're tired, we can stay here and relax. Nap. Sit by the pool. Have a few drinks."

Her eyes pop open. "Are you going to nap with me?"

"I could nap."

The doors open on our floor, and we step out. Once inside our suite, Aubrey kicks off her sandals and collapses onto the couch. A quick glance at my watch tells me it's only noon, and we didn't go to bed that late last night. She looks like she's taken part in a full day's worth of events.

"What's going on?" I ask, sitting down next to her.

"My mother exhausts me. Clara exhausts me. Scratch that, this whole wedding exhausts me."

"So why did you come?" *Shit.* I probably shouldn't have said that out loud, but I couldn't help myself. I hate that she feels like this after spending a few hours with them. I hate that this trip is exhausting her.

She opens her eyes, blinking rapidly a couple of times before staring down at her hands. "I had to come. She's my sister. They're my family."

She knows my situation and how I feel about family and being obligated to do things with them. I haven't spoken to my parents since I graduated from high school. My father didn't approve of me playing hockey, he wanted me to follow in his footsteps and join his investment firm. Had it not been for my granddad who was a hockey player himself back in the day, although he never made it past the AHL, I wouldn't have played. He was the one who bought me my first pair of skates and taught me to skate. He paid for all my coaches and training camps too.

My middle brother, Bryon, and my sister, Chelsea, stopped talking to me about the same time my parents did. I'm sure it's because dear old dad told them to break contact with me *or else*. The only people I consider my family these days, besides Aubrey, are my older brother, Brantley, his wife, and my nephew.

I blow out a breath. "I hate to see you put yourself through this stress. For what, Aubrey? Your mom is never going to be happy, no matter what you do. For Clara?"

"You wouldn't understand, Brody," she says, crossing her arms.

I nod, accepting her answer because the last thing I want to do is get into an argument with her. "Why don't you lie down for an hour or two? We can decide what to do when you get up."

She huffs out a breath, dropping her arms. "Okay."

She gets off the couch and shuffles into the bedroom, closing the door behind her. I pull out my phone and try not to think about her in the other room, lying in bed.

In the bed we shared last night.

Where I woke up, curled around her.

The bed we'll share again tonight.

Chapter Sixteen

Aubrey

I jolt awake, sitting up in bed and throwing the covers off. *Shit, I'm late for work if it's that light out.* Wait, my bedroom doesn't get this much sunlight, not even in the late afternoon.

Where am I? I rub my face, the room slowly coming into focus.

That's right. I'm in Key West. For Clara's wedding. Sharing a bed with Brody, who is pretending to be my boyfriend.

Taking a few deep breaths to calm my still racing heart, I swing my feet over the side of the bed and get up.

"Hey," I say as I make my way into the living room.

"Hi," he says, turning to face me, muting the television as he does. "Did you have a good nap?"

"Yeah." I take a seat next to him. "I'm surprised I fell asleep. Apparently I needed it after this morning's *excitement.*"

Brody smirks. "Which part are we calling the excitement? Brunch or before brunch?" His gaze darts to my mouth. I bite down on my lower lip, remembering him kissing me.

I swallow, forcing myself to focus on his question. "I was referring to brunch," I croak out. "What do you want to do for the rest of the day?" I need to change the subject before I start thinking and overthink our kiss . . . kisses.

Plural.

Many.

Multiple. Because there was more than one.

"I found a charter company that'll take us out to snorkel the reef." He frowns. "You're changing the subject, aren't you?"

"Changing the subject?" I repeat, my heart racing, hoping that my face isn't giving me away.

"About what happened before brunch."

"You're going to have to give me more, Brod. A lot happened before brunch. My suitcase arrived. We ate. My mother showed up."

"Aubrey." He levels a look at me that says he knows what I'm doing.

"Fine. You want to talk about this. Let's do it. You kissed me on New Year's Eve and didn't tell me."

Brody's gaze darts back and forth over my face. "How did you not know it was me?" My heart drops at the hurt in his voice.

I let out a breath. "It was dark. I couldn't see much of anything with where you were standing. We'd never kissed. How would I know it was you?"

"Fine. It's fine. Now we know." Brody leans back against the couch, closing his eyes. His shoulders sag, and I feel like shit.

"Why didn't you say something, Brod?" I whisper, leaning over and putting a hand on his cheek.

His eyes flutter open, and he leans further into my touch. He turns his head and kisses my palm before pulling back, his chocolate eyes searching my face for something. What, I don't know, but he must see it because he finally says, "What was I supposed to say? You ran. I thought"—his voice breaks, and he clears his throat before continuing—"I thought you didn't want me."

"What. No. I freaked out. I—" Now it's my turn to clear my throat and gather myself. "I enjoyed the kiss. I freaked out when it dawned on me that I'd kissed who I thought was one of your teammates. And enjoyed it as much as I did." I stare down at my hands folded in my lap.

"Aubrey." Brody whispers my name, and I peek up at him to see his face marred with emotion that I can't quite place. "Fuck, Aubrey." He runs a hand through his hair, getting to his feet, and begins to pace. "I thought you didn't want it. Didn't want me. I've been beating myself up for ruining our friendship. I'm such an idiot. I should have talked to you. Fuck." He's running his hands through his hair and tugging on the ends so hard that I'm afraid he'll pull some of it out.

"Brody." I'm on my feet and by his side as fast as I can. Is this why his game was off at the end of the season? Why he missed that goal? Because he was so focused on us? On what he thought he'd messed up? "I'm sorry I didn't talk to you about it. It's my fault too." My hand lands on his bicep, and before I can take another breath, he's spinning me around and pulling me into his arms. I think he's going to kiss me, but he surprises me by crushing me to his chest in a hug. I relax into him, wrapping my arms around him.

We stand in silence for a few minutes before he pulls back, looks down at me, and says, "Can we agree to talk to each other next time?"

"Yes, please." Talking to each other probably would have solved this whole thing a lot sooner, wouldn't it.

Are we good?" he asks after a few moments of silence.

"We're good, Brod."

"Friends? Or?" He wags his eyebrows at me.

"Or what, Brody?" I ask, meeting his gaze.

"Can I kiss you again?"

I shrug, a grin tugging at my lips. "You are my fake boyfriend, so I suppose it's expected."

I swear I hear him mumble thank fuck before his mouth crashes into mine, and I get lost in the feel of his lips. He seeks entrance with his tongue, and I open for him. He deepens the kiss, and the rest of the world fades away. It's just him and me in our little bubble. I sink my fingers into his scalp, which elicits a moan from him.

Does he moan like that when he's coming? My core clenches at the thought, and now I'm even more turned on. Eventually, he ends the kiss, pulling away from me. Breathlessly, I stare at him—his lips are swollen, and his hair is standing on end, which makes him look even hotter. If that's possible. And it's all because of me. It's a self-esteem boost knowing that I did that to him. That I have that effect on him.

He stares at me silently for a few minutes before saying, "Do you still want to go snorkeling? As much as I want to keep kissing you, Aubs, and I do, if we're going to go, I should call the charter company and make sure they can still take us out today."

I take a deep breath. Part of me wants to say screw snorkeling, let's kiss more, but the rational part of me knows we need to slow down and think about what we're doing before we go down a road we can't come back from. I opt to go with the rational part of my brain and say, "We don't need to charter a boat. I saw a sign for a company that does snorkeling trips. We can do one of those."

Brody shakes his head, pinching his lips together into a tight line. "Aubrey, I don't want to go on some company's boat on their schedule with a bunch of other people."

"Yeah, but—"

"But what? Let me do this. This is my vacation too, you know."

I smirk at him. "Who said this was a vacation?"

He barks out a laugh. "Fine. Fine. But if we're supposed to be dating, don't you think this is something your hot, rich, hockey boyfriend would do for you? Charter a boat so we can go snorkeling and boating in peace. On our schedule. Not pay a hundred dollars to be on someone else's timetable."

"Yeah, okay," I concede. "Call the charter company." I step back from him and turn toward the bedroom.

"So, you agree I'm hot?"

"Don't push your luck, sir." I peek over my shoulder and wink at him.

"Aubrey," he growls, scanning me up and down.

"I'm going to change into my bathing suit and pack my beach bag," I say, needing to get away from him and cool down before I do or say anything that I'll regret. Because that kiss. That kiss was something else.

I head to the bedroom and make quick work of changing and pulling on a cover up.

"It's all booked." Brody's voice comes from behind me. "They'll pick us up at the marina in an hour. They'll provide a meal too. Nothing fancy, but at least we won't be hungry."

"Perfect. I packed some stuff in my bag. If there's anything else you need, just add it."

"Okay. Let me get changed and we can go," he says, dropping a kiss on my neck before walking away.

Twenty minutes later, we're heading toward the elevators. I'm giddy with excitement. This is something I've wanted to do since I discovered that Florida has a reef. The weather is perfect too—warm and slightly breezy with not a cloud in the sky. Hopefully that means the visibility in the water is good too.

"I arranged a driver to pick us up, and we can call him when we're ready to come back to the hotel," Brody says, glancing down at his phone. "He's waiting for us out front."

"You think of everything," I say, reaching over to take his hand as the elevator doors slide open and we step out into the lobby.

"I don't know about this," Brody says from his spot by the side of the boat where he's staring down at the water.

The captain dropped anchor, and we're waiting for the first mate to bring us the snorkeling gear so we can go out.

"What do you mean, you don't know about this?"

"I mean I didn't think this through when you suggested it. We're out in open water." He gestures to the ocean in front of him.

"Yeah . . ."

"Like, deep open water," he mumbles, clearing his throat.

"That's correct." Is my big bad hockey-playing best friend nervous? Shit. Did not see that coming. "You don't have to if you don't want to. You can stay on the boat."

Brody finally tears his gaze from the ocean and looks at me, swallowing before saying, "No, I'll go. The guys will never let me live it down if they find out I chickened out."

"I won't tell them." I walk closer to him and go up on tiptoes to kiss him on the cheek. "You don't have to do anything you don't want to."

"I know."

"Here you go, folks," the first mate says, walking up to us. He hands us snorkel masks, fins, and two life vests. "I also brought pool noodles.

If you put one between yourself and your vest, it'll act as a floatation device."

"Thanks," I say as we take the gear from him.

"I'm going to go set up the ladder"—he hooks a thumb over his shoulder—"and grab my gear, and we can go down." He turns and walks away. Leaving us to get ready.

"You good?" I reach for Brody's hand as we make our way to the stern of the boat where the first mate is waiting for us.

"Yeah. Fine," Brody says, entwining our fingers before giving me a small smile. I'm not entirely convinced he's not putting on a brave face for me, but I take him at his word and get ready to snorkel.

"That was so much fun," I gush an hour later, wrapping my towel around me and taking a seat across from Brody in the bow of the boat.

We ended up seeing quite a few schools of fish along the reef. I wish I knew what they all were, or had an underwater camera, but at least I have the memories. Brody relaxed once we got into the water and started swimming. Or if he was still nervous, he didn't say anything, although I asked him a couple of times. Now we're heading to watch the sunset before going back to the marina.

Brody smirks at me. "Told you this was the way to do it," he says before taking a sip of beer from the bottle in his hand.

"You were right," I agree.

I watch his Adam's apple bob as he swallows, and my gaze drifts to his lips, shiny with beer. My face heats as I think about his lips on me a couple of hours ago. How did we go from being friends, close friends, to kissing? Multiple times.

Oh, yeah, I remember. Because I finally found out who my New Year's Eve kiss was, and he's sitting across from me with a grin on his face.

Isn't it ironic?

I find out that the best kiss of my life came from my best friend, and it's repeatable, but—because there's always a but, isn't there—it comes when I'm on the cusp of moving thousands of miles away for a job.

Why couldn't we have had this revelation a few years ago? At least then we could have possibly had a chance. Now, we're screwed.

"It's so nice out today. The weather is perfect," I finally say, breaking the silence.

"Yeah, it is. Today's definitely a day I won't forget." There's something in the way he says it that makes me turn toward him, and I catch him staring at me. He shifts closer to me on the bench seat and I hold my breath, wondering what he's going to do. "You got a little red." He runs a finger along my shoulders and collarbone.

A trail of goosebumps follows his fingers as they trace across my skin. He sucks in a deep breath. I open my mouth to ask him to kiss me again, but the first mate interrupts me.

"We're almost to the place where we'll drop anchor for the sunset."

"Perfect. Thank you," Brody says, sliding back to his spot.

I wish he'd stayed closer to me but I don't say anything, letting the moment pass. It's probably better this way. We've already blurred the lines between fake and real with the kisses we shared this morning, probably best not to blur them even more.

Ten minutes later, we're pulling up to the spot where we'll watch the sunset. We're surrounded by a bunch of other boats, including a couple of larger catamarans, probably the tour boat companies I found earlier, with live music and groups of people on them. The first mate comes back, bringing us another round of drinks, and asks if we need anything else. I could get used to this.

"It's beautiful," I murmur, watching the sky turn orange as the sun sets over the sea. I pull out my phone and snap a few pictures. We stay for a while longer, watching the sun disappear over the horizon, before the captain pulls up anchor, and we go back to the marina.

"Incoming," Brody hisses, grabbing my hand and lacing our fingers together as we walk through the lobby of the hotel. Not thirty seconds later, Clara is striding over to us, Chet trailing behind her.

"Sister." She beams at me, coming to a halt in front of us. "Brody. Can I borrow Aubrey for a moment?" She flutters her eyelashes at him and beams at him. I furrow my brow. She's up to something. Brody lets go of my hand.

"Over here," Clara says, marching over to a couch set in an alcove off the lobby. Brody mouths *you good* at me, but all I can do is nod.

"What's up?" I ask her.

"Sit. Sit," she says, smoothing down her dress and patting the cushion next to her.

"I know it's all a ruse," she says with a gleam in her eyes once I'm seated.

"What's a ruse?" I ask, my heart racing. I try to school my features, hoping she's not talking about what I think she is.

"You and Brody." She gestures toward him leaning against a pillar across the lobby, staring down at his phone. "There's no way someone like that"—she checks him out, and it takes all my restraint not to snap at her—"would date someone like you." She turns her gaze back at me.

"What's that supposed to mean?" I ask, crossing my arms. "I hate to break it to you, but we are dating. So I guess you're wrong," I say hoping my voice is calm, trying not to act like I'm freaked out.

"Pshh," she says with a shake of her head, her perfectly curly blonde hair bouncing over her shoulders. "Come on, Aubs, be serious."

"I don't know what to tell you, Clara." I glance over at Brody and notice he's staring at me. When I meet his gaze, he pushes off the wall and walks our way.

"Mom is going to love this," Clara says, putting her hand on my arm. "I can't wait to tell her."

I shake her off and stand as Brody reaches us.

He slips his arm around my waist and pulls me close. My hand lands on his chest as he leans down and kisses my cheek. "Are you about ready, babe? We should probably change out of these swimsuits." I sag against him. "I got you," he whispers in my ear, his hot breath tickling my neck, and I shiver. "Yep, come on beautiful. Let's go upstairs and take a hot shower. Bye, Clara."

"Good night, you two," Clara says, tilting her chin and looking at Brody's arm wrapped around me.

"Night," I say before spinning on my heel, taking Brody's hand, and striding toward the elevators.

"What the hell was that?" he asks when we're safely inside our suite a few minutes later.

"Just Clara insisting that we aren't really dating. In her words, someone like you wouldn't date someone like me."

Brody growls.

The man *fucking growls*.

I raise my eyebrows at him but remain silent.

He runs a hand down his face. "Why does she care?"

I lift a shoulder in a half shrug. "Because that's the way she is now."

"I don't remember her being like this."

"She wasn't. I'm not sure if it's this wedding, her spending even more time with Mother, or what," I scoff.

Brody nods, opens his mouth to say something, but then closes it. We stare at each other for a few seconds before I say, "I'm going to go take a shower."

"Okay."

I turn and walk into the bedroom, my heart hammering. What the hell have I gotten myself into, and why do I have a feeling that we're playing with fire? I say a silent prayer that Clara won't actually say anything to mother.

Chapter Seventeen

Brody

I exhale when I hear the click of the bathroom door. Shit, Aubrey's family is difficult. I drop onto the couch, close my eyes, and rest my head against the cushions. But the minute I do, my mind starts to run through the day, and all the times I touched Aubrey when I didn't have to.

What she looked like in her bikini.

How she felt when I wrapped my arms around her and she relaxed into me.

What it was like to kiss her this morning.

How soft and supple her lips are.

How much better those kisses were than the one we shared on New Year's Eve.

The discussion we had this afternoon. Her confession that she felt the same way about the kiss that I did.

The gut punch that came with the realization of how much time I've wasted this year by not talking to her about the kiss sooner. Let alone how much time we've wasted not talking about *us*.

I wonder if she'll let me kiss her again. Touch her. Taste her. The thought has my cock springing to attention.

I groan, opening my eyes. That's the last thing I need—for her to get out of the shower and see me on the couch sporting a half hard-on. Now I'm thinking about Aubrey in the shower. Naked. Soapy. That has me standing and pacing the room, trying to think of anything else.

Get it together.

"All done." Aubrey's voice comes from the bedroom. I take a deep breath, running plays in my head so I don't march in there, toss her on the bed, and kiss her senseless again. Explore her body. I want to. Oh boy, do I want to, but that's probably not the right move.

"Hey," she says when I step into the room. She's sitting cross-legged on the bed in a pair of gray shorts and the Storm shirt I lent her last night. Fuck, she looks good in it. Her wet hair is piled on top of her head in a messy bun.

"I'm going to take a shower." I point toward the bathroom like she doesn't know where the it is.

Smooth, Brody, smooth.

"Okay," she says, and I hurry to the bathroom and shut myself in before I change my mind.

"Whatcha doing?" I ask, walking back into the bedroom ten minutes later, slightly more relaxed after taking a cold shower.

She glances up at me. "I was hoping I could order some wine from room service, but there's nothing on the menu."

"I'm sure you can." I take a seat on the edge of the bed. "If not, I'll go down to the bar. Anything else you want with it? Dessert?"

Her eyes light up. She can never resist dessert. "Maybe some chocolate cake."

I pick up the phone, push the button for room service, and order a bottle of wine and a large slice of chocolate cake for us to share. It's not something I eat often, but after Aubrey mentioned it, the sweet tooth I don't normally have reared its head.

"You didn't get anything to drink," Aubrey says when I hang up.

"Wine's fine," I say, getting more comfortable on the bed. "What are we watching?" I pick up the control and turn the TV on.

A few hours later, there's a half-empty bottle of wine on the nightstand along with the empty dessert plates, and the empty dishes that held the hamburgers and fries we ordered after we decided dessert wasn't enough.

"So," I say, picking up my glass of whiskey. I had two sips of wine, promptly handed the rest of the glass to Aubrey, and called room service to order a bottle of bourbon. She thought I was crazy and wanted to know how I was going to drink it all. I shrugged and told her not to worry about it. I figure I'll share whatever's left with Devon, Arthur, or Thad.

"So," she parrots back, sipping her wine.

"Are we going to talk about the elephant in the room?"

"What would that be?"

"The kisses, Aubrey."

"I thought we already did." She stares down at the comforter, picking at the threads.

"We talked about the kiss on New Year's Eve but not the other ones." I drain my glass and set it on the nightstand.

"What's there to talk about?" she whispers, still staring down at the duvet.

"Aubrey." I reach over and tilt her chin so she meets my gaze. "What's going on in your head? Talk to me."

"We kissed. Multiple times."

"I know. I was there."

"Are things going to be awkward between us now? Because I can't stand to lose my best friend," Aubrey whispers, her blue eyes fixed on me.

Her best friend

Is that how she sees me? Still? Even after the kisses? The confessions? I thought we were moving toward more than friends. I suck in a deep breath, afraid to ask, but we need to have this conversation. I know Aubrey, if I don't start the conversation, it will never happen. "Is that all we are?"

"What else can we be? I'm moving to Hawaii in the fall." She moves closer to me.

"I'll be whatever you want me to be, Aubs," I answer honestly.

She's silent for a few seconds before getting on her knees and gently cups my cheek. I take a shaky inhale, closing my eyes, and sinking into the feeling of her hand on my face. "I enjoyed kissing you," she finally whispers.

My heart skips a beat. Before I can do or say anything, she removes her hand, and I hear her shift even closer. I hold my breath, keeping my eyes closed. Afraid if I open them, this will turn out to be a dream.

"Brod," she whispers. I finally open my eyes to see her staring at me. "Will you kiss me again?"

Kiss me again.

It takes a second for my brain to catch up, but when it does, I reach for her and pull her into my lap so she's straddling me. I groan, feeling her warm center connect with my dick, which is suddenly raring to go.

"Anything you want," I murmur before pulling her into me and fusing our lips together. I lick at the seam of her lips, and she opens for me. She sinks her hands into my hair, her fingers against my scalp, and I groan, my eyes rolling into the back of my head. She tastes like chocolate and wine.

Fuck, I'm addicted.

All too soon, she tears her lips away. She goes to move off my lap, but I hold her in place.

"Fuck," she says, chewing on her bottom lip.

"What is it?" I ask softly, fighting the urge to pluck her bottom lip out from between her teeth. Lean in and kiss her again.

"What about after?" She asks, finally meeting my gaze.

"What do you mean, after?"

"After this trip. This was supposed to be fake between us. This doesn't feel fake anymore. I feel like we're crossing a line. Maybe it's the alcohol. We're not thinking straight. I don't want to do anything that's going to ruin our friendship," she gestures between the two of us.

"Aubrey, I've had one glass of whiskey. I know what I want. What I've wanted since New Year's. Since before that. But if you're going to regret any of this in the morning, we can stop. I don't want you to have any regrets. Do you feel this?" I flex my hips, pushing my erection into her. Not that there's any way she could have missed it, but just in case she wasn't sure, she's sure now. "If you want to cross the line I'll happily cross it with you."

It feels so good to say the words out loud, to finally admit my feelings.

She whimpers, bracing her hands on my shoulders. "Brody, I've dreamed of you. Of this. For years. I . . ." She drops her gaze to stare at the bed.

"Tell me. Please." I whisper the last part, desperately wanting to know what she's thinking.

"I didn't think you wanted me. You didn't want me in high school."

"Aubrey." I suck in a deep breath, about to admit out loud how pathetic I am. "I did." I take another deep breath, willing the emotion out of my voice. "I never thought I was good enough to date you. I spent so many years denying my feelings for you and telling myself that you were better off with me as just a friend. That you deserved a partner who could match you in intellect. I'm sorry, Aubrey. I don't . . ." I rake my hand through my hair. "I convinced myself that it was better this way. That I was married to my career. That I didn't want anyone." I take a deep breath, trying to build up the courage to tell her.

She stays silent, stroking her hands up and down my arms, waiting for me to speak.

I meet her gaze, ready to pour my heart out. "Seeing Hunter fall in love this past year . . . I don't know. It stirred something in me. Seeing Cole and Caleb starting families. It made me reevaluate things. Aleksi is talking about retiring when his contract is up. He's younger than I am. It's made me realize that I have regrets. That I've missed out on things because I convinced myself that I was better off alone. Something changed this year. Call it an early midlife crisis. But I realized that I do want someone to share the rest of my life with. I've always wanted that. Somewhere along the way I convinced myself that I didn't. That I didn't deserve it. But I look at those guys, and they have partners, someone they can lean on, someone they go home to at the end of a road trip or a game. And I want that too. Is that ridiculous? Because it feels like it is."

"It's not, Brod." She rubs her hands along my arms again.

I take a deep breath, steeling myself to tell her the whole truth because we agreed to be honest with each other. "You know my contract was up with the Storm at the end of this season."

She nods.

"I don't think they're going to offer me a new one."

"What? Why?" she asks, her mouth falling open.

"I failed the team." My chest tightens as I admit to her the things I've been thinking about for weeks. "I missed a shot that got us eliminated from the playoffs. It was all my fault. I'd been having a rough end of the season, and that was the icing on the cake. I don't think they'll want me back."

"Was it because of me? Because of the kiss? Because shit, Brody, I don't know how you could forgive me. Still want to be with me if it was." She goes to climb off my lap, but I hold her against me.

I take another deep breath. "No. I'd been having issues on and off with my game before the kiss." I shake my head, trying to put into words how I feel. "I think it's me. I'm getting older. Thirty-five isn't exactly a spring chicken in the NHL. Hockey's not the same for me anymore."

"You didn't fail the team, Brody. Yeah, you're the one who missed the shot, but there's how many other guys on the ice with you? It's not all on you to win the game."

"That's what Caleb said," I mumble.

"He's a smart man," she says with a grin.

"Probably shouldn't tell him that. It'll go to his head." I huff out a laugh.

Aubrey leans forward and wraps her arms around me. I wrap mine around her and inhale deeply.

"Fuck. This wasn't how I wanted to tell you all of that. Now you probably think I only want you because my career is over."

"No, of course not." She pulls out of my arms and leans back so she can look up at me. "But now what? I want you. I've always wanted you. Except it doesn't seem fair to say that because I'm not going to be living in Florida soon. I can't offer you anything serious."

I don't like that answer, but maybe I can change her mind. Prove to her that we can work. I feel like my reality has been rocked this season. My goals and dreams are changing, but to what I don't know. What I do know, is that I want her.

"You can have me. Any way you want me." I lean forward, trailing kisses along her throat and across her jaw. She hums and sags against me. "You taste so good, Aubs."

She shivers.

"What was that for?" I want to know what I said or did to make her shiver so I can be sure to do it again.

"You called me Aubs. You've never done that until this trip." She moans, circling her hips. "Why do you always call me Aubrey? I've never asked."

I grip her waist to still her because she's driving me out of my mind. "It started"—I take a deep breath—"as a way to get a rise out of you. And then it turned into a way to remind myself that we had to keep our distance. That we were just friends."

"And now?"

"Now I want to kiss you again. Taste you." I say, searching her face for a sign that she wants the same thing.

"Yes. Please."

That's all the permission I need to crash my lips to hers. We get lost in each other for a few minutes. Kissing her feels so damn good.

"Touch me." Aubrey's voice is raspy as she pulls away from me. "Please."

My brain short circuits for a second, but I recover quickly. "Anything you want," I say, flipping us so she's flat on her back and I'm hovering over her.

"Hi," I whisper as I lean down and pepper kisses along her neck, jaw, and down her collarbone. Shifting onto one hand, I palm one of her breasts through her shirt, groaning when I realize she's not wearing a bra.

"Take off your shirt," I demand, moving so she can sit up and pull it over her head. She lies back down, covering herself with her arms. "No." I knock them away gently, wanting to take her in.

"Brody."

"Aubs, you're beautiful. Let me look at you." I gaze down at her, my dick getting hard at the vision below me. Her hair spread out over the pillows, chest flushed, nipples hard and waiting for attention. I salivate at the thought of tasting them but force myself to slow down. Savor the moment. I commit the sight of her half-naked stretched out below me to memory before leaning down and kissing her. Touching her everywhere I can.

It feels so good to finally be able to.

I nip at her bottom lip only to swipe my tongue over it, soothing the pain. I lift my head and meet her gaze. Her pupils are blown out, and her chest is flushed a pretty pink color. I kiss my way down her body, circling closer and closer to her nipples before finally sucking one into my mouth, lavishing it with attention. I make sure to do the same to the other. Aubrey digs her hands into my scalp, pushing my head down. I chuckle against her skin.

"Brody," she says, her voice breathy and full of need.

My dick gets harder hearing her say my name like that.

"What do you need? Where do you want me to touch you? Taste you?"

I wait for her to answer, but she doesn't. I lift my head to look at her, and I'm shocked at what I see. She's got her eyes closed and her eyebrows scrunched down. "Aubrey," I prompt. "What's wrong?"

"N-nothing," she says, shaking her head.

I rock back onto my knees. What the hell is going on? "Open your eyes, Aubrey. What's going on? Did I do something wrong?"

She does as I ask but diverts her gaze, glancing around the room, anywhere but at me.

I furrow my brows. I don't like this. "Talk to me. Please."

"I—I . . ." She crosses her arms over her chest, turning even redder.

I move so I'm sitting against the headboard of the bed and spread my legs out. "Come here," I say, motioning for her to sit between my legs, her back to my front. She does as I ask.

"What's going on?" I ask wrap my arms around her. Fighting the urge to play with her breasts that are pressed against my arm. If she's having second thoughts about us, about this, I want to know, so I force myself to take a few deep breaths and ignore my hard cock.

She huffs out a breath and sags against me. "You're going to laugh."

"Never, Aubrey. Never."

"I'm not used to being the center of a guy's attention like this. Your question threw me off. I froze."

"What the fuck?" I bite out.

"I'm—I—" She shifts in my arms and starts to pull away.

"That's not what I meant. I'm not upset at you. I'm trying to figure out how you've never been the center of attention for any of the guys you've dated."

"Maybe this was a bad idea," Aubrey says, trying to pull herself out of my arms again.

"If you really mean that, I'll respect it. If you're only saying it because you feel embarrassed or whatnot, then I think we should talk about it."

She takes a few deep breaths before finally saying, "I want you, Brody."

Thank fuck.

She turns in my arms until she's kneeling in front of me, topless, her breasts pressing against me. I fist my hands at my side so I don't reach out and touch her, letting her take control.

"This is all new to me. Not sex, because I've had sex." She blushes, shaking her head before continuing. I fight a grin at her words but remain silent. "It's new to me being with someone . . . Someone who clearly wants to put my needs above their own. So be patient with me."

"Always."

She leans in and kisses me but pulls back far too quickly. "Touch me," she whispers.

I'm happy to oblige and in one swift movement, she's flat on her back, her chest heaving, and I'm hovering over her. I kiss down her neck and chest, sucking one of her nipples into my mouth. I'm not a breast man, but fucking hell, are Aubrey's perfect.

She's perfect.

All of her.

And I. Can't. Get. Enough.

Already.

And I haven't even had all of her.

"Brody," she whines. "More." She moans, her fingers tangled in my hair.

I lift off her and prop myself on my side. "May I?" I ask, skating my fingers along the waistline of her shorts.

My heart is in my throat as I wait for her to answer. We've crossed so many lines tonight, but this one is the biggest. Finally, after what feels like an eternity, she nods, and I slowly lower her shorts and underwear, tugging them off and tossing them over the edge of the bed.

"Beautiful," I say, staring down at the woman below me. My eyes trace over her gorgeous naked body.

She's fucking beautiful.

"What did I do to deserve you?"

Chapter Eighteen

Aubrey

I hear the emotion in his voice as he asks the question, and I don't have an answer. Because I'm wondering the exact same thing. How did I get so lucky? Brody leans down, brushing his lips against one of my nipples.

I shiver.

He lifts back up, watching me through hooded eyes as he runs his fingers across my stomach and down my hip before dipping a finger between my legs. I widen them further, starting to blush under his gaze. He swipes a finger through my aching center, and if I wasn't so turned on I would probably be embarrassed by how loudly I moan at the contact.

"Please," I whine. "Touch me."

"Is this what you want, beautiful?" Brody slowly thrusts one of his fingers inside of me. I bite back a moan, my eyes fluttering shut.

"So good. So tight." Brody groans, sliding his finger in and out before pulling all the way out. I whine at the emptiness. He runs his fingers over my clit, and I almost shatter. He repeats the process, playing me like an instrument, and I feel my orgasm build.

He must too because he says, "Look at me. I want to see you when you come."

I take a deep breath and do as he says. "Fuck." I moan seeing him watching me, watching where his finger disappears inside of me.

Brody looks up and meets my stare. That's the final blow. Him staring down at me like that, something akin to fire in his eyes. His hand between my legs. The shape of his hard dick pressing against his shorts. Easily the hottest thing I've ever seen. I see stars as I call out his name as my orgasm rips through me.

My toes curl.

"That's my girl," Brody says as he continues to pump his finger in and out of me. He slips a second finger inside, and I groan.

"What are you doing?" I mumble, even though I'm well aware of what he's doing. What he's trying to do.

"Giving you another orgasm."

"I can't." I pant as my hips ride his hand on their own. I'm a one and done girl. Always have been. I count myself lucky to even have one orgasm. Normally, it's not this easy. Normally, it's not him, a tiny voice pipes up in the back of my head. I shove that thought away.

"Your body says otherwise, Aubs. Look at you riding my fingers like a good girl."

Fuck me. I didn't know I was into praise, but hearing him say *good girl* has me climbing the hill of another orgasm. "I can't," I repeat.

"Oh yes you can. Just feel." Brody leans down and sucks my clit into his mouth.

"Holy shit," I yell out, my eyes rolling to the back of my head as he licks and sucks my clit, continuing to move his fingers in and out of me.

"Yes! Brody," I shout, fisting the sheets, as my second orgasm barrels through me. This one is more intense. So intense it leaves me shaking. I whine at the loss of contact as he removes his fingers, but suddenly he's lying next to me, pulling me into his arms. I'm the little spoon to his big spoon.

"You're so fucking sexy when you come like that, Aubrey. Fuck, I almost came in my pants," Brody whispers into my hair, thrusting his hips forward so I feel his hardness against my ass.

I moan. Wetness pools between my legs at the thought of Brody's cock. How am I ready to go again?

"Seems like you need another," Brody whispers, wrapping his arm around me and slipping his fingers between my legs so he can play with my sensitive clit.

"Brody." I groan, thrusting against him, his hard cock digging deeper into my ass. His answer is to slide first one finger and then a second one inside of me.

"You like it when I fill you up, don't you?" he asks, stroking in and out of me.

"Yes." I pant so close to coming again.

"Come for me, beautiful. I know you want to. I can feel your insides fluttering and squeezing my fingers," Brody whispers into my hair as he adjusts his hand that's between my legs, so his palm brushes up against my clit. That's all it takes for me to explode.

"Brody. Yes." I hiss, riding his hand.

Brody slowly removes his hand from between my legs and I close my eyes, suddenly exhausted. Being in his arms is something I used to dream about but never thought would happen. And exactly like I imagined, it feels right.

"We should get up and brush our teeth," Brody mumbles, his arms tightening around me.

"In a minute," I whisper, my body heavy with sleep from the mind-blowing orgasms.

The alarm goes off far too early for my liking. I groan, my body sore from sleeping in one spot all night. We did get up and brush our teeth eventually. Once we were done, we got right back into bed and cuddled the same way we had been. Except I'd pulled on my underwear and shirt, much to Brody's chagrin. Once the orgasm euphoria wore off, I was back to being uncomfortable naked in front of someone.

"I think my whole right side is dead," Brody says, rolling onto his back. I nod although I'm not sure if he can see me. "I'm too old to sleep in one position all night."

"Okay, old man," I say, chuckling.

"Hey now." He sticks out his bottom lip, pretending to pout. "And you're not that much younger than I am," he says, pointing at me.

"Still not as old as you."

He glares at me before breaking out into laughter.

I shake my head at him, getting out of bed and making my way to the bathroom. I return as Brody hangs up the phone.

"I ordered some coffee and breakfast," he says as he sets the menu down. "I got a little bit of everything."

"Sounds good. We're supposed to meet in the lobby at nine thirty."

"What are we doing again today?" he asks as he stretches, lifting his arms above his head. It takes everything in me to keep my mouth closed and not drool at the sight of him—his abs rippling and flexing as he moves, his tattoos that I love on full display.

"The Southernmost Point. The Hemingway House. I think the Truman Museum. Lunch at one of the seafood restaurants near the marina. I think it's called Alonso's. It's supposed to be fantastic. A few hours of downtime and then dinner." I say, tearing my gaze away from his naked upper body. I wave my hand around, already exhausted thinking about spending the day with my family and the wedding party.

"Can we bail?" Brody asks as he gets up and makes his way to the bathroom.

"Unfortunately, I can't. But you can. Clara wants pictures with the entire wedding party." I furrow my brow. "Well, I'm not sure if it's her or Mother who wants it, but either way, I have to go."

He raises an eyebrow at me but stays silent.

"I know. I know. It's a million degrees out. But there's an air conditioned trolley that will take us to all the locations."

"Sounds wonderful. I'm gonna go shower."

"You can stay here," I repeat.

"I know I can, Aubrey. But if you have to be there, I'll be there with you." Brody levels me with an expression that tells me I shouldn't argue with him. I nod, and he walks into the bathroom, shutting the door with a click. I sag back into bed, then grab my phone and scroll through social media.

"Coffee and food's here," I yell a few minutes later after the room service cart has been wheeled in and the bellhop sufficiently tipped and sent on his way.

I grab two mugs and pour us both coffee while lifting the lids on the plates. A smile plays on my lips when I see a large fluffy Belgian waffle. He knows me so well. As if I had any doubt. I grab the syrup and bowl of fresh berries and fix the waffle the way I like it. I'm settled on the couch with my food when Brody strolls into the living room.

His hair is wet, and he's wearing a different pair of athletic shorts, slung low over his hips, and no shirt. I've seen him shirtless countless times, but there's something different about it today that makes it hard to stop staring.

I'm captivated, watching the way his biceps flex as he fixes his coffee and the way his back muscles move as he reaches across the cart to select his breakfast. For fuck's sake. His body is a work of art, all the lines of muscle from years of hard work on and off the ice. How did I get so lucky to have this hot as sin man interested in me?

"Like what you see?" Brody asks, glances over his shoulder at me. My face heats from being called out.

"Yes," I mumble, going back to my waffle.

He laughs a deep rumbling laugh that does things to my lady bits and comes to sit next to me. I shake my head at him and focus on my breakfast, saying a prayer that today's events won't be as terrible as they sound. Maybe we will have time to properly see the places we're going. Although knowing my mother, she'll have us on a tight schedule.

"Smile, ladies," Gene, our photographer, says, giving us a fake grin as he peers around his camera. His face is red from the heat. His Hawaiian shirt drenched with sweat.

This is the third location we've been to today, and Gene is definitely earning his pay. But based on the scowl on his face when he thinks no one is looking, he's wishing he hadn't agreed to this gig regardless of how much he's earning.

Can't say I blame him.

Mother and Clara have inspected every photo to make sure there's one they both approve of before we move on. At the Southernmost Point we had to redo the photos three times, first because Clara didn't like the way she was standing, then because Bri's eyes were closed, and the last time because one of the bridesmaids was fixing her hair. I'm pretty sure the family waiting to take their pictures was silently cursing at us to hurry up.

I take a deep breath before plastering on yet another smile. Gene has us arranged in front of the Truman Museum. It's a beautiful yellow colonial style home with palm trees flanking the walkway. Truthfully, it's a gorgeous building, and I don't fault Clara for wanting to take photographs here. Thankfully, this is our last stop of the day before we head to lunch. Gene takes a few shots and steps over to where my mother is waiting so she can approve them.

"I'm dying," Bri hisses at me out the side of her mouth as we wait to see if we're going to get the okay from Mother that we can head inside. "My feet are killing me, and I've got sweat in places I shouldn't." She pulls her dress away from her chest in an attempt to cool herself down.

I stifle a giggle and nod my head. I'm sweating too. I'm going to need another shower after this.

"You okay," Brody asks, walking over with two bottles of water. "Here," he says, handing me one of the bottles before passing the other to Bri.

"Thanks. You're a lifesaver." Bri flashes Brody a grin. Devon stayed back at the hotel today because the sitter they had lined up had to cancel at the last minute.

"Thanks, babe." I take a swig of water.

Brody moves closer to me, and I stiffen, unsure of what he's going to do. "Relax, beautiful," he says, brushing his lips against my cheek. Before I can respond, Mother is telling us to head into the museum.

I heave out a sigh of relief as cold air hits my skin. We're greeted in the foyer by a young woman with a name tag that reads Maria, a tour guide I assume, who starts to tell us about the house.

"We don't have time for a tour. I was informed that we could take pictures inside," Mother barks out, interrupting her.

"Oh, yes. Of course. Right this way," Maria says, gesturing for us to follow her.

"You okay?" Brody asks, falling into step next to me, grabbing my hand and lacing his fingers through mine.

"Fine. Just hot. And tired. Ready to be done."

"You think they're buying it?"

I glance around at the rest of our party. "Yeah. Although I think that everyone is so hot at this point, they're barely noticing what's going on."

"That was exhausting." I flop down onto the couch, kicking my sandals off a few hours later. It's only a little after three, but I feel like I've been on my feet for the past twenty-four hours.

We didn't even walk that far—the trolley drove us around to all the locations and dropped us at the door. But I spent the past five hours with my family. In ninety degree weather and a ridiculous amount of humidity. Something I'm not used to.

"And we still have dinner."

"Don't remind me." I groan, leaning back against the cushions and closing my eyes.

"At least lunch was good."

"Yeah. It was," I say, thinking about the delicious freshly grilled mahi mahi and shrimp I had. "I'm jealous that you got to actually see everything. I had to stand there for countless pictures," I say, looking over at him.

My phone dings with a text message.

Summer: You alive?

I huff out a laugh and text her back.

Me: Yeah, I'm alive. Barely.

She texts back quickly.

Summer: Barely? Call me later. I need the details.

I send her a thumbs up, and set my phone on the coffee table.
Brody studies me. "Summer?"
"Yeah. She was checking in."
He nods but doesn't say anything, pulling my feet into his lap in-
stead.
I let out a moan as he gently starts massaging the sole of my foot.
"That feels so good."
"Good."
I watch as he massages first one foot and then the other. How did I
get so lucky to have a best friend like him?
"I don't know. You just did." Brody looks up at me, smiling, his eyes
twinkling with mischief. I realize I said what I was thinking out loud
and clamp a hand over my mouth. "You'll have to find a way to pay that
friend of yours back for the awesome foot massage he gave you." He
wiggles his eyebrows at me, and I let out a bark of laughter.
"Oh yeah. How do you suggest I pay him back? Cash? A check?
Something else?" I tease.
His expression grows serious, and he's quiet for a moment before he
says, "Kiss him."
"I can do that." I slide my legs off his lap and lean in toward him.
"Wait. Let me wash my hands," Brody says, holding them up be-
tween us and all but jumping to his feet. I rub a hand down my face as
he heads into the bedroom.
What the heck is going on?

Chapter Nineteen

Brody

I'm about to kiss my best friend.

Again.

The woman of my dreams.

I need a moment alone to collect myself before I do something like blurt out that I'm falling in love with her. Because I realize that's what's happening. Maybe I've always been in love with her and was too blind to see it. I close the door to the bathroom and take a deep breath. I'm still reeling from what happened last night. I know we need to talk more about it. What it really means. What it means for our friendship.

For us.

I don't want whatever this is between us to end when this trip is over. I want to see what happens between us. Bracing myself on the counter, I take deep breaths, trying to calm my racing heart.

I'd never really thought about my life after hockey. My plan was to play until I couldn't anymore. Then I'd buy a house somewhere far away from everyone and live out my life in peace and quiet. Alone. I'd find somewhere that no one knew me so I could hide out. Disappear. So there was no one I could let down.

Thinking about it now, I realize that was a ridiculous idea. That as much as everyone thinks I'm a loner, that I keep to myself, I'm not really. I want to be around people. Maybe not the people who I was around today. Or at least, not all of them. But there is one woman who I'd like to be around all the time.

Pushing those thoughts aside, I focus on the task at hand—washing my hands, which are trembling slightly now. I can't remember the last time I felt this way. I'm always calm and composed, on and off the ice, no matter the situation. It's what everyone on the team has come to expect of me.

This is new—feeling off my game. Like the normal rotation of my life has changed. I close my eyes, slowly counting backward from ten.

"You okay?" Aubrey's voice comes from the other side of the door. I should probably go back out there. I've been gone for a long time for someone who was just meant to be washing their hands.

"Yeah." I open the door and walk over to where she's perched on the edge of the bed.

"What do you think about going down to the pool? We've got a couple of hours before dinner," she suggests, and I heave out a breath, grateful she didn't ask me why I was in the bathroom for so long.

"Sounds good to me."

Aubrey riffles through her suitcase, pulling out a bathing suit. I try to focus on changing my clothes, pulling a pair of board shorts from the dresser. But I'm distracted by the sight in front of me, my dick instantly getting hard, as she peels her dress off, her back to me.

"Aubrey," I say and take two steps until I'm standing directly behind her, my hands settling on her hips. Keeping enough distance between us that she doesn't feel my hard on, even though all I want to do is rub it against her, sink into her, feel her heat wrapped around my dick like I felt it wrapped around my fingers last night.

"Yes," she says, peeking over her shoulder at me, a coy smirk on her face.

She knows exactly what she's doing teasing me. Fucking hell. How did I get this lucky that she's interested in me? I will never stop thanking my lucky stars that I'm here with her doing this, whatever this is.

"I never collected on my kiss." I growl, leaning closer to kiss the exposed column of her neck.

"Oh, really," she mumbles, spinning in my hold so she's facing me. "I did promise you a kiss, didn't I?"

I suck in a breath at the sight of the woman in my arms, dressed in a beige bra and matching underwear. Fuck. I really am so gone for her. Aubrey blushes at my perusal, her arms coming up to cover herself.

"Don't." I hate that she's so self-conscious. It bothers me that she thinks she needs to cover herself up around me.

"I—I wasn't expecting to get naked in front of you when I picked these out. I don't . . ." Her gaze drops to the floor.

"Hey," I say, leaning down so she's looking into my eyes. "There's no reason to hide from me."

She gives me a small smile and takes a deep breath. "I feel so inadequate in my boring underwear. I've gained some weight this last year—one more fun part about being in your mid thirties, I guess."

"Aubrey," I say, letting go of her hip so I can stroke her cheek. "Please don't put yourself down. You're beautiful. Exactly the way you are. You always have been. I'm going to kiss you but if you don't want me to you, you need to tell me."

She bites down on her bottom lip, and a growl rumbles in my chest, but I wait for her answer. I don't want to do anything she doesn't want.

"Please," she finally whispers, and I close the distance between us and kiss her.

I grip her hip with one hand and caress her cheek, neck, shoulder and any bare skin I can touch with my other hand. I deepen the kiss, sweeping my tongue against her lips and she opens her mouth for me. Our tongues dance together. She moans and it goes straight to my cock. She reaches up and sinks her nails into my scalp. Her other hand grips my shirt holding me close to her as if she can't get near enough to me.

"Fuck." I groan, tearing my lips from hers. I kiss along her neck, noting the way she shivers and pushes herself closer to me when I reach the spot right behind her ear.

"Brody." She groans as I reach up and cup one of her breasts through her bra.

"Yes, beautiful," I whisper against her neck.

"Take it off."

It takes me a second to realize she means her bra, and I fumble with the clasp before it finally comes loose and I push the straps off her shoulders.

"Hold on," I say as I lean down, gently pick her up, and toss her on the bed. "That's better." I climb across the comforter and hover over her.

"You're wearing too many clothes." She tugs at the hem of my shirt. I sit back and peel it over my head in one swift movement, noting how her pupils dilate even more as she takes in my naked chest, her gaze dancing over my tattoos. I've caught her staring at them a few times recently, and I love that she seems to love them.

"These too," she says, sitting up and fumbling with the button on my shorts before turning to push the comforter down the bed and laying back down again watching me.

My heart races as I stand up, undo my shorts, and pull them off, leaving me in only my black briefs.

This is the moment of truth.

She's going to see it and know.

"I thought we were going to the pool," I say with a laugh as I climb into bed with her.

"This is so much better," Aubrey says, reaching for me, her fingers dancing along the top of my briefs and closer to the secret that I've kept hidden for years. My cock gets harder every time her finger slips under the waistband. I take a deep breath, steeling myself not to pounce on her.

"Take them off." She bats her eyelashes at me like she needs to convince me to do what she's asking.

"You first," I say, gesturing at her underwear, moving back so she can take them off.

She sits up and pushes them down, kicking them off her ankles before motioning for me to do the same. I take a fortifying breath before standing and pushing my briefs down. My cock jumps to attention as her gaze rakes down my body.

I see it. The moment she registers my tattoo.

"Brody." Aubrey says, point at my hip. "What's that?" Her voice is barely above a whisper. She reaches out and traces the constellation on my hip. The one I consider *our* constellation. The one I always try to find when I'm away from the city lights and can see the stars.

"Aubrey." My voice is cautious. She hasn't freaked out yet, so that's got to be a good sign, right?

"Is that Ursa Major?" she asks, finally locking eyes with me.

"Yeah." I climb back into bed, lie down on my back, and tuck my hands under my head.

"How long have you had it?"

"A long time." I reach for her and pull her toward me until she's half on top of me and half on the bed. My cock aches for her, but he's going to have to wait.

"We saw that constellation the night I told you I wanted to be an astronomer," she whispers.

"I know."

I remember that night perfectly. We were sitting in my backyard looking at the stars after a grueling Algebra 2 tutoring session. She'd been tutoring me for a few months by that point, and we'd become friends. An unlikely pair—the jock and his tutor, for lack of a better way to describe us.

Contrary to what everyone thought, I didn't have a lot of friends in high school. Much like I do now, I kept to myself.

Aubrey had pointed out Ursa Major. And then proceeded to point out more constellations. Some I recognized by name and some I didn't. But she knew them all. That was the night she told me she wanted to be an astronomer and study the stars.

"You also told me that night that I should never stop dreaming and that anything was possible," I whisper, running my hand along her back. She pulls away and sits up, her hand resting on my chest.

"Because you told me you were worried you wouldn't get drafted after high school." She blows out a breath. "You said you were afraid your father was right and you were wasting your time. Right after that we saw a shooting star, and I told you to make a wish."

"I remember." I remember that night like it was yesterday, not eighteen years ago. This isn't exactly how I pictured having this conversation with her—naked in bed together—but it's long overdue.

"What'd you wish for?" she asks, tucking a piece of hair behind her ear.

I run my hand along her cheek. "I can't tell you."

"Brody."

I pull her toward me, and as I kiss her, I breathe out the one word that could change everything. "You." She doesn't say anything, so I add, "I wished I could be good enough to be worthy of you."

She stiffens above me, and I wait for her to pull away, but she doesn't. She runs her tongue along the seam of my lips, seeking entrance, and I grant it to her. I let her take control of the kiss, groaning as her tongue enters my mouth. All too soon, she's tearing her lips away.

"You have me, Brody," she says, her chest heaving, her lips swollen from our kisses, and her pupils dilated with desire. "You've always had me. I want you. All of you." She reaches between us and wraps her hand around my cock, stroking it a few times.

"Aubs," I rasp out, closing my eyes and reciting plays in my head so I don't explode from her touch alone. "Stop," I say, stilling her hand.

She pulls back and tries to climb off me.

"Where are you going?"

"I— You—" She points at me, her face turning red.

"Aubrey. I. Want. You." I inhale a deep breath. "If you kept touching me like that, I was going to come."

"Oh." She nibbles on her lower lip, her cheeks getting redder.

"What do you want, Aubs?"

"You," she whispers, peering down at me.

"You have me," I say, using her words. "How do you want me?"

"I want you to fuck me. I need you, Brod. I've needed you for so fucking long, and I can't take it anymore."

Her confession lights up something in me, and I can't hold back anymore. I wanted to let her control the pace, but I don't know if I can. "Are you aching for me? Are you wet for me?" I ask, pulling her back down to my chest, slipping a hand between her legs.

I groan when I feel how wet she is. My dick gets harder, if that's even possible.

"So wet," Aubrey says, rolling onto her back and widening her legs.

"Look at you. So beautiful. Your pussy spread out for me." I stare down at her, thanking my lucky stars that my wish came true. That I finally get to touch her, taste her, and make her come until she can't remember her own name.

I dip down and take one of her breasts into my mouth, then suck it and kiss it as she squirms below me. I chuckle against her chest as I move to the other one and give it the same attention. I let go of her nipple with a pop and kiss down her stomach and along her hip bones.

"Brody." She lets out a breathy sigh.

I smile against her skin and continue my quest, kissing up her thigh and finally reaching my destination—her pussy. Where I bury my tongue inside her. She gasps and thrusts her hips up to meet me, her hands sinking into my hair. I lick, suck, and nip at her like she's my last meal on earth, and she just might be. I could die right now, and I'd go a happy man.

I know she's getting close when her legs start to shake and her moans get louder and louder. Shifting slightly, I slip first one finger, then a second inside her and suck her clit back into my mouth. I glance up at her from between her legs, and our gazes meet.

"Fuck. Brody. Yes. Right there. Yes," she yells, her hips fucking my fingers as she rides out her orgasm. When she's sated, I pull my fingers out and stand up.

"Where are you going?"

"Condom." I walk over to my pants and pull out the one condom I keep tucked into my wallet. I make a mental note to find a place to buy more since it's the only one I have with me. I should have prepared better, but I didn't expect this to happen.

"Hurry," Aubrey rasps out, tracking my movement across the room. "I need your cock inside me. Now."

Fuck me.

Her talking dirty to me is making me even harder. I tear the wrapper open and sheath myself before crawling back onto the bed and aligning myself with her opening. My eyes roll to the back of my head as I stroke my dick along her hot center before I start to slowly sink into her.

She lifts her hips and pulls me in deeper. "Yes," she hisses.

"I'm not hurting you, am I?" I ask through clenched teeth, wanting to start moving but wanting to give her time to adjust to me.

"No, but I need you to move. Please." The last part comes out on a whimper. I pull all the way out and piston back into her. Then do it again and again, reveling in her tight heat wrapping around me every time I re-enter her.

"Harder," she demands, wrapping her arms around my shoulders.

I pull out of her, grab a pillow, and tug her down the bed so her ass is on the end. I shove the pillow under her so she's slightly elevated and lift her legs onto my shoulders.

"What are you— Fuck." She hisses out as I slam into her. This new position allows me to go deeper, and based on the noises she's making, I'd say she's enjoying it too.

"Look at us." I stare down at my dick disappearing into her pussy. "Look at how well you take me, like the good girl you are." I slip my finger between her legs and strum her clit as I hammer into her. Her pussy tightens around me, and I know she's close.

"Come for me, beautiful." I command and she moans, falling over the edge, pulling me with her. "Good girl," I rasp out as I piston my hips a few more times before filling the condom with my release.

I groan, pulling out of her and slumping over the bed, careful not to crush her. My chest is heaving like I ran five miles.

I'm ruined.

Absolutely fucking ruined.

She's ruined me for any other woman.

Not that there's any other woman that I could want after I've had her.

Chapter Twenty

Aubrey

Holy shit.

Holy fucking shit.

I had sex with my best friend.

Hot, amazing sex.

Probably the best I've ever had.

"Have I died and gone to heaven?"

Brody chuckles next to me. "No, you're not in heaven. This is real life, beautiful."

My face heats as the realization of what we did washes over me. Suddenly self-conscious, I roll away from him and move up the bed pulling the covers over myself.

"Aubrey?" Brody says, standing up, a questioning look in his eyes. He watches me for a few beats before gesturing toward the condom. "I'm going to go take care of this, and then we'll talk."

We'll talk.

Great.

Famous last words.

He's already regretting what we did. I got lost in the moment. In the fairy tale. In seeing that tattoo on his hip and discovering he remembers that night as vividly as I do. In his confession of what he wished for. I take a deep breath, trying to stop my spiraling. The bed dips as Brody climbs in next to me.

"What's going on?" he asks, reaching for me. But I shake my head, wrapping my arms around myself, careful to keep the sheet over my body.

"Aubrey. Talk to me. Please."

"You tell me." I take a deep breath before continuing. "You said you wanted to talk."

"I wanted to know why you pulled away from me. What happened?" His gaze darts around my face.

"I thought you were having second thoughts."

"Never, Aubs. Never." This time when he reaches for me, I let him pull me into his arms and bury my head in his chest, inhaling deeply.

"Why have we waited so long to do that?" he asks after several moments of silence. "I was such a fool to not tell you how I felt sooner. I'm sorry, Aubrey."

"Why are you sorry?" I ask, pulling back so I can look him in the eyes. His gaze darts back and forth, and he swallows a few times before speaking.

"Because I've been missing out on you all these years. On this. On us."

"Brody, you know it would never have worked out. We live over a hundred miles apart. We both have demanding jobs." I take a deep breath. "Yes, the sex was amazing. The best I've ever had. But I'm moving, and we'll be thousands of miles apart. We should enjoy this week together."

"My contract is up with the Storm. I have nothing tying me to Florida anymore. What happens if we weren't going to be thousands of miles apart?"

I open and close my mouth a few times before finally saying, "There are no hockey teams in Hawaii, Brody. Besides I'm sure it's only a matter of time before the Storm call with a new contract." Why is this so hard? My heart wants one thing—Brody—but my brain wants another thing—this job in Hawaii.

Everything in me is at war.

He runs a hand down his face blowing out a breath before saying, "I don't think they will. I'll be an Unrestricted Free Agent on the first. That's only a few weeks away. They would've called by now."

"Maybe," I say, my heart racing. "Or maybe they'll call you tomorrow. Or another team could offer you a contract."

Brody opens his mouth to speak, but the room phone starts ringing. *Saved by the bell.*

Hello," he says, answering it. He's quiet, listening to what's being said on the other end. "She's in the shower," he says after glancing over at me. "Yep. Will do. Okay. Bye." He hangs up the phone with a sigh.

"My mother?"

"The one and only. She wanted to make sure we weren't going to be late to dinner. Had to remind me three times that it starts promptly at six and that we need to be there on time. Speaking of which"—he glances over at the clock—"you should get in the shower if we're both going to freshen up before dinner and be on time."

I nod, getting up. For once in my life, I'm glad for my mother's incessant need to remind me about being places on time because it ended the conversation Brody and I were having.

"This discussion isn't over though," he says as I climb out of bed and make my way to the bathroom.

"Okay. Fine," I concede although I don't know what else there is to talk about. The Storm will offer him a new contract and the possibility of us being anything more than friends after this week is over will be moot. And if they don't, I'm sure another team will want him.

"Your turn," I say ten minutes later as I walk out of the bathroom, wrapped in a towel. Brody makes his way to the shower. Once I hear it running, I grab my phone and slip out of the bedroom.

"Hey," I whisper when Summer picks up.

"Why are we whispering?"

"Because Brody's in the shower, and I don't want him to hear." I lean against the counter in the kitchen. Hopefully the walls are thick enough that if he gets out, he won't hear my conversation.

"What happened?" Summer's voice gets serious. I can picture her turning off whatever she was watching—probably Grey's Anatomy—and giving me her undivided attention.

"What makes you think something happened?"

"You're calling me while on vacation with that hot as sin fake boyfriend of yours."

I bark out a laugh at her description of Brody. She's the only one who knows our relationship isn't real. She would have seen right through me, so I told her the truth. Not surprisingly, she was all on board with the fake relationship. Told me it was about damn time.

"It's not a vacation," I protest, readjusting my towel.

"Aubrey!"

"Fine. Fine." I huff out a breath. "We had sex."

Summer squeals, and I have to pull the phone away from my ear so I don't go deaf. "Are you done?"

"Freaking fin-a-lly. What was it like?"

"It was good."

"Good, Aubrey? Just good? Is there something wrong with him? Does he not know how to use his goods? Pleasure a woman? Is he small? Because that man has big hands, so I figured . . ."

I snicker. I hear a beeping in the background on Summer's end followed by what sounds like a microwave. "Are you making popcorn?"

"Duh, woman. Now give me the details."

"I don't have time for details," I hiss.

"Okay, so tell me the details later. Why are you calling me anyways? Shouldn't you be waiting for him naked in bed for round two or three?"

"I'm calling because I'm freaking out."

"Why are you freaking out?"

I take a deep breath, trying to put into words how I feel. I hear Summer moving around on her end, fixing her bowl of popcorn, I assume. I've never liked talking about my feelings, probably because of my family. It always takes me a little while to articulate everything, but I don't have all day. Brody could be done with his shower any minute and come out to find me on the phone, so I say the first thing that comes to mind. "Because it changes everything between us."

"How so?"

"Because— Because— It just does. And I don't know what to do about it," I answer.

"You like him, and he likes you, right?"

"Yeah." I nod although she can't see me.

"You're both consenting adults who aren't in another relationship, right?"

"Yes." Where is she going with this?

"What's the big deal? Enjoy the sex. That man adores you. Let him shower you with orgasms and attention." She says it like it's common sense. Like of course that's what I should do.

"What happens after this trip is over? He hinted at moving to Hawaii with me. I can't let him give up hockey for me. But how could we do long distance? That would be crazy with the time difference plus his schedule is chaotic. We'd never talk let alone see each other."

"You'll figure it out. If it was meant to be it'll work out. Stop worrying about it, and live in the moment," Summer says, like it's that simple.

It's at that moment that I hear the bathroom door open. "I gotta go." I hang up the phone before she can say anything else.

"What are you doing out here?" Brody asks, walking toward me.

"I—I, ah . . ." I clear my throat. Why do I feel the need to lie to him? It's not like he's going to care who I was talking to. "I was talking to Summer. My friend from work," I hastily add, my heart racing. What if he asks me why I was talking to her?

"I know who Summer is. I've met her. Remember? That time you two came to a game?"

"Right. That's right." I shift from foot to foot. "I should probably get dressed." I step around him and all but run into the bedroom. I frantically pull on underwear and a bra and hurry to the closet. I fling the door open and start rifling through my clothes for something to wear tonight.

"Hey. What's going on?" Brody asks, coming up behind me, his hands landing on my shoulders. He gently spins me around, studying my face before wrapping his arms around me and pulling me into his chest where I relax into him.

"I'm sorry. I'm panicking."

He rubs my back in small circles. "Because of dinner? I think we have plenty of time to get ready and get there on time."

I shake my head. "No, I'm panicking because we had sex and I don't want it to ruin our friendship," I admit.

"Hey. It won't, Aubrey. I promise. Look at me." He pauses and I do as he asks, meeting his gaze. "I promise you I will not let it ruin our friendship. How about we get through dinner and we can talk about it."

"Okay."

Brody leans in and kisses me gently before pulling back and walking over to the dresser to pull out clothes.

I can't help staring at him, at the way his muscles flex and move as he pulls on a pair of jeans and a button-down shirt. At how it felt earlier having his dick deep inside of me, filling me up. The dirty things he said to me. The sounds he made when he came.

"Is this outfit okay?" he asks, spinning back around to face me. His eyes widen when he sees me still standing in my bra and underwear. "Were you watching me, beautiful?" He stalks over. "I thought you were going to get dressed, but you're over here still half naked," he says before kissing me.

"I—I got distracted."

"Whatever you were thinking"—he dips down so he can whisper in my ear, his warm breath giving me goosebumps—"save it for later. If you tell me now, we won't make it to dinner."

"I—I wasn't thinking anything."

"You were blushing, which means you were thinking something dirty. I'd ask you to share it with me, but we have somewhere to be. The last thing I want is for your mother to flip if we don't make it or we're late." With that, he steps back, and I immediately miss his warmth.

I whirl around and resume my hunt for something to wear. I settle on a navy sundress with cap sleeves and tiny flowers all over it. It comes down to mid calf, but it has a slit up the side that makes me feel sexy. Not something I'd normally wear, but Summer insisted I try it on when we went shopping, and I fell in love with it. It takes me ten minutes to apply some light makeup, braid my hair, and add a pair of small silver studs and a matching necklace. I grab a clutch, shove my room key, ChapStick, driver's license, and a credit card into it, then find Brody, who's on the couch engrossed in SportsCenter.

"You ready?" I ask, slipping into my sandals.

"As ready as I'll ever be," Brody says, turning off the television and finally looking up at me. "Hot damn, Aubrey."

I blush under his gaze.

"You okay?" he asks a few minutes later, his hand on my lower back as we step off the elevator and make our way toward the ballroom where we had brunch yesterday.

"Fine. Fine."

"I'm right here," he says, removing his hand from my back and entwining our fingers. The sight of his much larger hand wrapped around mine makes me grin.

"Let's do this."

We turn the corner and walk inside. I'm taken aback by the complete transformation. It doesn't feel like we're in the same ballroom as yesterday.

The lights are dimmed, and a string quartet plays in the corner. The large round tables have been replaced with smaller, more intimate tables of varying sizes, which are scattered around the room. Each is adorned with a light pink tablecloth, a vase of flowers, and tea candles.

"Wow," Brody whispers under his breath.

I don't have time to respond as Clara comes toward us, dressed in a knee-length pale-pink dress, her blonde hair twisted up into a fancy updo.

"Hi, Aubrey. Brody. I'm glad you're here. I hope you both enjoy tonight." She sweeps her arm around the room. "You're at table twelve." She points to a table for two situated in the corner. Bri and Devon are seated nearby.

"This is beautiful, Clara. Not at all what I expected," I admit, watching wait staff dressed in black uniforms flit between the tables bringing guests drinks.

Clara laughs. "Mom about shit her pants when I told the wedding planner what I wanted. She wasn't thrilled. But this was important to Chet and me. We wanted to recreate the place we had our first date. One of the waiters will take your order. Dinner menus are on the table."

Before I can pick my jaw off the ground and reply, Chet walks up and pulls Clara into his side, kissing her.

"Hello, Aubrey." He greets me with a smile before turning his attention to Brody. I hold my breath, waiting to see what he's going to say. Brody told me what happened at brunch, and I laughed so hard when he recounted Arthur and Thad's comments. Chet clears his throat and puts his hand out to Brody. "I want to apologize for the way I spoke to you yesterday. It was out of line."

Brody jerks his head back slightly before letting go of my hand and shaking Chet's. "Apology accepted."

"You caught me having a bad morning. But that's not an excuse for how I treated you. I'm sorry."

Brody looks over at me, and I shake my head slightly, silently telling him that I have no idea what happened.

"No worries," Brody says.

"Okay. Well then, right this way," Clara says, spinning on her heel and grabbing Chet's hand as she beckons for us to follow her to our table. Once we are seated, they excuse themselves to greet more guests. A waiter appears and we order some drinks.

"Are we in the twilight zone?" Brody whispers, leaning across the table.

"I don't know. Maybe." I huff out a laugh, glancing around the room. I spot my mother sitting next to Aurthur at a table with Chet's parents. She's scowling even more than usual and sitting stiffly in her seat. I glance over at my little sister, and for the first time in a long time, I really look at her. She's glowing. Without our mother hovering around pushing things on her, Clara seems like a different person.

"What are you thinking?" Brody asks me after the waiter comes back with our drinks and asks us what we'd like for dinner.

"That all of this"—I gesture around—"is not what I was expecting. And that maybe I unfairly judged my sister. I kind of wonder how much of this week was her idea and how much of it was Mother's because she likes to put on a show."

"But what about what Clara said to you last night? That isn't exactly something you can blame on your mom. That was all her."

"Maybe you're right. But also, do I really know her anymore? She's been around our mother a lot longer than I ever was. Maybe that's her coping mechanism . . ." I suggest while watching Clara and Chet talk to their friends at another table.

"Don't make excuses for her."

Before I can say anything, the waiter returns with our food, and we dig into our meals. I contemplate what Brody said, but I also start to wonder if there's more going on with Clara and Mother than I know. I make a mental note to pull Bri aside later and ask her what's really going on. And to talk to Clara more.

Chapter Twenty-One

Brody

I sneak glances at Aubrey during dinner, trying to figure out how to approach the topic of us being together after this week. I was just going to go for it and tell her how I feel, but after I overheard her on the phone with Summer, I realized I need a plan—a way that we can make it work between us—for her to even consider us staying together. Something more than *I'm going to retire and go with her wherever she goes even if that means moving to Hawaii.*

Now that I've had her, I don't want to let her go. I don't want anyone else. Aubrey has always been special to me, but now it's on a whole other level. We've skipped the whole awkward getting to know each other and figuring out if we're compatible because we've been friends for so long. Somehow, I instinctively knew her body and what would make her feel good.

I didn't know what I was missing until I had her, and now I don't ever want to go without her again. I hope she feels the same way. Because if she doesn't, I don't know what I'm going to do. I hope her reluctance for us to be something more is only because she doesn't know my plan to retire.

I open my mouth to ask if she wants to dance but am interrupted by the buzzing of my phone in my pocket. I pull it out and see it's Bruce, my agent. I hit Ignore, sending him to voicemail.

"Everything okay?"

"Yeah. Fine." I shove my phone back into my pocket. "It was Caleb. I'll call him later." The lie rolls off my tongue. It feels easier than telling her the truth. I glance up to find her studying me.

"Let's dance." I gesture toward the small dance floor set up in front of the string quartet.

"Oh, I don't think . . ."

"Come on," I say, getting to my feet and holding out my hand.

"No one else is dancing," Aubrey protests, glancing around the room at the rest of the guests who are all either still eating dinner or standing around in small groups talking.

"Who cares." I reach for her hand, gently tugging on it, hoping she'll come with me. "I want to dance with you, Aubs," I whisper, leaning down to press my lips against hers briefly. She inhales shakily but finally stands and takes my outstretched hand. I lead us toward the dance floor and pull her into me as we start to sway.

What the hell am I doing?

I don't dance. Especially not when there's no one else dancing. But it felt right when I asked her. Like everything else we've done together these last few days. I regret nothing. The only thing I regret is not doing these things with her sooner.

The awkwardness of being the only ones on the dance floor fades as I get lost in the way she feels nestled against my chest. I lean over and capture her lips in a kiss, pulling back before it gets heated because this is not the time nor the place. I'd hate to give her mother more ammunition. I hear rustling next to us and turn my head to see Brielle and Devon joining us on the dance floor. Brielle flashes us a knowing smile before Devon pulls her into his arms and they start swaying.

"We started a trend," Aubrey whispers a few minutes later as other couples join us.

"See, aren't you glad I had this idea?" I whisper back. We dance through a few more songs before the string quartet takes a break. I reluctantly let go of Aubrey, and she steps back out of my arms.

"Want to go get a drink with us after this?" Brielle asks as we walk back toward our tables.

Aubrey hesitates, looking at me.

"Sounds good to me," I say.

"Me too," Aubrey agrees.

"I haven't had this much fun in a long time." Brielle giggles, a few hours later as she leans back against the booth in the hotel bar where the four of us retreated after dinner ended.

"That's kind of sad," Aubrey says, draining her glass of wine.

"That's what happens when you're a parent." Brielle giggles again. She's on her second pina colada, and if I had to guess, definitely feeling it.

"Anyone want another drink?" I ask, finishing the rest of my bourbon in one sip.

"Yes, please," Aubrey says.

"Just water for us," Devon says. "If you don't mind."

"You got it." I slide out of the booth and walk over to the bar. The bartender is busy, his back to me, so I lean against the bar waiting my turn.

"Buy me a drink?" I hear next to me. I don't answer, assuming whoever the woman is she's talking to someone else, but suddenly a hand lands on my sleeve, and I start. I turn toward the woman who is touching me.

She winks at me before saying, "Buy me a drink, hot stuff."

"No," I grind out, attempting to shake her hand off. Why do people think they can touch someone they don't know without permission?

"Oh, come on," she purrs, moving closer to me.

"I'm not interested," I repeat, finally freeing my arm.

"There you are, hunny," Aubrey says from my other side.

"Hi beautiful," I say, flashing her a relieved look as she takes my hand in hers.

"Thank you for keeping my fiancé company while I was in the ladies room," Aubrey says, leaning around me to address the woman on my other side before kissing me.

Her tongue darts out, and I open for her, conscious that we have an audience but not caring. We kiss for far longer than is probably appropriate for the middle of a bar. Distantly, I hear a throat clearing, and I break our kiss to find the bartender staring at us. But the woman who was hitting on me is gone.

"That was hot," I whisper to Aubrey once I've placed our order. What I don't tell her is how much I liked it when she called me her fiancé.

Aubrey winks.

"What did we think about tonight's dinner? I for one wasn't expecting it," Aubrey asks once we're back at the table.

Brielle drinks some water before speaking. "Mom wasn't happy. I had to hear her opinion about how silly the whole thing was. Apparently, she wanted to rent out a restaurant downtown, but Clara refused. Sounded like it was a whole argument."

"Arthur said that Beatrice threatened to not pay for the whole wedding. He had to step in and smooth things over," Devon adds.

"I'm shocked he has that much pull over her." I take a sip from my drink.

"Yeah. They're an interesting pair," Brielle says with a shake of her head. Everyone nods their agreement.

"So," Brielle says. "Is it true what they say about hockey players?" She smirks at me over the rim of her glass.

"What's that?" I brace myself for what's about to come out of her mouth. I don't know the adult version of Brielle very well, but I have learned, in the few hours we've been sitting in the bar, that the more she drinks, the less of a filter she has.

"That their stamina is through the roof. That they can go All. Night. Long." She punctuates each word with a waggle of her eyebrows. I choke on my bourbon and have to inhale deeply a few times before I can breathe again.

"For fuck's sake," Aubrey mumbles, shaking her head at her sister, her face flushing.

"What?" Brielle asks, raising a shoulder in a half shrug. "Is it true?"

Well things just got *interesting*.

Did not see the conversation going this way tonight.

"Bri," Devon hisses. "Sorry." He directs his apology at us.

I chuckle into my glass and take another sip, waiting to see what Aubrey's answer is.

"None of your business." Aubrey says, glaring at her sister.

Thankfully, the conversation shifts after that. Eventually, Brielle and Devon decide to call it a night, so we pay our bills and head to the elevators.

Even though we were up much later last night than nights past, my eyes still pop open at seven. I lie in bed for a little while trying to fall back to sleep, but it's no use. With a sigh, I get up and pull on my gym clothes and running shoes. Might as well get a run in if I can't sleep.

An hour later, having run six miles and stretched, I head back to our suite. As I'm opening the door, my phone vibrates with a text from Bruce. I knew ignoring his call last night wasn't going to stop him.

Bruce: Hey Brody. I know you're on vacation, but I wanted to talk to you about the offer I got from the Storm.

My mouth falls open. The Storm want me back? I scrub a hand down my face, inhaling sharply as I step into our suite. Didn't see that coming. Before I can respond, another message comes through.

Bruce: Three years. Eight million a year.

My eyes dart toward the still dark bedroom where Aubrey is sleeping. That's quite an impressive offer. In any other situation, I'd be jumping to tell Bruce to accept it, but now, after the events of the past few days, I don't know. I want to explore whatever is starting between Aubrey and me. But she's moving to Hawaii in the fall. I can't take the deal without seeing where things are going between us. Without talking to Aubrey about where we might be headed. I take a deep breath and then type a message back to Bruce.

Me: Not sure. Let me think about it.

Bruce's response comes quickly. He must be glued to his phone.

Bruce: I don't know that the Storm can do any better with the salary cap they're up against. But maybe another team might.
Me: It's not that. Let me think about it.
Bruce: Okay, but I need an answer before July first.
Me: Okay.

I stare at my phone long after it goes black, thinking about the Storm's offer. Is this real life? I've spent the past two months convincing myself that my career was over, which wasn't as terrifying as it ought to be. And now here they are asking me to come back. I just don't know if I want to.

Especially if it means giving up Aubrey.

Chapter Twenty-Two

Aubrey

The sound of a door closing and the squeaking of wheels wakes me up. A glance at the clock tells me that it's probably time to get up if I'm going to be ready by eleven to head to the spa. I'm sitting up in bed when Brody pokes his head into the bedroom.

"Good morning."

Even sweaty from a workout, he's gorgeous. I'm sure I look like a wreck with my hair a rat's nest from sleeping with it loose. As I'm gathering the energy to get out of bed to brush my teeth Brody sits down and leans toward me.

"Morning," I mumble, scrunching up my nose.

Brody steps back. "Sorry, I probably smell."

He's worried about smelling bad? I gesture to my mouth. "No. Morning breath."

"Aubrey, I don't give a fuck about morning breath." He leans closer to me again.

"But I do." I put a hand to his chest to stop him. He sighs and shakes his head but moves so I can get out of bed.

"Ready for today?" I ask as a few minutes later, my teeth brushed and hair tamed.

Brody's reclining against the back of the bed, sans shirt and shoes, scrolling on his phone.

He lifts a shoulder in a half shrug, and says, "Sure."

I raise an eyebrow. While the bachelorette and bachelor events today are just for the wedding party, Chet extended invites to both Brody and Devon since they're the only ones whose partners are in the wedding and they aren't.

"You could always back out," I offer, knowing full well how Brody feels about golf.

"It's fine." Brody gets to his feet. "There's food in the living room. And coffee. I'm going to take a shower."

He leans down and brushes his lips against mine, and it takes all of me not to protest when he pulls back and saunters into the bathroom, closing the door behind him. I wait until I hear the shower turn on before pulling off my shirt and underwear. I leave them in a pile by the bathroom door. Taking a deep breath, I step inside, hoping Brody's actually in the shower and not going to the bathroom. I can't help but stare at the sight in front of me—Brody naked, his back to me as he soaps up his hair.

"Aubrey?" Brody says as he turns to catch me staring at him, a smirk on his face. "Did you need something?"

"I, ah . . ." I'm at a loss for words, my bravery having disappeared the minute he caught me in here. What happens if I overstepped? Maybe I shouldn't have barged in on his shower. My eyes drift down his body to his cock, which gets harder the longer I stare at it.

"You coming to join me, beautiful?" Brody asks, and my gaze moves up to meet his. I see the desire I feel reflected back in his expression. All I can do is nod, pull open the glass door, and step in. He moves back, and I get under the hot water.

"Fuck, you're so sexy like that," Brody rasps.

"Like what?" I turn to look at him. He's standing in the corner of the shower, watching me as he strokes himself.

"All wet. The water running down your body. Hell, Aubrey, I could come watching you take a shower."

I let out a bark of laughter, moving closer to him. "Oh yeah." I reach out and run my hands over his body, and he groans, tipping his head back.

"Touch me," he says, letting go of his cock and gripping my hips to pull me closer. I oblige, wrapping my hand around him.

"Like this?"

Brody hums in response, his hand tracing my hip bone, making me shiver, before dipping between my legs and swiping across my clit.

"Brod," I rasp out as he sinks a finger inside me.

"Hmmm?" he mumbles, leaning closer to me and kissing along my collarbone and up my neck as he pumps his finger in and out of me. It's all I can do to hold myself upright and stroke him.

"I'm so close, Aubs."

"Me too," I grit out. He uses his thumb to stroke my clit, and I combust, yelling out his name as I come. He removes his fingers from me and wraps his hand around mine, helping me stroke him. I look down, mesmerized by his bigger, stronger hand wrapped around mine, guiding me back and forth over his cock.

"Fuck, this is hot," Brody says, thrusting a few times before shooting hot white ribbons of cum all over the shower wall. We stroke him a couple more times before he removes his hand and I let go of him. Needing a moment, I step back under the spray of the shower as he sags against the wall.

"Damn, woman," he says a couple of seconds later. "What a way to start the day."

I smile, moving out of the way so he can rinse off, but I have to agree with him. What a way to start the day. We're silent as we shower although he steals a few kisses and touches as he helps me wash. I can't help but stare at him as he rinses the soap off his body, and much to my delight, his cock starts to get hard again under my gaze.

"If you keep looking at me like that, we'll be heading back to bed when we get out of here, and there won't be any spa or golf happening today."

"Yes, please."

Brody smirks as he turns off the water. "Up to you."

I take the towel he hands me and start drying off. "We probably shouldn't. But I want to."

"Me too," he says, leaning over and kissing me before wrapping his towel around his waist and stepping out of the shower. I follow him back into the bedroom, glancing at the clock on the nightstand to see if we have time for a quickie before we have to get ready. Before I can decide, my phone dings from the nightstand. I grab it, holding my breath and hoping that it isn't my mother because I haven't had coffee yet. Thankfully, it's not, it's Summer.

Summer: Checking in to see how things are going. The office is quiet without you.

I snicker. The office is always quiet.

Me: Going okay. Clara was strangely nice last night. IDK. It's a long story. I'll fill you in after I get back.

Summer: I can't wait to hear what she did now. How's your sexy boyfriend? Is he giving you all the orgasms you can ask for, or do I need to talk to him?

I choke on nothing. Leave it to Summer to ask that question. Again.

"You okay?" Brody's voice comes from behind me.

"Fine. Fine," I say between deep breaths. "Went down the wrong pipe."

Brody smirks, his eyes darting to my phone. "Tell Summer I said hi," he says finally.

Busted.

"Hey, Bri." I greet my sister at the table she's sitting at in the hotel café. "What are you doing over here? I thought we were meeting out front." This isn't like her. Usually, I'm the one who doesn't want to socialize.

"I wasn't ready to face them." She tilts her chin toward the lobby behind me. I turn and see Clara holding court with her friends surrounding her, giggling about something.

"Are they really that bad?" I ask with a raise of my shoulder, turning back to Bri.

She takes another deep breath, and on an exhale, says, "My head is pounding. Anabelle woke up three times in the middle of the night. Devon got up with her so I could sleep, but it still woke me. Why did I think pina coladas after multiple glasses of wine was a good idea?" She pinches the bridge of her nose, wrinkling her forehead.

"At least there won't be much chatting while we're at the spa. Should give you plenty of time to recover. Did you take anything?"

"Yeah." Bri gets to her feet. "Advil. And I drank what feels like a gallon of water. And had a Gatorade for good measure." She tips her head toward the others. "We should probably go over there."

I hook my arm through my sister's, and we make our way to Clara and her friends. "Sisters," Clara squeals as she hurries over and throws her arms around us. Bri and I exchange looks over the top of her head.

"You okay?" I ask Clara.

"Perfectly wonderful now that you're here. Ready to go?" Her words are slightly slurred.

"Where's Mom?" Bri asks.

"She isn't coming," Clara answers, pulling back and turning toward her friends. Weird.

"Oh." My eyes widen at the revelation, and I wait for Clara to elaborate, but she doesn't. Bri simply shrugs her shoulders.

"Limo is here," one of the bridesmaids yells. We make our way outside. Once seated, I pull out my phone and text Brody.

Me: In the limo. Clara's already tipsy. Surprisingly, my mother's not here.

I don't have to wait long for a response.

Brody: At least you won't have to worry about her criticizing everything you do. Try to relax and enjoy.

I exhale and tuck my phone away. Of course he sees it. I think everyone sees the way my mother treats me. I am glad she's not here, but it still surprises me. At brunch on Tuesday, she said she was looking forward to the spa. I make a mental note to ask Brody if Arthur played golf with them.

Four hours later, I'm nicely relaxed after a Swedish massage, a mud wrap–which was as gross as it was relaxing–a manicure, a pedicure, and a few glasses of champagne.

"You excited for the big day?" I ask Clara as we sit waiting for our manicures to dry and for the rest of the group to finish getting their nails done.

"I guess," Clara whispers, studying her nails.

"You guess?" I repeat. "I thought you were excited to marry Chet." I pull my hands out of the nail dryer and inspect the light pink polish that matches my maid of honor dress.

Clara peeks up at me, and I wonder if she's drunk enough alcohol today to loosen her tongue. I sit silently, waiting for her to elaborate.

"I am. But this wasn't how I imagined it," she finally says with a resigned sigh.

Well, color me shocked. Clara's been talking about Key West and this wedding since they settled on a date. I open my mouth, but she cuts me off.

"Don't get me wrong, I'm excited to get married here. I just pictured something . . . different." She picks up her water bottle and takes a sip, as if what she told me is no big deal.

"Oh?" Is all I can come up with?

Clara blows on her nails although I'm sure they're dry by now. "It wasn't my idea to have such a huge wedding party. Or to do just about everything else we've done."

"Whose idea was it?" I ask, even though I already know the answer.

Clara levels me with a look that says *take a wild guess* before saying, "Mom's."

"What are we talking about?" Bri asks, taking a seat on the other side of Clara.

"The wedding," Clara says, staring back down at her nails. "I hate my dress. It's ugly."

Shit.

Shit.

I suck in a deep breath, shocked at my sister's revelations.

Bri interjects. "Why didn't you say anything?"

Clara stares down at the floor. "She insisted that I looked the best in that dress. That it was the one I should get. And since she's paying for the wedding . . ."

I meet Bri's gaze, silently asking her what to do.

"I don't—" I start, but Clara interrupts me, glancing at both of us.

"There's nothing to be done now. It is what it is. It'll be over in a few days, and I can move on with my life."

I hate that answer, but there isn't much that can be done now about her dress. I wish I had known how she felt sooner. So I could do what, though? It's not like I could have swayed my mother. But maybe I could have supported Clara more during the planning. If I had, maybe she would have had the strength to stand up to Mother.

There's one thing that's been bothering me since the change in Clara's demeanor and attitude toward me last night. No time like the present.

"Why were you so adamant about proving that Brody and I aren't really dating?"

Clara studies me for a minute before saying, "I figured telling Mom that you two were fake would get her off my back and back to meddling in your life. It would take her focus off me. Make me feel better about my shitty wedding. I'm sorry."

The rest of the bridal party comes pouring in from the room where they were getting their nails done. Clara is swept away by her friends, and I'm left alone with Bri.

"Did you know about Clara's feelings toward the wedding?" I ask her.

"Not all of it. I knew she wasn't happy, but I figured it was because Mom was taking over."

Clara calls us over before I can ask any more questions, and we head to the limo.

"Well," Clara says once we're all seated, "We're going to meet the guys for lunch. After lunch, we're heading to the Southernmost Bar. We rented out the back room there."

The group cheers. I pull out my phone for the first time in a few hours and see I have a couple of missed calls from a number in Hawaii. My heart starts pounding as I unlock my phone and navigate to my voicemail. Thank goodness for the automatic transcription because there's no way I could hear the message with how loud it is.

My heart is in my throat as I read, *Hi, Dr. Fairchild. This is Angie from the Observatory. I wanted to call and let you know that you passed the background check. Welcome to the team. I'll be sending over some paperwork and information about what you can expect in the next week via email.*

I let out a little squeal that's drowned out by the noise in the limo.

As we drive toward downtown, it starts to sink in that I really am moving to Hawaii in a few months. That Brody and I really are going to have to end things when this trip ends.

Chapter Twenty-Three

Brody

The limo pulls up to the restaurant downtown where we're meeting the bachelorette party for lunch. I was relieved when Chet announced that this was our next stop. Golf was fine. It's just not my thing. I hung out with Devon, Thad, and Arthur, all of whom looked as excited about golf as I felt. We played six holes before deciding we'd had enough and headed to the clubhouse.

While we waited for the rest of the bachelor party, I enjoyed a leisurely cup of coffee while staring out at the ocean. Really social, I know, but it's not like there was much conversation happening. Thad and Devon both had their noses buried in their phones, and Arthur fell asleep.

As we pile out of the limo, I spot Aubrey off to the side leaning against the wall of the restaurant.

"Hey, Brod," she says when I walk up to her.

"Hey beautiful." I tug her into me and give her a quick kiss. "Have fun at the spa?"

"Yeah. I actually did. Got my nails done." She wiggles her fingers at me. "Had a nice massage. It was really relaxing."

"Good." I take her hand and we walk toward the entrance.

"How was golf?"

"Eh. We played six holes and then some of us went up to the clubhouse until everyone else was done. It's right on the ocean, though, so the views were magnificent."

"Everyone was nice to you?" Aubrey asks, tilting her head toward me.

I huff out a laugh. "Yes, everyone was nice to me."

"Good. Because otherwise we would have had a problem."

I shake my head at her. It's sweet and kind of a turn on that she asked if everyone was nice to me. The thought of her defending me makes my heart swell, although I'm not sure what she'd do or say, but it's the thought that counts.

I hold the door open for her. The hostess shows us to the private room, where we slip into two of the three empty chairs around a large, long table. Who's missing?

"It's my mother," Aubrey whispers. "I still don't know why she didn't come today."

I wait silently for her to elaborate but she just shrugs before handing me a menu. Two waitresses arrive to take our drink orders.

Aubrey gets pulled into a conversation with Bri and one of Clara's friends, and I sit back, watching everyone talking and enjoying themselves. Once we place our food orders, we don't have long to wait before we're being served.

"Everybody ready?" Chet asks twenty minutes later, chugging the rest of his drink as he stands up. "The limos should be outside waiting to take us to the Southernmost Bar."

Everyone gets to their feet slowly. Some have sobered up during the meal, and others have gotten more drunk. And here we are heading to a bar in the middle of the afternoon. I'm not entirely sure I'm ready to witness whatever wildness is bound to happen.

"Want to go back to the hotel?" Aubrey whispers, as if she can sense my discomfort.

"Yeah," I mumble out the side of my mouth as we trail behind the group.

Before she can say anything, Arthur pipes up, "Well kids, it was fun." He claps his hands together, glancing around at everyone and smiling before saying, "But I think I'm going to head back to the hotel."

"Us too," Brielle says, much to my dismay. "The nanny's been with Anabelle all day. I told her we'd be back in an hour two hours ago."

"Us as well," Aubrey says, slipping her hand into mine.

"Oh, come on," Clara groans, shooting her sisters a look.

"Sorry, I've got some work things that I need to take care of." Aubrey shrugs her shoulders. Is that true? Or is she using it as an excuse to get out of going to the bar?

"Fine. Fine," Clara huffs out, coming over to hug her sisters. The group going to the bar gets into the limos, leaving those of us who are going back to the hotel standing in the hot sun outside the restaurant.

"I need a nap," Brielle announces as we wait for our Uber.

"Me too," Aubrey agrees.

I look over at her and she winks, the corner of her mouth quirking up into a grin. Come to think of it, I could nap too. Although, with the way Aubrey was looking at me, I'm not sure if she meant a nap as in the kind where you actually sleep or if she was implying something else. The thought of something else with her has my cock stirring to attention. Our Uber pulls up, and we all pile in for the short ride back to the hotel.

"So," I say as we part ways with the rest of the group.

"So," Aubrey repeats, looping her arm through mine as we walk toward the elevators.

"Do you really need a nap or were you implying you needed something else?"

Her lips quirk up in a half smile leaning against the elevator wall as we make our slow ascent up to the sixth floor.

"Aubs," I growl, caging her against the wall.

"Was this, the something else you were referring to?" she asks coyly as she reaches up and wraps her arms around my neck before kissing me.

I groan, dropping my arms and tugging her into me as her tongue darts out, seeking entrance. Our kiss is short-lived as the elevator comes to a halt on our floor. With a huff, I step back, letting her exit first. She reaches for my hand as we walk the short distance to our suite. She toes off her shoes inside the door before glancing over her shoulder at me with a smug grin and making her way to the bedroom, dropping her purse on the couch as she walks by.

"Aubs," I repeat, stalking after her.

By the time I reach the bedroom, she's tugging her shirt over her head, her shorts a heap on the floor. Turning so her back is to me, she reaches up and unclasps her bra, and with a glance over her shoulder at me in the doorway, lets it fall to the floor.

"Fuck." I grit out, my cock hardening at the sight in front of me—Aubrey naked except for her underwear.

"I told you I needed a nap," she says with a smirk before climbing into bed. I laugh, yanking off my shirt and shorts before climbing in after her.

"Do you need some company?"

"Mmmhm," Aubrey says, her eyes raking down my body.

Two can play this game. I push back the covers and make myself comfortable.

"You know what? I think I've got too many clothes on." I push my boxers down, my cock springing out. "That's better."

With a grin, I fist my hardening cock and stroke myself a few times. What the hell has gotten into me? I'm not usually this . . . playful. Aubrey brings it out in me.

"I don't think I'm tired anymore," she whispers.

"Oh yeah?" I turn to look at her, and she's staring at my cock, licking her lips.

Goal, Brody.

"Something else you'd like to do instead?" I continue to stroke myself, glancing over at her.

"Touch you."

"Go right ahead." I tuck both of my hands behind my head as she reaches a tentative hand out and strokes first one finger then another over my cock and around the sensitive head.

"Fuck," I grit out as I get even harder. Aubrey giggles and continues her barely there touches. "Harder," I beg. Yeah, I'm not above begging at this point because my cock is starting to ache for her touch, for release. "Please."

She does as I ask, wrapping her hand around me. *Shit, that feels good.* I close my eyes and take a deep breath, trying to stave off the orgasm that's already tingling at the base of my spine as she strokes me. My hips pump reflexively. Suddenly, her hand is gone, and I open my eyes as she leans over me, running her tongue along the underside of my cock before sucking me into her mouth.

"Shit." I grunt as her warm mouth strokes up and down my length. "What are you doing to me?"

She pulls away, and I almost cry at the loss of contact. "Making you feel good. Do you not like this?" she asks, blinking up at me.

"Like it, Aubrey? I about came the minute you put your hands on me. Then you put me in your mouth." I ball my fists up as I get harder at the memory.

"Oh" is all she says before wrapping her lips around me again.

It doesn't take long before I feel my orgasm building once again, and this time, I won't be able to hold it off. "Aubrey. I'm going to come," I grit out. She looks up, locking eyes with me as she continues to suck and stroke me. "Are you going to be a good girl and swallow my cum?"

She nods. *Fuck me*. I thrust into her mouth a few more times, my orgasm barreling out of me. I see stars as I yell out her name and other, incoherent, things as she drinks every drop of my cum. Breathing hard from that life altering orgasm, I reach down and tug her into my arms.

"Shit, Aubrey," I huff out. I pull her up to me and kiss her, tasting myself on her lips, running my hands along her back.

"Was that good?"

"Good? That was the best blow job of my life."

She blushes. "That was my first one."

"What?" I ask, pulling back to look her in the eyes. Fuck, it somehow makes it even hotter that I was her first.

And only, if I have it my way.

She stares down at the comforter, twisting her hands. "My sex life has been fairly boring." She blanches. "I've had sex, but that's been it. I've hardly ever done other things. Like this."

Well, fuck me.

Chapter Twenty-Four

Aubrey

I can't believe I told him that. I was so in the moment, proud of making him feel good, that my filter was temporarily gone. My face heats up at the admission, and I turn away from him. Ready to run and hide.

"Hey. Where are you going?" Brody whispers. With a sigh, I meet his eyes. I told my *best friend* about my sex life. We've never talked about sex. Hell, I gave my *best friend* a blow job.

"Can we not talk about it anymore? Please?" The last part comes out in a whisper. I shift on the bed, ready to move away.

"Aubs." Brody's voice is soft, and he gently tugs me down until I'm lying on his chest again. "Talk to me."

"I'm so embarrassed," I whisper, tracing his chest muscles with my finger. At least from this position, I don't have to look him in the eyes.

"There's nothing to be embarrassed about. It's me." He runs his hand over my back a few times.

I take a few deep breaths. Brody stays silent, rubbing my back. That's what I love about him. He knows I need a moment to collect myself sometimes, and he doesn't rush me. He never has. Unlike other guys I've dated who hated waiting for me to speak my feelings and would usually change the subject or walk away before I could figure out the right words to say how I felt. But not Brody. Even when we first met in high school, he was always patient with me. Never judging. He's somehow always understood me.

Been my person. That thought has my heart racing. But it's also what finally gives me the courage to speak.

"I'm embarrassed because you're, well, you." I wave a hand over him. "You've probably had way better blow jobs. Way better sex than with me. And here I am telling you all this."

"Aubrey, look at me," Brody commands, and I lift my head, making eye contact with him. He visibly swallows before saying, "I wasn't lying when I said that was the best blow job I've ever had. *Because* it was you."

"I—What?" I open and close my mouth a couple of times. "What do you mean, *because it was you?*"

"It means . . ." Brody takes a deep breath, and I think I hear him mumble *fuck it* before he says, "I'd be lying if I said I never dreamed about this moment with you. Because I have. Many, many times. Not only this moment but all the moments we've had together on this trip. Just being with you. I want you. For real. I want there to be an us when this trip is over. Whatever it takes, I'm willing to do it. I'm all in, beautiful."

I stare at him, my brain short circuiting. "I want that too. But . . ."

"But what, Aubrey? I know you're moving to Hawaii. That doesn't stop me wanting this to be real."

I open my mouth to protest. To tell him we can't. But I don't. I want to enjoy us being real for a little bit. Live the 'happily ever after' for a little bit, the one where I get the guy, and the job. "Okay. But once we get back to Orlando, we need to talk about the reality of the situation."

"I know. But I'm serious, Aubrey, I want you. I want us," he says before pulling me down to him. Our lips crash together, like all the pent-up feelings are finally set free. He tugs at the waistband of my underwear. "Take them off." I do as he says.

"You're beautiful. I don't know if I'll ever get over seeing you like this, spread out, and naked for me," he rasps out, staring down at me.

He kisses his way down my body. He runs his tongue around one of my nipples, lavishing attention on it before moving to the other one for a few seconds, then continues his quest down my body, kissing up one thigh, then the other. I can't do anything but lay there and feel, moaning as he gets closer to where I need him. Finally, he makes contact with my aching clit, groaning as he does. I almost combust at the sound. He sucks, licks, and lavishes his attention on me, making me see stars.

"Ple-ase, Brody." My voice is needy, almost whining. "I'm so close."

"I know, beautiful." He stares up at me from between my legs, giving me a devilish grin before working first one finger, and then a second into me. He eats me like a man starved until my legs start to shake, and I come, yelling out his name. He places one final kiss on my swollen, pulsing clit before rising to his knees.

He stares at me for a few seconds, before leaning down and kissing me. I groan against his lips, tasting myself, and his cock nudges against my entrance.

"I need to be inside you," he says, resting his forehead against mine and peering down.

"Yes, please." I snake my arms around him and pull him toward me, desperate for him to be inside me.

"Condom." Brody grunts, trying to extract himself from me. "Shit. I don't have any more."

"I have an IUD. I got tested at my last appointment, all negative. Haven't been with anyone in . . ." I trail off. "A long time."

He pulls back and peers into my eyes. "I was negative the last time I was tested too. Haven't been with anyone since. Are you sure?"

"Yes," I whisper, thrusting my hips up toward him, needing him inside me.

"Watch me slide inside you. Bare. Watch your pussy take all of my cock." He fists himself and runs the head of his cock through my arousal.

I groan, panting at his words. "This is the cock that you had your mouth on before." He's stroking himself as he speaks. "Do you want it in your mouth again before I bury it in your pussy?"

I'm usually timid in bed, but the way Brody looks at me, speaks to me, makes me feel wild and uninhibited. So, yes, of course I want his cock in my mouth. I think I might combust if I don't. "Yes. Please," I pant.

Brody growls, moving off me and crawling up the bed until he's kneeling next to my head. "Open wide," he commands, running his glistening, hard cock along my lips and my jaw. "Make me nice and wet before I slide into your pussy."

I moan, feeling myself getting even wetter for him. I open my mouth and run my tongue along his cock. Sucking him in as far as I can at this angle.

"You take my cock like a good girl. Fuck, that's a beautiful sight."

I run my tongue along the head and feel him get harder. I reach up and cup his balls. His head falls back, and he groans before pulling out of my mouth.

"That's enough," he groans and I whine in protest. He moves over me and lines his cock up with my entrance.

"Yes," I rasp out breathlessly. Brody meets my gaze as he sinks in, inch by glorious inch, and I groan, loving the feel of his cock inside of me, stretching me out. He leans down, capturing my lips with his when he's fully seated inside me.

Pulling back, he studies me as he rocks slowly in and out. The mood changes as he strokes my face and slowly pulls out before sinking back in. Over and over and over again.

"You feel like heaven."

I nod because that's all I'm capable of as I chase another orgasm, feeling it building. Knowing exactly what I need he reaches down and strokes slow circles around my clit.

I detonate.

He pumps in and out a few more times before calling out his own release.

"Fuck, Aubrey," he mumbles, his face buried in my hair. "That was . . ."

"Yeah," I agree, stroking his back. That was something.

Something scary.

Something big.

Something I didn't anticipate.

Eventually, he pulls out, rolls off the bed, and walks into the bathroom, coming out a minute later with a wet washcloth.

I reach out to take it from him. "I can do it," I mumble.

"Let me take care of you," he whispers before bending down and kissing the inside of my thigh.

I'm speechless, unable to take my eyes off this gorgeous man.

My best friend.

Who has suddenly turned into more.

The thought scares me.

I'm moving to Hawaii. Why couldn't our timing be better? How am I supposed to pick between him and my dream job? Am I going to have to be like the rest of my family, sacrificing part of myself for love? My thoughts have me sitting up and moving off the bed.

"Where are you going?" Brody asks, his eyebrows furrowed as he watches me.

"Bathroom," I rasp out, trying to tamper down the emotions that have suddenly surfaced.

Shutting the door, I take a few deep breaths, trying to calm my racing heart. The woman staring back at me in the mirror isn't someone I recognize. Her hair is mussed, her face flushed, and there's a glow in her eyes. She looks . . . happy. Which immediately makes me sad. Because that happiness won't last.

I hope I haven't screwed up our friendship. That's the last thing I want to do. Brody means the world to me, and I'd be devastated if our friendship ended over this.

With a shake of my head, I use the bathroom, wash my hands, and brush my teeth for good measure. When I come out, Brody is sitting up in bed, staring down at his phone in his hands.

"You alright?" I ask when he looks up at me. He opens his mouth and closes it a few times before running a hand through his hair and dropping his phone on the bed. I sit next to him, waiting for him to talk to me.

"Fine," he finally says with a shake of his head. "The guys being"—he waves his hand around as if he's not sure what to call it—"their usual selves."

I quirk an eyebrow at him. I feel like there's something more going on that he's not telling me, but I won't push him. At least not right now.

Our conversation is interrupted by a knock at the door. I glance over at Brody, but he shrugs and shakes his head. I move to get off the bed, but he's already on his feet, yanking his shorts on. As I'm putting my shirt on to go see who's out there, he comes back into the room.

"That was Devon." He inclines his head toward the door. "He wanted to know if we fancied hanging out by the pool with them."

"I thought Bri was going to take a nap."

"Maybe they changed their minds like we did. What do you want to do? I told him you'd text Brielle."

"I'm game if you are," I say, grabbing my phone from the nightstand.

It's probably a good thing that Devon came by because it gives me something to do instead of worrying about what will happen after we leave. I don't want to think about that right now. I don't want to worry about what our friendship will be like when we go back to reality. I want to live in the moment, pretending that we can have a real relationship once we leave here.

Chapter Twenty-Five

Aubrey

"You almost ready to go?" Brody asks, peeking his head into the bathroom where I'm putting the finishing touches on my hair and makeup for the rehearsal and dinner.

"Yep," I answer, pinning the last piece of stray hair into place and surveying myself in the mirror. I watched at least a dozen YouTube videos on how to do a French twist, and it didn't turn out half bad.

"I'm not too dressed up, am I?" he asks, tugging at his collar.

I turn around to take in his whole outfit—black shorts and a maroon collared shirt. "Nope, your outfit is perfect. I'm ready, just need to grab my purse." I smooth a hand down the pale-blue strapless dress and straighten the strap on my left sandal.

Brody nods and backs out of the bathroom. After one last glance at myself in the full-length mirror on the back of the door, I walk out to find him sprawled on the couch, sipping from a bottle of water.

"Want some?" He holds the bottle out to me.

"I'm good," I say, and he caps the bottle and gets to his feet. We head out of our suite and toward the elevators.

In the lobby, I spot Bri and Devon standing off to the side with a few of the others that are in the wedding. We make our way over, but before we reach them, the wedding planner—Maggie—is calling for us to follow her outside to where the ceremony will take place.

"Where's Mother?" I ask Bri, glancing around as we follow Maggie.

She grimaces before saying, "No idea. This isn't like her."

Maggie comes to a halt at the edge of what I can tell is the aisle, chairs already set out on either side for tomorrow. I'm surprised they set everything up already. She claps her hands together, but before she can say anything, the door to the hotel is flung open, and my mother comes charging outside. Arthur hurries after her.

"This won't work," Mother says as she marches over to Maggie.

"I'm sorry. What won't work, Mrs. Fairchild?" Maggie asks, turning her attention to my mother.

"This. All of this." My mother waves her hands around. "This is not what I asked for. This beach is not big enough. That hideous arch will not do for an altar." She points at the arch decorated in pink flowers at the end of the aisle.

Bri snorts out a laugh next to me, quickly pretending to cough to cover it up. I shoot her a look and she shakes her head, her hand over her mouth.

"Mrs. Fairchild, this was in the email I received last week with updated requests for the ceremony."

"Well, I didn't send it. This will not do," She repeats, crossing her arms.

"I sent it, Mom," Clara says, stepping up to them. "I'll take care of this," she says to Maggie before putting a hand on Mother's arm and attempting to guide her away.

Mother glares at Clara, ripping her arm away. I look over at Brody who's watching the scene, wide-eyed. A quick glance around confirms that the rest of the wedding party is as transfixed as Brody is. I feel like crawling into a hole and disappearing. Talk about secondhand embarrassment.

"Maybe we should talk about this somewhere else," I say, glancing over at Bri who dips her chin at me and we walk over to Mother and Clara who seem to be having a silent battle. Maggie stays silent, her face red as she wrings her hands. Thad appears out of nowhere and stands next to me.

"It's alright, Maggie. Why don't you go over the order of events with everyone else. We'll sort this out and let you know if anything needs to change," I say.

Maggie gives me a small smile, looking relieved to be given an out as she steps away from us and asks the rest of the wedding party to follow her. When it's just my family, Brody, Chet, and Devon left, I turn to my mother. "What is going on?"

"Oh, butt out, Aubrey. No one asked you," she snaps.

Brody growls next to me, and before I can so much as blink, he's wrapped his arm around me, tucking me into his side, and is facing down my mother who's glaring at me.

"Mrs. Fairchild, with all due respect. Actually"—he clears his throat and glances over at me before turning back to my mother—"scratch that. Since you can't show Aubrey respect, why should I show you any?" He shifts against me, standing taller, his body vibrating with anger as he continues. "How dare you talk to her like that? I've stood by all week and watched you talk down to her. Aubrey is trying to help the situation. You don't deserve your daughters. Not with the way you treat them."

It's only because I'm watching my mother closely that I see her jerk back slightly at Brody's outburst, blinking a few times as if someone threw water in her face. It's satisfying to see.

Good. For a second, I think she's going to apologize, but she doesn't, recovering and turning her gaze to Clara instead. I sag into Brody, and he tightens his grip on me.

"And you." She points at her. "How dare you?"

Clara rears back. "How dare I? This is my wedding, Mom. Or did you forget?" Chet wraps his arm around Clara's waist but wisely says nothing.

Before Mother can say anything else, Arthur steps in. "Beatrice, let the girl have it the way she wants it."

"Stay out of it," She snaps at Arthur. "These are my children. I'll deal with them how I see fit."

"Mother," Thad growls, glaring at her. I stare at my brother—he's never been one to raise his voice.

"Go back to your phone, Thaddeus. No one wants to hear what you have to say," She bites out.

"Beatrice!" Arthur snaps, grabbing my mother by the arm and practically dragging her away toward the hotel entrance.

Bri and I exchange looks, her mouth hanging open. I'm sure I look just as shocked. *Holy fuck.* I have never known Arthur to be anything but calm, timid, and submissive to Mother, so to see this side of him is great, actually.

"Are you okay?" Brody asks. All I can do is nod. Chet pulls Clara, who appears to be near tears, her face red, her chin shaking into him and wraps his arms around her. She buries her head in his chest. He leans down and whispers something to her.

"What the fuck," Bri says, finally breaking the silence.

Thad shakes his head. "This is ridiculous. I don't know what's gotten into her." He turns to Clara. "I'm going to go talk to her. Someone's got to talk some sense into her, and I don't know that Arthur's up for the job. At least not alone." With that, he turns and walks back toward the hotel.

Better him than me.

"I wanted to have a few things the way I wanted them, and this is what happens . . ." Clara says, pulling back from Chet so she can speak. "I don't know why I bother anymore. She's going to overrule everything we want."

"I'm sorry," I whisper, my voice cracking. And here I'd always thought I was the only one Mother treated poorly.

"It's not your fault. Either of you," Bri says, glancing at me before turning to Clara. "We've got your back, Clara. Whatever you need."

"I'm sorry, Clara. If I'd known this was how it was going to turn out, I wouldn't have let her pay for the wedding," Chet says.

Clara takes a deep breath before looking over to where the rest of the bridal party is huddled with Maggie, their backs to us. "We should probably get the rehearsal started if we're going to make dinner."

"Clara, is any of this what you wanted? What did you and Chet want from your wedding?" At this point, I have no idea how much of this week was at Mother's insistence and how much of it was what Clara and Chet wanted. I know Clara is unhappy with her wedding dress and the parading around Key West we did the other day, but I assumed she was okay with everything else. I mean, she has to be, right? It's her wedding day. I can't see her letting Mother dominate all of it.

Clara slips her hand into Chet's, and they exchange a look before she turns her attention back to me.

"Kind of. Do I wish there were less guests? Yes. We wanted an intimate beach wedding." She nods her head at everyone around us. "This isn't exactly what we wanted, but at least we're getting married on the beach. A lot of the other things that Mom insisted on we couldn't care less about, so we let her do it. But I couldn't stand the set up for the ceremony. What she wanted was hideous."

"As long as you both are happy. Because if you aren't"—I glance at Bri, and she dips her chin in agreement, indicating we're on the same page—"we could easily call this whole thing off. You two could get married the way you want to. When you want to."

"It's okay. We'll make the best of it," Clara says.

Chet grins down at Clara. "As long as Clara's happy, I'm happy. But, babe, if this isn't what you want, we can postpone it."

"I want to be married to you," Clara mumbles, staring up at Chet.

"Well then. Let's get the show on the road." I step out of Brody's arms, grab his hand, and walk toward Maggie and the rest of the wedding party.

Maggie sees us approach and announces that the rehearsal will start now.

"You okay?" Brody whispers.

I shrug because I don't know. I feel like everything I thought I knew about Clara and her relationship with our mother is incorrect. Part of me is angry that Clara didn't tell me before what was really going on, and part of me is relieved that it isn't me feeling our mother's wrath. I don't have time to explain that to Brody, though, as Maggie whisks me away to my spot in line to walk down the aisle.

We run through the ceremony once, and as we're lining up to go through it one last time, Arthur comes striding out of the hotel, making his way to Maggie. I can't hear what he whispers to her, but she glances at the rest of us before replying.

Arthur nods at Maggie's response and walks over to Clara who he speaks to in hushed tones. I wish I could hear what they are saying. Bri catches my eye and inclines one shoulder as if to say she's as confused as I am. Arthur hugs Clara before walking over to Bri. My brows knit together as they exchange words, and soon, he's making his way to me.

"Aubrey, darling," he says, putting a hand on my arm. "I want to apologize for how your mom reacted earlier. She's not feeling like herself today and won't be coming to dinner tonight. I'm going to stay here and take care of her. But you all go and have a good time."

I arch a brow at him before saying, "That was inexcusable behavior, Arthur. She should be apologizing. Not you. You have nothing to apologize for."

He heaves out a breath. "I know, Aubrey girl. But, unfortunately, that's not how things work with your mom, is it?" He stares at me for a moment before adding, "Things are not always as they seem."

"What do you mean?"

Arthur takes a deep breath, and I hold mine, hoping he's going to elaborate. What the hell is going on?

He pats my arm and says, "It's nothing you need to worry about."

I open my mouth to argue, but he shakes his head and walks toward Thad who's been watching the whole exchange silently. They exchange words, and Thad glances over at me before nodding at Arthur. Arthur pats Thad on the back and walks back toward the hotel.

"Let's run through this one more time and then I'll let you all get to dinner and the rest of your evening," Maggie says with a clap of her hands.

We line up and proceed to walk through the ceremony one more time. My mind is spinning. What the hell is really going on? Have I stepped through some crazy wormhole into an alternate reality?

Chapter Twenty-Six

Brody

"What are you thinking about?" I whisper, leaning closer to Aubrey. She blows out a breath before turning from where she's been staring out at the ocean to face me.

"That this wasn't what I expected. Ya know?" She tilts her head, studying me. "All these years I thought it was just me she treated like that," she adds in a whisper. If I wasn't standing so close to her, I wouldn't have heard the words. "I always wondered what I did to make her hate me so much." She sighs, glancing around.

I move so I'm standing next to her, our backs against the railing of the catamaran, watching everyone drink and laugh as the boat glides through the water. I slip my arm around her and pull her close to me so her head is resting on my chest. We stand in silence for a few minutes as everyone parties around us. The band starts playing again, and I nudge her gently so she looks up at me.

"Dance with me?"

"Okay," she says, stepping away from me, and I immediately miss her.

I lead her to the dance floor and wrap my arms around her. My best friend. The woman I've fallen in love with. The woman I've probably always been in love with but never admitted it to myself.

"This was definitely not the way I saw this week going," Aubrey whispers as we slowly sway back and forth even though the band is playing an upbeat song.

"Do you think they'll still get married tomorrow?"

It's something I've wondered since the scene with Mrs. Fairchild. And after, when Clara said that a lot of this wedding isn't what she and Chet wanted. I've never given any thought to my own wedding, but I sure as shit know I wouldn't want anyone, other than my fiancée, taking over. Changing things like Mrs. Fairchild did.

"Why do you say that?" Aubrey stops dancing, pulling out of my arms so she can peer up at me.

I shrug one shoulder, pulling her back into my arms. "You can't tell me the thought hasn't crossed your mind."

"Oh, it has," Aubrey mumbles. "I don't think Clara has it in her. Even if she's livid at Mother, she still wants to make her happy. Make us all happy. It's who she is. Who we all are. Living to make other people happy."

The words give me pause. This time, it's me who pulls back from her so I can stare down into her eyes. "I hope you don't do that with me. I want you to be happy. Don't think you need to make choices that will make me happy."

Aubrey studies me for a few seconds before saying, "I know. Want to go get another drink?"

I stare at her for a heartbeat. "Yeah, sounds good, Aubs." I intertwine our fingers and lead her toward the bar.

A few minutes later, drinks in hand, we move away from the crowd at the bow of the boat.

"So—" Aubrey starts.

"Do we really have to talk about this now?" Clara's voice comes from the other side of the wall that Aubrey's leaning against. Aubrey turns to look at it as if she can see what's going on on the other side.

"I think that's one of the bathrooms," I say, glancing around. It's really the only thing that makes sense. There are no other private places on the boat.

"Now's my last chance. When we get off this boat, the guys are going to whisk me away, and I won't see you until we're at the altar," Chet answers, his voice muffled by the wall.

"Do you not want to get married? Is that what this is?" I can picture Clara crossing her arms and rolling her eyes at Chet as she says that. I hold my breath, wondering what his response is going to be.

"Of course I want to get married to you, Clara. I love you. But is this wedding going to make you happy? Or will you look back on it in fifty years and regret it?"

"What are you saying?" Clara's voice is quieter.

"All I'm saying is that we don't have to do this tomorrow if it's not what you want."

"I don't know what I want," Clara finally says.

"I just want you to be happy. And that stunt your mother pulled today was unacceptable. I'm done not saying anything and letting you handle it. If she does it again, she and I are going to have words. You're about to be my wife, and no one talks to my wife like that."

Aubrey and I exchange glances, and she puts a hand to her heart. I find myself smiling too.

"Chet . . ." Clara's voice breaks off, and muffled sounds come from the bathroom.

"Ahhh, maybe we should move now," Aubrey says, glancing between me and the wall where I can make out low moaning.

I cough out a laugh. "Yeah, probably a good idea." I take her hand, leading her back toward the dance floor.

"Want to sit down? Or dance some more?" I ask, staring down at her.

"Dance," she whispers before kissing me. I groan against her lips when she rubs against me, my cock hardening at the feel of her.

"Aubs. Beautiful." I break our kiss and step back from her. I take a deep breath, silently reciting plays in an effort to calm my now hard dick. Everything back under control, I take her hand, and we make our way back out to the dance floor.

"How are you feeling?" I ask Aubrey as we wait our turn to get off the boat a few hours later. Thankfully, there was no other drama for the rest of the night, well, aside from some drunken dancing by the groomsmen. But luckily, no one fell overboard or got sick. I'd call that a win.

"Fine. I didn't drink much," she answers.

"Me neither. Anything you want to do when we get back to the hotel?"

Aubrey peeks at me over her shoulder, her gaze drops to my crotch, her tongue peeking out to swipe along her lips. Fuck me. My cock starts to get hard, and I'm thankful that everyone around us is too drunk or focused on getting off the boat to notice. We pause near the gangplank, waiting our turn, and I step closer and grip her hips.

"Feel that?" I whisper into her ear, pressing into her. "That's what you do to me with only a look."

She grinds back against me, and I have to bite down on my lip so I don't groan. I still her hips with my hands. Well, that backfired.

Everyone starts to move forward so I have no choice but to let go of Aubrey and follow her off the boat. Some of the group opts to go down to Duval Street to continue the party, but most of us, including all of Aubrey's siblings and their partners, get on the charter bus to go back to the hotel.

"Did you see what I saw?" I whisper to Aubrey when we're seated on the bus.

"No." She whips her head around to look at everyone. "What did you see?"

"Clara's definitely been crying; her nose is red and her mascara is smudged. Chet seems distraught."

"Shit," Aubrey hisses. "I thought they were fine. After everything."

"Me too."

"I need to talk to her," Aubrey says once we're back at the hotel. "You don't have to wait for me." Before I can say anything, she crosses the lobby to where Brielle is and the two of them make their way to Clara and Chet.

"What's going on?" Devon asks, gesturing toward the sisters huddled in the corner. Chet has walked a few feet away and is surrounded by his groomsmen.

"I'm not really sure. Clara was crying and Chet looks like he's seen a ghost." Chet's now sitting on one of the couches, his head in his hands, one of his groomsmen talking to him.

Devon crosses his arms, watching the ladies chat in the corner. He glances around before leaning closer to me and saying, "I'm sure it was Mrs. Fairchild."

"Wouldn't surprise me." I say, half expecting her to show up and cause more chaos.

"Right? Why else would they look like that?"—he dips his head toward the pair—"on the night before their wedding."

Before I can answer, Brielle and Aubrey walk over to us, leaving Clara with one of her bridesmaids.

"Well, that was interesting," Aubrey says.

"What happened?" I ask, taking her hand in mine and pulling her closer. She sags against me.

"Mom called Clara while we were on the boat. Left her a voicemail and told her in no uncertain terms that she was getting married tomorrow. Or else," Brielle says.

"Well, shit." Devon whistles, shaking his head. "What do you think they'll do?"

"Or else what?" I ask.

"We don't know. Clara's mostly worried it'll cause a rift in the family. Bri and I told her that we're on her side. And we're sure Thad is too, given what he said earlier," Aubrey answers.

"She said she's going to stay with her bridesmaid, and Chet's going to stay with his groomsman tonight like they planned. They agreed to talk in the morning," Brielle says. "We're going to head up to the room and relieve the babysitter," she continues, glancing at her husband. "If she calls you and needs us, call me. I'm going to sleep with my phone on. I'll let you know if I hear from her."

"Guess I'll see you in the morning for, hopefully, a wedding," Aubrey says, hugging her sister. Brielle and Devon wave and head for the elevators, and we make our way to the elevators on the opposite side of the lobby.

"What do you think will happen?" Aubrey asks.

"I don't know." I scrub a hand over my face. "I'm sure it depends on how much Clara wants to keep the peace. They'll have to talk about it, that's for sure. Would your mother really do something if they don't get married tomorrow?"

"Who knows. Maybe Arthur can talk to her. But I don't really know how much sway he has over her." Aubrey takes my hand as the elevator comes to a halt on our floor, and we walk down the hallway. As soon as we step into the suite, Aubrey flops down onto the couch.

"I'm exhausted," she says with a yawn.

"Me too." I gesture toward the bedroom. "Don't get comfortable, let's get ready for bed."

She climbs to her feet and silently follows me into the bedroom. A few minutes later we crawl into bed and I pull her into my arms.

As crazy as this evening was, any day that ends like this, with Aubrey falling asleep in my arms, is a good day.

Chapter Twenty-Seven

Aubrey

Voices I can't distinguish coming from the living room are the first thing I hear when I wake up. Brody's side of the bed is empty and cold, so he must have gotten up quite a while ago. The clock on the bedside table shows that it's a little after eight. Guess I might as well get up since I need to meet my sisters and the rest of the bridal party at noon to start getting ready. That is, if this wedding is still on.

Stretching, I climb out of the bed, then head to the bathroom. I quickly use the toilet, brush my teeth, and run a brush through my hair before pulling it into a bun. I put on a bra and swap my tiny sleep shorts for a pair of black leggings because who knows who's out in the living room. I grab my phone off the nightstand and see I have a text message from Summer.

Summer: Big day today. Have fun. Don't stress too much, and don't let your mother piss you off.

I let out a bark of laughter, if only she knew, and text her back.

Me: Big day might not happen. Long story. Tell you later.
Summer: Oh boy. Call me when you can. I'll have my popcorn ready.

Locking my phone, I take a deep breath and head out to the living room. My steps falter when I see both of my sisters sitting on the couch. My gaze flickers to Brody who is leaning against the wall, sipping a cup of coffee.

"Hi—Morning," I sputter. Brody meets my gaze before pushing off the wall and walking over to where I'm standing in the bedroom doorway.

"There's coffee." He gestures toward the room service cart. Leaning closer, he whispers, "They showed up a few minutes ago. I was about to come to wake you." He kisses me on the cheek before stepping back.

I remain silent, fix myself a cup of coffee, and take a sip before turning back to my sisters who are watching me from the couch, Bri's arm wrapped around Clara. I can't quite figure out what's going on, but it can't be great news if they're here now—we're supposed to see each other in a few hours.

"What's going on?" I ask, sitting in the armchair across from the couch.

Clara clears her throat and glances over at Bri who gestures for her to explain. "Chet and I aren't going to get married the way we were originally going to."

The air whooshes from my lungs, and I try to digest her news. My face must give me away because Clara gives me a thin smile before continuing. "What you said to me last night about getting married the way we want really sank in. Chet and I ended up talking about it again. Neither of us wants this big of a wedding." She takes a deep breath before saying, "I called Maggie this morning and asked her if she could throw together a smaller ceremony on Smathers Beach instead. I told her we'd pay whatever the cost is."

"Mother is going to flip."

"I don't care what she thinks. I talked to Arthur, and he's on our side. As are Chet's parents. We're going to get married tonight at sunset, with just you all." She gestures to the three of us. "And of course Thad, Devon, and Chet's parents. Plus Arthur and Mom, if she wants to come and promises to be on her best behavior."

"What about the other guests? The reception?" My mind is spinning with all the things that will have to be done now she's canceling the wedding.

"Maggie is drafting a note that she'll distribute to all the guests letting them know what's going on. The reception will still happen. We moved it by a few hours. We'll take pictures beforehand. While everyone is at cocktail hour, we'll go to the beach for the ceremony. It's a bit unorthodox." Clara shrugs before continuing. "But it's the best we can do on such short notice. And honestly, Chet and I don't really care about doing things the *right way*. After the ceremony, we'll come back for dinner and all the rest," Clara explains. Wow, she's really thought this through. Good for her.

"I think it's a grand idea," Bri says, beaming at Clara. "Don't you, Aubs?" She turns to me.

"Yes, of course." I take a sip of my coffee. "What do you need from me?"

"Nothing. Chet and I are going to go talk to Mom with his parents. We figured having them there might mean she'll be on her best behavior and won't go off the rails."

"Highly doubtful. But it's a good idea." I lean forward in my seat, glancing from one sister to the other. "Do you want me to come too?"

Clara shakes her head. "No, I don't want her to think we're ambushing her. It'll only make her more defensive."

"At the end of the day, it doesn't matter what she wants. This is your wedding," Bri says.

"Except she's paying for it all," Clara points out, giving Bri a tight-lipped smile. "I doubt she's going to be thrilled about all of this. Imagine how it's going to look." She rolls her eyes, and I have to pinch my lips together to suppress the laughter that wants to escape.

"But it's all already paid for, right? If you and Chet offered to pay the extra costs for the changes, what's she going to do?" Brody asks. "Cut you out of the will?"

"It's not like there's anything to inherit," Bri mumbles.

I blink rapidly. This is the first I'm hearing of this. "What do you mean?"

My sister's exchange looks before Bri says, "Aubrey, besides the business, which we all know Mom's share goes to Thad, and the house, there's nothing left. All our inheritance was spent when Dad got sick."

"Wait? How did I not know this?" I ask, glancing from sister to sister. What the hell? How did this go on and no one told me. I knew Dad was really sick and tried a bunch of different treatments, but I never stopped to think about how everything was paid for.

"You were in school. You rarely came home. We didn't want to burden you with it," Bri whispers.

"Burden me with it? I'm the oldest." I point to myself. "If anyone shouldn't want to burden someone, it should be me not wanting to burden you with this information."

"Drop it, Aubrey," Clara bites out, and I rear back.

"Does this have anything to do with why Mother got married to Arthur so quickly after Dad died?" I ask. It's something I've always wondered about. I've never wanted to ask her or Arthur because it's not really any of my business, but now, knowing that the inheritance is gone, it's starting to make sense.

Bri clears her throat before saying, "Well, according to Thad, Mom and Arthur only got married so the family could keep control of the business." She pauses, taking a deep breath before continuing. "On his death, part of Dad's ownership reverted to Arthur and the two other partners. I guess it was the original business agreement they came up with, for who knows what reason. Thad thinks Dad assumed that since he was a good ten years younger than any of them, he would outlive them all."

How the heck does she know this, but I don't? That's a question for another time. I need to hear the rest of this story. I wave my hand at her to indicate she should continue.

"Anyway, after he died, Mom and Thad ended up with forty-two percent combined. Arthur and the two other partners own the rest, split evenly between them. This is the part that I don't understand. But Arthur agreed to marry Mom and give her the percentage she needed so she and Thad could have a majority share. Our guess"—Bri points to herself and Clara—"is that Arthur's been in love with Mom for years. I remember at Christmas parties he'd always bring her drinks and try to talk to her. Sneak looks at her when he thought no one was watching. I caught them kissing in the kitchen one New Year's Eve."

"Seriously?" That's a crazy story that I have a hard time wrapping my head around. "I mean, Arthur's so nice. He's been a great stepdad. I can't believe he went along with this whole crazy scheme."

"I think he really cares about her. But I don't know if she feels the same way. Even if Bri saw them kiss once." Clara shrugs. "She probably sees it as a business arrangement."

"How can it be worth it to marry someone you don't love? I mean, I thought she at least cared about him," I say.

Bri clears her throat. "I think it's something she had to sacrifice to keep the business in the family for Thad and whichever of his children takes over."

After a few moments of silence, Clara says, "I'm sorry we dropped that bombshell on you."

"I wish I knew all of this before."

"What would be the point in knowing?" Bri asks. "Not like you could have done anything. You were off doing your own thing."

I stare at my sister at a loss for words. I don't think she meant to be nasty, but her comment still stings a bit.

"I'm sorry," I say, although I'm not really sure why I'm apologizing.

"Nothing you can do. I better go meet Chet and his parents so we can talk to Mom," Clara says, getting to her feet. Bri also gets up from the couch.

We hug, and Bri promises to text me when the hair and makeup people are in her room. Clara didn't want to cancel them with such short notice, so she told the rest of her wedding party to still come get their hair and makeup done.

When the door finally shuts behind them, I blow out a breath and sag back into the chair. Brody sits down on the coffee table in front of me, taking my hands in his.

"What can I do?" he whispers, squeezing my hands.

I shrug. I don't know. I'm overwhelmed, and I don't know where to start in sorting through my feelings.

Chapter Twenty-Eight

Brody

Did not see that coming. I try not to dwell on all the new information or the change of wedding plans and focus on the woman in front of me instead.

"What do you need?"

"I don't know," Aubrey finally says, rubbing a hand over her forehead and down her face. "I think I need something to eat. And maybe a stiff drink." She grimaces. "It's probably too early for alcohol, but after all of that." She waves her hand around.

"I understand." I get to my feet. "You want your usual waffle, fruit, and eggs?"

"Yes, please. And a mimosa."

"Got it." I walk into the bedroom and call down to room service. When I step back into the living room, Aubrey has moved to the couch where she's hunched over her phone, typing furiously.

"Your phone was going off." She gestures toward it sitting on the coffee table, not even looking up at me.

"Thanks. Food will be here in . . ." I unlock my phone and my stomach drops as I see multiple text messages from my agent.

Bruce: Hey, Brody. Not sure if you're still on vacation.

Bruce: Still waiting on your thoughts of the offer from the Storm.

Bruce: If you could give me a call in the next few days. They're waiting on us.

I glance up at Aubrey, wondering if she saw the messages. As if sensing that I'm watching her, she peeks up at me, her blue eyes flashing between me and my phone before meeting my gaze.

"It nearly vibrated off the table. I had to catch it before it fell." Her voice softens. "They want you back, don't they?"

"Yeah. Seems that way." I run a hand through my hair.

"That's great, Brody. You should take it."

"I don't know if I want to," I say, stepping closer to her.

"Oh?" Aubrey looks up at me. "Why not?"

I take a deep breath before saying, "I made peace with being done. With the end of my career. Besides, there's something I want more than hockey now."

"What's that?" She tilts her head, studying me.

"Us. You. I want you."

"Us?" she repeats.

"Yeah, us, Aubs. You know I want there to be an us after this trip is over. I thought you did too." I drop to the couch and reach for her. She draws away from me.

What's that about?

"I thought we'd agreed to be real while we were here and figure everything else out after the trip ends," Aubrey says, studying her hands.

"We did." I slowly shake my head. "But I'm still going to want there to be an us." I stare at her, willing her to look at me.

"But the Storm want you back now. You have to take it," she says, picking at her fingernails.

"No, I don't." Why isn't she getting it?

"I can't talk about this with you now," she whispers, finally peeking up at me. "There's too much going on with the wedding."

Before I can answer, there's a knock at the door.

"That's probably room service. I'll get it." She all but sprints for the door and pulls it open.

I rake a hand through my hair, sighing in frustration as I get to my feet to serve myself breakfast. I understand her not wanting to talk about it now, so I won't push. But we're going to talk about it. She needs to understand that if I have to pick between my career and her, I'll pick her. A million times over.

I can't lose her.

I refuse.

Maybe it's the fact that I've shared such a small space with another person for a week, pretending to be in a relationship, or maybe it's the fact that there's a wedding happening today, but I've come to realize I want that too. I want a partner. Someone to go through the rest of my life with. Someone to share the ups and downs with. I want her. I only hope Aubrey wants that too.

"Brody. Earth to Brody," Aubrey says from next to me.

"Sorry, I got lost in thought."

"I know. I could tell." She studies me for a moment before asking, "want to talk about it?"

I heave out a breath. Do I want to talk about it now? I mean, I want to, but will Aubrey be receptive to what I have to say, or will she immediately shut it down? She already told me she didn't want to talk about us until after this trip so maybe I shouldn't say anything.

But I can't help myself, so I say, "thinking about everything going on recently. Caleb and Cole both starting families. Getting older." I lift a shoulder in a shrug before taking a bite of scrambled eggs.

Aubrey is quiet for a few seconds before saying, "I think about that too. The getting older part. Definitely feeling the aches and pains now more than I used to in my twenties. Don't even get me started on how many times I've woken up with back pain from sleeping wrong. Or sneezing and hurting my neck. Getting old sucks."

I let out a bark of laughter. "My recovery time isn't what it used to be, that's for sure. Takes me way longer to get over hits that I would have shaken off in a day or two before. Makes me wonder if it's time to hang up my skates. Maybe not for good, just professionally."

"You've still got a lot of years left in you. Didn't Gretzky skate until he was thirty-eight?" I nod. "You've still got years of your career ahead of you."

"True. But I wonder if I'm going to shorten my overall lifespan by five, ten years because I play another three years and end up needing hip surgery? Or break my back? Or take a hit to the head that affects my memory?" I stare down at my empty plate, unable to look Aubrey in the eyes because I don't know what I'll see there.

"I don't know, Brod. I don't have all the answers. I don't think anyone does."

"I know." I finally meet her gaze. "Sorry to bring the mood down."

She tilts her head, watching me. "Do you regret still being single? Not having kids or a family?"

"Regret? No." I shake my head. "Hockey has been my life for so many years that I don't think I could have given a partner the attention she deserved."

"And now?" she whispers, her gaze dropping to the floor.

"Now, I could. I've lived my dreams. I've gotten to hoist the Cup. Multiple times. This past season, it started to feel like my time on the ice is coming to a close. That this chapter of my life is ending, and it's time to start a new one." My heart beats wildly at that admission. I want to say *'because I finally understand what it means to be in love. Because I love you. I've always loved you.'*

The air whooshes out of my lungs as that realization hits me. I study Aubrey, willing her to look up at me. Hoping she'll see the love that I know is written on my face. I feel like a part of me is unlocked now that I've finally acknowledged, although not out loud, that I'm in love with her. That she's the one I want. I want to tell her. Heck, I want to scream it from the rooftops, but judging from the way she still hasn't met my gaze, I'd say she's not ready to hear it.

We're interrupted by the ringing of her phone, and she snatches it up, answering it with a hurried hello. Her expression changes, and she gets to her feet and paces the room as she nods at whatever is being said on the other end.

"Okay, I'll be right there," she finally says, hanging up the phone and turning to me. "That was Arthur."

"Okay?" Why is he calling her?

Aubrey pinches the bridge of her nose. "My mother's missing."

"She's what?"

She lets out a strained laugh. "Exactly. I don't know." She waves her hands around. "Something about her saying she was going down to the restaurant in the lobby for breakfast after Clara and Chet left but never showing up there. No one can find her."

"She's a grown woman. Who's fully capable of making her own decisions, right?"

"Yes," Aubrey says, dropping back down onto the couch and tucking her legs up under her.

"Maybe she doesn't want to be here anymore. Can't say I blame her after the way she acted yesterday and all the other times this week. Maybe she finally realized that no one really wants her here if she's going to behave that way, so she left."

"I don't know, but Arthur's in the lobby and I told him I'd be right there," she says, picking at her nails.

"Okay," I say even though I want to tell her not to bother. Would her mother do the same thing for her if she suddenly left? But I don't say those things. The last thing I want to do is make Aubrey even more anxious than she already is. "Want me to go with you?"

"No, that's okay. I'm going to change and go." She gets to her feet and walks into the bedroom.

With a groan, I drop my head against the back of the couch and close my eyes. This is not how I saw this trip going, heck, it's not even how I saw today going, even after Clara and Brielle came by.

Chapter Twenty-Nine

Aubrey

The next few hours pass quickly as I help Arthur search for my mother. We finally get some information about where she might have gone when the concierge comes back from his break. He tells us she tipped well, which is why he remembered her, and that he got her a car to the airport earlier this morning.

I'm not sure why Arthur didn't do it before, but as soon as he heard that, he called their bank and discovered that a one-way ticket to Orlando had been booked this morning. We assume she got on the flight. Arthur was beside himself the whole time, apologizing profusely to me for the hassle. I'll give him credit for the way he handled the situation. He's a good man in an awkward position. I don't know what I would do if I were in his situation. But I don't have time to dwell on that because now I have to meet my sisters and break the news to Clara.

As I make my way to Bri's suite, I replay the last few hours, trying to figure out how I'm going to tell Clara that Mother's gone. As much as I'm angry at her for the way she acted yesterday, I still expected her to show up to the wedding. And now she's not. Today is turning into a shit show. I hope for my sister's sake that everything else goes smoothly.

Bri must see the stress written on my face because when she opens the door to her suite, her smile drops.

I step inside, taking a deep breath. When Clara sees me, she starts to get up from the couch, but I shake my head and sit down next to her. I take one of my baby sister's hands in mine and stare into her eyes. The couch dips behind me as Bri sits down, but I don't turn to face her.

"Mother's not coming." Might as well rip the Band-Aid off.

"Wha-what do you mean?" Clara chokes out, her eyes filling with tears. "She was fine when Chet and I left her earlier." Her gaze darts from mine to Bri's as if Bri will have an explanation.

"Clara," I say gently. "A car drove her to the airport a few hours ago. Probably right after you talked to her."

"Maybe she went to pick someone up," Clara suggests, wiping away the tears that are now freely flowing.

It breaks my heart to see my sister so broken up about our mother not coming to her wedding. I don't know if I'm more angry that Clara is so upset about it even after the way Mother treated her, or the fact that she had the audacity to leave.

I shake my head. "No. Arthur called the bank, and there was an airline ticket purchased this morning."

"That doesn't mean she's actually not coming. Maybe she'll change her mind," Clara protests.

"Maybe," I say gently, rubbing a hand over my sister's arm. "Arthur was calling the airline when I left to come here. To see if she boarded the flight."

"For fuck's sake," Bri hisses out behind me. "Of all the days for her to throw the biggest tantrum ever, she chooses today."

"What do you mean?" I ask, my forehead furrowed.

"Don't you see." Bri waves her hand around. "She's doing this because she knows Arthur will be frantic trying to find her. That we'll want to help him, and Clara's big day won't get the attention it deserves. It's her way of still being in control of the situation."

"Well, let's not let her have that control. To hell with her. It's Clara and Chet's day. Not hers," I say. Bri stares at me, her mouth open, and all I can do is shrug.

"Fuck it all," Clara says, laughing. I turn to look at her. "Aubrey's right. It's her choice not to be here. I'm getting married with or without her at this point. I've sacrificed enough because of her demands and what she wanted for me. But no more."

I twist my head back to look at Bri.

"I'm in. Let's get the show on the road," she declares.

My mind whirls at Clara's statement. I want to ask her what she sacrificed, but before I can say anything else, there's a knock at the door. The bridesmaids come streaming in, bringing with them multiple bottles of champagne, followed closely by the makeup artists and hair stylists.

Since I'm not one of the first to get ready, I wander into the second bedroom, needing some peace and quiet. I peer out the window, gazing down at the adults and kids playing in the pool.

"You okay?" Bri asks, coming into the room and shutting the door behind her. Before I can answer, she's wrapping her arm around my waist and giving me a half hug.

"Why wouldn't I be?"

"Because of everything going on. It's not your fault, you know."

"Who said I was blaming myself?"

"Oh, come on, Aubrey. I know you. I know you think it's your fault that you somehow didn't see what was going on with the wedding. Or know everything that went down with Mom and Arthur after Dad died. It's not your fault."

"Why didn't you ever tell me?"

"Because what were you going to do about it?" Bri asks. "Speaking of not telling each other things, are you finally ready to admit how in love with Brody you are?"

"I'm not in love with him. We're faking it."

Bri rears back, studying me. "Well, yeah, I knew it started off as fake, but it's not like that now. Is it?"

My mouth gapes open. "We are. Well, we were. Now we're . . ." I pause. What are we doing now? "Having fun," I finally settle on. "You saw Mother pushing me to have a date. She was going to set me up with the son of one of her friends. Brody offered to be my date, and that's it."

"Okay, sister, if that's what you say," Bri says, crossing her arms and giving me a look I can't quite place.

"What do you mean?"

"It's not fake now. Not with the way he looks at you, and watches you when you're in the same room. That man is in love with you. And more than as a friend, even a best friend."

"I don't . . ." I shake my head.

I'm saved from explaining more when one of the bridesmaids peeks her head into the room to tell us that it's our turn for hair and makeup.

The rest of the afternoon passes in a blur, and before I know it, I'm making my way back to my suite to get into my dress.

"Hi," Brody greets me when I walk in the door. "Your hair looks nice."

"Thanks," I say, touching the braided updo the stylist did for me. Some of the girls went with fancy hairstyles, but I wanted to keep it simple.

"How are things?" Brody asks, walking over to me. He wraps his arms around me and pulls me into a hug.

"Watch the makeup," I mumble, patting him on the shoulder.

He chuckles, and the sound rumbles through me right to my core. I can't help the shiver that runs down my body. Brody's hands wander down my back until he's gripping my hips.

"Kiss me."

I do as he asked, sealing our lips together. He nips at my bottom lip before his tongue soothes away the ache. He swallows my groan, then tears his mouth away to ask, "How long until we need to be somewhere?"

"An hour."

"Perfect. Come on." He takes my hand and leads me toward the bedroom.

"We should be getting ready," I protest.

He stops just inside the bedroom doorway, pulling me to him and brushes his lips against mine before he leans over and kisses down the column of my neck. Pulling back, he stares at me.

I all but groan at the loss of contact, but before I can do or say anything, he says, "Are you telling me that you're not wet for me? I mean, if that's the case"—he drops his hands and goes to step back—"we can get ready."

"No. No. Brody."

He smirks, a sparkle in his eye. If I wasn't this turned on, I'd probably be pissed because he knows exactly what he's doing.

"Are you going to stop protesting and let me give you what I know you need?"

"Yes," I all but whine. "But no lying down, my hair will get wrecked," I add.

Brody kisses me again before pulling away. "Clothes off. Turn and bend over the bed."

I do as he says, my arousal growing knowing he's watching me. He doesn't make a move to take off his clothes, just watches me. When I turn and face the bed, placing my hands on the edge, he steps closer and runs his finger through my wet, aching center.

"Fuck, beautiful. Is this for me?"

I nod, at a loss for words. He swipes another finger through my wetness before I hear what sounds like his clothes hitting the floor.

Peeking over my shoulder, I see him stroking his cock from root to tip. He winks at me and continues to stroke himself. My mouth waters watching him. Suddenly, he steps up behind me, his heat engulfing me, wraps one arm around me so he can play with one of my breasts, and with his other hand, guides his hard cock along my wet center.

"Brody," I say, aching for him.

"Yes, Aubs," he says as he continues to tease me.

"I need you inside me." I'm panting now. So close to coming. Already.

Without warning, he pushes all the way inside of me. I groan, dropping my head down toward the bed, rocking my hips against him, loving the way his cock fills me up. Fuck, maybe Bri was right. None of this feels fake. It never did if I'm being completely honest with myself.

"Brody, I need you to move," I half groan, half moan.

His reply is to pull almost all the way out before slamming back in. He grips my hips, pistoning into me. I meet him thrust for thrust. The sound of our skin slapping together and our groans is the only sound in the room. It's erotic.

"I'm so close."

Brody reaches around and strums my clit, which sends me over the edge of my orgasm. He thrusts into me a few more times before yelling my name and a mix of incomprehensible curses. Spent, he collapses on top of me, catching himself with his hands at the last second so he's not crushing me. We stay like that for a few minutes before my legs and hips start to cramp.

With a groan, he moves off me, and I collapse onto the floor, my back against the bed.

"You okay?"

I glance up, mesmerized by the sight of him standing above me naked, somehow still half hard. I try to memorize the way he looks in this moment so I can remember it when we're not together. When I'm in Hawaii and he's here in Florida. When he starts dating someone else, because I know that's going to happen. Now that he's finally realized he wants a partner, he'll find someone. He's drop dead gorgeous, sweet, and thoughtful. He's a catch. He's bound to meet someone who makes him happy.

My stomach sinks at the thought of Brody with someone else. But there's nothing I can do. Not without sacrificing my career and the job I worked so hard for. Not without doing exactly what I swore I'd never do.

Chapter Thirty

Brody

I hadn't intended to pounce on Aubrey when she came back to the room. I wanted to finish our earlier conversation. I wanted to talk about us. About what we're going to do. I spent the morning researching moving companies and houses for sale in Hawaii. I even picked up the phone and called Bruce. He didn't answer, so I left him a voicemail asking him to call me back on Monday. I plan to tell him that I'm not taking the Storm's offer. That I'm hanging up my skates. That I'm retiring. I haven't worked up the courage to call Caleb or Coach yet, but I will. I want them to hear it from me and not from the media or the front office.

But when she stepped back into the room, my lizard brain took over, and once I touched her, that was it. Do I regret it? Nope, I sure don't. Especially not with the way she's gazing up at me right now from her spot on the floor. My cock takes notice of her heated stare and starts to harden again. Doesn't help that she's licking her lips, and it makes me think about the feel of them wrapped around me, her tongue licking along my shaft. . .

I give myself a mental shake, then reach down and lift her up by her waist. "Can we talk?" I ask as I set her down gently on the edge of the bed.

"We need to finish getting ready," she says, her eyes darting around the room, anywhere but at me. What's that about?

"Everything okay?"

She finally meets my eyes. "Yeah. Everything from today is catching up with me. And from this week. It's been a lot."

I sit on the bed next to her and reach for her hands. "Want to talk about it?"

"We don't have time now. We need to finish getting ready." She doesn't give me time to respond, getting to her feet and walking around the bed to gather her clothes.

She dumps them on the dresser before selecting underwear and a bra from her drawer. With a sigh, I get up and pull my briefs back on. It won't take me long to get ready, and I doubt it will take her long, either, but I don't argue. She needs time to process everything. When she's ready, she'll tell me what she's thinking.

A few hours later, we're gathered on Smathers Beach, waiting for Clara to make her appearance. I reach over and take Aubrey's hand, happy to have her standing next to me. Clara decided she didn't want anyone walking down the aisle or standing at the altar with her.

Music starts from somewhere, and everyone turns to watch as Clara walks down the sand toward us. Except for me. I'm watching Chet. I know the minute he sees his soon-to-be-wife because his eyes light up and his smile grows bigger. He shifts on his feet, adjusting the cuffs of his suit jacket, and my lips tip up into a grin. I can't help it—I love weddings. I look over at Aubrey. Has she ever thought about her own wedding?

That's when I see it.

Flashes of me standing under an arch with the ocean at my back watching her come down the aisle. The image is so vivid I can see glimpses of Caleb, Cole, and the rest of the Storm in the crowd. My breath hitches as the realization hits me that I want this with her.

I want forever with her.

I want to stand up in front of our friends and family and promise to love and cherish her for the rest of our lives, like Clara and Chet are doing right now.

"Brody," Aubrey whispers, a hand on my arm.

I blink, inhaling, and realize that Clara has now joined Chet in front of the Justice of the Peace, and they're saying their vows. I smile at Aubrey and force myself to pay attention to what's happening in front of me instead of the scene that's lingering in my mind of what I want to happen in the future. Now, I have to hope that she wants it too.

That she wants *me*.

"Want to dance?" I ask Aubrey a few hours later, setting down my empty whiskey glass.

After the ceremony and a few more pictures, we headed back to the hotel for dinner. Everything has gone flawlessly so far. Well, except for the drama with her mother this morning. None of the guests batted an eye at the change of plans. Or if they did, they did it in private. It probably helps that they've been kept occupied by alcohol, food, and live music.

Aubrey places her hand in mine. I lead us out onto the dance floor, picking a spot on the edge, away from everyone. The band is playing some fast-paced pop song, but I pull her close and wrap my arms around her.

Aubrey tips her head back to look up at me. "You know this isn't a slow song."

"But it gives me an excuse to hold you close," I whisper, pulling her further into me as we sway. This is the most I've ever danced in my whole life, and I'm actually enjoying myself. Probably because it's Aubrey I'm dancing with.

When the song ends, she steps away. "Want to get a drink?"

"Sure," I say, even though all I want to do is pull her back into my arms and never let go.

At the bar, she asks for a glass of wine, and I order a whiskey, neat. Drinks in hand, we head back to our table.

"Aubrey," Brielle yells, prancing over to us.

I can't help but laugh. She's clearly had a few drinks and is thoroughly enjoying herself. I glance around for Devon and see him a few steps behind her with a smirk on his face. He catches my eye and shrugs, as if to say *I can't contain her*.

"Bri!" Aubrey matches Brielle's enthusiasm, pulling her sister into a hug. "You seem like you're having a good time." Aubrey pulls back to look at her sister. Now that we're close enough, I see that Brielle's eyes are glossy, and her face is flushed. Yep, she's definitely far past tipsy.

"Here." Devon thrusts a glass of water at Brielle.

Brielle turns to him, crossing her arms and surveying the glass in his hand. "I thought you were getting us more drinks."

"I did. Here. Drink this. I don't want you to feel like crap tomorrow for the drive home." He thrusts the glass at her again. This time she takes it with a resigned sigh, but she does as she's told, drinking half the water in one gulp. I can't help but grin at Devon taking care of her.

"What's up, Bri?" Aubrey says when her sister has finished taking a drink.

"Nothing. I came to see you. I feel like we haven't seen each other all night."

Aubrey giggles. "I saw you a little while ago during dinner. We sat at the same table."

Brielle waves her hands around before turning to me. "When are you going to tell my sister that you're in love with her?"

I nearly choke on my whiskey. How does she know? This is not how I thought this was going to go down.

"Oh, come on." She pats me on the arm. "Being in love isn't all that bad. Look at me and Devon."

"Bri," Aubrey hisses, shaking her head at her sister.

"Come on. That's enough." Devon mouths sorry to us before taking Brielle by the hand and leading her away. Before I can say anything to Aubrey, the emcee announces that Clara and Chet are cutting the cake.

Thirty minutes later, I'm pushing my empty cake plate away from me.

"I'm exhausted," Aubrey says, leaning back in her chair.

"Me too. At least our flight isn't until the afternoon," I say, thankful that we have a late checkout and can sleep in. "Want to go back to the room?"

Aubrey nods, stifling a yawn.

I get to my feet and help her up so we can say good night to everyone. Finally, we're on the elevator, heading up to our suite.

"I had fun tonight," Aubrey mumbles, leaning against me. "I had fun on the whole trip. Thank you for coming with me, Brod. Making things bearable."

"No problem," I murmur as we get off the elevator. "Come on, let's get ready for bed."

Ten minutes later, she's lying on my chest, my arm wrapped around her. I lean down and kiss her on the forehead. She mumbles something that I don't quite catch, but before I can ask her to repeat it, her breathing slows down, and she's asleep. I lie awake for a while listening to her even breath, unable to sleep.

I'm not ready for this trip to end. At least she's staying with me this week. Hopefully, when we get back to Orlando, we can have a conversation about us.

I can tell her I'm in love with her.

That I want to have a future with her. I hope she feels the same way.

Chapter Thirty-One

Aubrey

Groaning, I roll over as Brody's alarm blares. I nudge him, and he finally reaches over and turns it off. "What time is it?" I ask, rubbing a hand down my face.

"Nine," he says, his voice laced with sleep.

"I thought we were going to sleep in," I say as I sit up, stretching my arms over my head.

"This is sleeping in," Brody mumbles as he gets to his feet and heads into the bathroom.

I reach for my phone to see if I have any text messages. I don't. Not that I was expecting any. Although I'd kind of hoped I'd hear something from my mother. Or have a message from Arthur saying he'd heard from her. But no such luck.

I open my email, and my breath catches in my throat when I see an unread one with the subject line *Urgent: Start Date Update*. Why are they emailing me on a Sunday?

I click on the message and read it. They're asking me to start in a month instead of October. The outgoing director has decided to retire earlier because his wife has some health issues. I type a quick response saying that I should be able to start when they want me to.

"You okay?" I glance up to find Brody studying me from the other side of the bed. "Something with your mom? Your sister?"

I shake my head. "They want me to start next month."

"Well, that's good. Right?" Brody asks.

"I suppose." I set my phone down and get out of bed. "I'm going to shower," I mumble, slipping past him and into the bathroom.

As I'm showering, it hits me that I probably can't work remotely from Brody's next week like I'd planned, and I should change my flight back from Orlando to tomorrow so I can start packing and talk to my boss. I probably won't get to see Brody again before I move. I push the tears down that threaten to fall as I finish my shower and get dressed quickly. When I come out of the bathroom, I see that he's already started packing his suitcase. I find him on the couch drinking a cup of coffee and watching SportsCenter.

"Shower's all yours," I say as I make myself a cup of coffee.

"Aubrey, we need to talk."

"Not here, please. Can we talk about this when we're back at your place?" I peek at him over my shoulder and see him watching me. I think he's going to argue, but he just nods before getting to his feet and walking into the bedroom.

I'm mid packing when Brody ambles out of the bathroom in only a towel. My breath catches in my throat when I see him drop it out of the corner of my eye. I can't help watching him bend down and pull a pair of briefs out of his suitcase. He must feel my eyes on him because he grins at me over his shoulder, the underwear still in his hand. He turns to face me, and my eyes travel down his body as if they have a mind of their own. My gaze catches on the tattoo on his thigh.

The one for me.

For us.

"Like what you see?" he rasps out.

My mouth gapes open, and he lets out a throaty chuckle, reaching down to stroke his hardening cock. He strokes himself from root to tip a couple of times. Just the sight of him has me aching for his touch. I blink a couple of times and take a few deep breaths, forcing myself to meet his gaze.

He smirks at me as he steps closer. Before I know what's happening, he's got me pinned against the dresser, his hard length nudging against my center. My shorts and underwear are the only barriers between us.

Brody leans down and ghosts his lips along my throat and chin before moving upward and pulling my ear lobe into his mouth, sucking on it gently. My hands fall to his shoulders, and I hold on to him, not sure what he's going to do. He lets go of my ear lobe with a pop.

"See what you do to me? And I think I have the same effect on you. If I slipped a hand down your shorts, would I find you wet and wanting?"

"Brod, we can't," I mumble.

"We have plenty of time before we have to leave for the airport."

But that's not what I mean. If we touch each other, fall into each other again, I don't know if I'm going to be able to leave him to go to Hawaii. I'll decide to give it all up for him and stay in Florida. I'll end up like every other member of my family and sacrifice myself for someone else. But I don't say that. I just shake my head and push gently against his chest.

Brody studies my face for a few seconds before stepping back. "What's going on, Aubrey?"

"We can't," I repeat, turning my back to him and pulling the rest of my clothes out of the dresser. "I know we said we'd talk after we got back to Orlando, but I think we should go back to being friends. And leave all the rest here in Key West. Chalk it up to a vacation fling." I cringe at the word but can't come up with a better one for what we had.

"Why?"

I take a few more deep breaths, and when my heartbeat has steadied, I whirl around to face him and am thankful that he's pulled on underwear and a shirt. "I'm moving to Hawaii, Brody. Next month. Even if it was still in the fall, what would we do? Long distance? I can't do that."

"But what if I come with you?" He cocks his head, studying me.

I cross my arms. "And how will you play hockey?"

"I wouldn't."

I shake my head. "I think we're better off agreeing that our relationship was fake and we go back to being friends."

"I thought we both agreed that we didn't want this to be fake. That we would talk about it after we got back to Orlando."

"Brody, I care about you. I do. You know that. You're my best friend. But that's all we can ever be. Our lives are on two different tracks. It was crazy to think that there could be anything more between us than friendship."

"Stop lying to yourself. What we feel for each other is more than friends. You and I both know that," he argues.

"Brody, I can't." I put up a hand to stop him. "I can't have this conversation with you now. We have to leave for the airport soon. Can we please talk about it later?"

He nods. I let out a breath and go back to packing my suitcase. Silence settles over us as we finish packing and get ready to leave. I try to ignore the thoughts swirling around in my head.

The things that Brody said.

There's no way we can make this work. But he's right—I do care for him as more than a best friend. But our lives are on different paths. Maybe if we'd figured this out five or ten years ago, things would be different, but now... now there's nothing either of us can do besides continue on the paths we're on. Me to Hawaii. And him, hopefully back to the Storm. He'll forget about all this once the season starts. I'm sure of it. He thinks he wants me now because we've been together nonstop. Because we crossed so many lines.

Chapter Thirty-Two

Brody

My chest is tight as I finish packing. I know what I did earlier probably wasn't the smartest move, but I couldn't help myself. I'd hoped that if Aubrey saw what she does to me, if she admitted to me and herself what she feels for me, maybe we could talk.

I don't want this to end.

I know we have to go back to reality and make some decisions about us, but I'd hoped she would be open to talking through things. I don't expect her to give up her job opportunity for me. I would never ask her to do that.

I'm in over my head. How do I make Aubrey see that I will do whatever it takes to be with her? I zip up my suitcase, wheel it into the living room, and take a seat on the couch. She's still packing, which gives me a few minutes to ask for help.

Taking a deep breath and silently praying I don't regret this, I pull out my phone, open the group chat, and type a message.

Me: First of all, if any of you say I told you so, I'll never speak to you again. But I've got a problem. A relationship problem.

I set my phone down and wait with bated breath for a response.

I groan silently, tipping my head back against the couch, imagining the guys giving me shit from now until the end of time when I admit that we were faking it. They'll never let me hear the end of it when they find that out. Aubrey's smiling face comes to mind, and I decide that whatever shit they give me is worth it for her. If I get to call her mine at the end of the day, it's worth it. When my phone dings, I open my eyes and pick it up. Hunter is the first to answer.

Hunter: What's going on? Finally get your head out of your ass and realize you're in love with Aubrey?

I chuckle before typing back a simple yes.

Wes: So what's the problem, Brod? Tell her.
Me: She's moving to Hawaii for a job. She's convinced that we're done. That we can't work.
Wes: Tell her you love her and that you're going with her. That's what you're planning to do, right? I assume that's the reason you haven't signed your contract.
Me: I tried to tell her that, well the part about going with her. It didn't go well. I don't think she believes me. Also, how'd you know that?
Wes: I hear things.

Before I can reply, Aubrey walks into the room, pulling her suitcase behind her, her overnight bag slung over her shoulder.

"Ready?" she asks, offering me a tight-lipped smile.

"Yeah. Our car is here."

I give the suite one last look before closing the door behind me. The clicking of the lock feels like the symbolic closing of the door to any relationship, outside of friendship, Aubrey and I could have.

I ignore that thought, choosing to believe that we'll figure things out. We're silent on the ride down on the elevator. I don't like it, but I don't know how to break the silence. I don't know how to fix the weirdness that seems to have come between us. The last thing I wanted was for things between us to get weird.

It's not until we're seated next to each other on our flight to Orlando that Aubrey finally speaks up. She leans closer to me and says, "I don't want things to be awkward between us."

I turn to face her and notice she's staring at the floor.

"I don't want that either." I put my hand on her arm. "Look at me, Aubs. Please." The last word comes out in a whisper. I watch her contemplate my request, and I start to wonder if she's going to ignore it, but she finally turns to look up at me.

"There's no reason for things to be awkward between us. There's also no reason for things to end between us." She opens her mouth to say something, likely another protest, but I hold up my hand, and she closes her mouth and gestures for me to continue. "Let's do what we said and talk about this when we get back to my place."

Is that what I wanted to say? No, of course not. But the flight is not the time nor the place to have the discussion we need to have. She nods and stares out the window. I try to relax, taking a sip of the coffee that the steward set in front of me a little while ago.

The flight is uneventful, and before I know it, we're descending into Orlando International Airport. Shockingly, by the time we arrive at the baggage claim, all the luggage from our flight is already coming down.

"First time for everything," I mutter, grabbing first my suitcase and then Aubrey's. "A car is waiting for us," I say, directing her through the sliding glass doors and out into the arrivals pickup area.

A little over an hour later, we're thanking the driver and walking into my building.

"Are you hungry?" I ask, pulling out my phone as we ride the elevator and seeing that it's a little after six.

I ignore the text messages from the guys, I'll deal with them later, and look at Aubrey who's standing across the elevator from me, her back resting against the wall, chewing on her bottom lip. I swallow, forcing myself to focus on her eyes and not on her lips. To not think about how much I want to lean over and pull her lip out from between her teeth before kissing her.

"I could eat. What were you thinking?"

"Sushi?" I frown, thinking back to all the seafood we ate in Key West. "Or are you not in the mood for more fish?"

The elevator dings, and the doors slide open. I shove my phone back in my pocket and hold the door open for her.

"I'm always in the mood for sushi. You know what I like. I'm going to go shower the plane smell off me," she says once we're inside my condo.

"Okay."

She continues down the hallway. I heave out a breath when I hear the guest bedroom door close behind her. I wish she was going into my bedroom. I wanted to tell her as much, but maybe a night apart will make her rethink her stance that things are over between us.

I grab my bag and head to my room. I pull out my phone and put in our order before unpacking. Once everything is put away or in the hamper, I hop in the shower.

As I'm getting out, Aubrey yells, "Foods here."

I make quick work of toweling off and getting dressed in black athletic shorts and a faded, worn Storm shirt before heading into the living room where she's laid out the food on the coffee table.

"Want to watch Seinfeld?" Aubrey asks when she sees me walking into the room carrying two glasses of water for us.

"Sure." I take a seat next to her on the couch, and she pulls up the show. We fall into a comfortable silence eating dinner and watching Netflix. I relax as, for the first time today, things feel back to normal between us. Now, if only I can convince her that we should try to make things work between us, that would be great.

"I'm so full," Aubrey says, setting her empty container down on the coffee table.

"That's because you polished off three rolls." I tease, setting my own empty container down and chugging the rest of my water. She playfully swats at me, and I can't help but chuckle. *There she is.*

"You didn't feed me all day," she says with an exaggerated sigh.

"Hey. I fed you breakfast." I protest, chuckling. "It's not my fault we had a midday flight."

"I know. I'm just joking," Aubrey says, getting to her feet and collecting the trash. I stand and help her, and we make quick work of cleaning up.

"Want to watch more Seinfeld? Or a movie?" I'd much rather be talking about us and where we go from here, but maybe that's a conversation for tomorrow.

"A movie sounds great." Aubrey grabs the bottle of wine and a beer for me out of the fridge. I nod my thanks when she hands it over. Glass of wine in hand, she follows me back into the living room where we make ourselves comfortable and pick a movie.

At some point during the evening, she shifts closer to me. I can't help but put my arm around her and pull her closer. I fear that she's going to pull away, but she doesn't, resting her head against my chest instead. Her breathing evens out after a little while, and I realize she's fallen asleep.

The selfish part of me wants to keep watching the movie with her curled into me, but I know I should wake her up and let her go to bed. So I do just that, leaning down and kissing her on the forehead.

"Aubrey. Beautiful."

"What?" she mumbles, her voice thick with sleep.

"You fell asleep. We can finish this tomorrow."

She rubs her eyes before getting to her feet. I shut off the television and the lights and follow her down the hallway. She pauses, glancing between the guest bedroom and my bedroom. I hold my breath, staying silent behind her. With one last glance in the direction of my room, she turns toward the guest room, walks in, and shuts the door.

My heart feels like it's breaking all over again as I get ready for bed. I lie in bed long into the night trying to come up with what to say to convince Aubrey that even though we may have started out as fake, we're not anymore, and we can make it work.

Chapter Thirty-Three

Aubrey

Even though we had a relaxing evening and things felt okay between us, sleep doesn't come easy. I might have fallen asleep on the couch during the movie, but that was one hundred percent because of Brody. As tired as I was on the couch, the minute I finished brushing my teeth and lay down in bed, my brain started going a mile a minute, and I was wide awake again.

When I walked down the hallway to go to bed, it felt like a test. A test I failed by choosing the guest room over Brody's. Part of me wanted to walk into his room, sleep in bed with him, but part of me, the rational part, knew I couldn't.

I knew that if I went into his room, we would fall back into the easy relationship we had in Key West. That in the morning... I wouldn't be able to leave.

As much as it pains me, I can't do that.

I can't sacrifice my dreams and goals.

I don't want to wake up in twenty years and resent him because I gave up my dream to be with him. Just like I don't want him to resent me because he gave up hockey to follow me. As romantic as it sounds, I couldn't live with myself knowing what he sacrificed for me. It wouldn't be fair to either of us.

With my mind made up, I close my eyes and try to think of something else so I can get some sleep. It's going to take all the strength I can muster to have this conversation with him. To tell him goodbye.

I toss and turn for a while and eventually fall into a restless sleep. And I dream of Brody. Because of course I do. Except in my dream, he's walking away from me. I chase him down roads and through streets that aren't familiar, always yelling his name. But somehow, he's always just out of reach. He never hears me. Never turns around or stops to wait for me.

I jolt awake, the blankets twisted around me, drenched in sweat. Taking a deep breath, I try to calm my racing mind. Tell myself it's only a dream. That it's not real. Running a hand down my face, I take a few deep breaths. Once my heart rate has slowed down and my mind has stopped whirling, lie back down. Luckily, I sleep the rest of the night without any more dreams.

The smell of bacon and coffee wakes me up. Stretching, I clamber out of bed and make my way into the en suite. I get dressed and throw the few items I unpacked last night back into my bag. I'm not sure when I'm going to leave yet since my flight isn't until this evening, but I'd rather be ready now. Once that's done, I make my way into the kitchen where I find Brody in front of the stove, cooking eggs.

"Good morning," he greets me over his shoulder. "There's coffee." He points toward the coffee pot with the spatula before turning back to the stove.

"Morning. Thanks," I mumble, grabbing a mug and pouring myself some. I fix it the way I like it before sliding into one of the barstools at the kitchen island. Taking a sip, I rack my brain for ways to bring up the topic of me leaving, but before I can figure out what to say, he's walking over to me with two plates in his hand.

"Here." He slides one of the plates, filled with scrambled eggs, a Belgian waffle, and fruit, toward me before setting the other one in front of the seat next to me.

His plate is almost the same as mine except he's got potatoes instead of a waffle. He went through all the trouble of making a waffle just for me. Didn't he? Of course he did. Why does he have to be so . . . perfect? I don't know whose heart is going to be more broken—his or mine—when this is all over. But there's not a whole lot I can do.

I give him a tight lipped smile as I take the knife and fork he hands me before he sits down next to me. When our plates are empty, he pushes his away and turns to face me. "I'm going to come out and say it. I don't want what we started in Key West to end. It feels like we are just beginning."

"I can't," I mumble, staring down at my empty plate, the waffle I ate feeling like a lead block in my stomach.

"Aubrey." Brody reaches over, and I flinch back.

I can't do this. If he touches me, if I end up in his arms, I won't want to leave. I won't be able to. I square my shoulders, take a fortifying breath, and stare up at him. "I'm not sacrificing this for you. For us. I'm sorry, Brody. This is my dream job. I can't, I won't give it up. Not even for you." The last part comes out in a whisper, and I wonder if he heard me.

Now I understand why everyone in my family made sacrifices for love. It was probably easy for them. Because it would be so easy for me to do the same. It breaks my heart to break both of our hearts, but I need to do this. I need to follow this dream. Even if it means giving up the one person that I love the most.

Brody shakes his head at me like he can't believe what I said. I lean back against the counter, the knot tightening in my stomach, bracing myself for what he's about to say. Bracing myself to hear him say that he can't be friends with me anymore.

I was stupid to think our arrangement could end smoothly after the wedding. Why did I think this was a good idea? Now I'm going to lose the one person that means the most to me. But it's either this or give up my dreams. Sacrifice myself for him. And I can't do that. I won't do that. It's taken me too long to get to this point in my career to throw it all away.

It's what he says next that I don't anticipate. That throws me for a loop.

Chapter Thirty-Four

Brody

I understand what she's saying. I do. I would never expect or ask her to give up her dreams for me. My mind is made up, and I know what I need to do, what I *want* to do. I think I've always known. "I love you. You don't have to give up Hawaii for me because I'm coming with you."

"You're what?" Aubrey rears back.

"I love you. I'm coming with you," I repeat.

"I can't let you do this," she says, crossing her arms.

"You're not letting me do anything. I'm choosing to do this."

"But hockey is your dream. The Storm is your family. You can't abandon them." She pushes her chair back and stands, her eyes wild.

"Aubrey." I run a hand over my face. "Hockey was my dream, yes. But dreams can change. The Storm is my family, yeah. They always will be. But you're my home. Hockey is my past, you're my present, my future."

"I'm not worth it," she whispers, her gaze dropping to the ground, and, fuck, my heart breaks.

"Yes, you are, Aubs. You're worth it to me."

"No. No. I'm not. You still have years of hockey left. I'm not going to let you give that up for me. I'm not going to let you sacrifice that for me. The Storm want you to sign another contract, right?"

"Yeah. For another three years." I run a hand through my hair and tug at the ends.

"Do it, Brody," she whispers, her voice breaking.

"Aubrey." I level her a look that I hope conveys how I feel. This is ridiculous. Why doesn't she see that I've made up my mind? That she's all I want. For me to have her, I have to give up hockey. That's fine. I've made peace with that. Hell, I made peace with it at the beginning of the summer when I was convinced the Storm weren't going to offer me another contract. When I didn't think I'd have anything or anyone to go to at the end of the day. But now, I can have her.

Why doesn't she realize that she's the ultimate prize? That I'd trade anything for her. Never in my wildest dreams did I think I'd be lucky enough to have her and have a great hockey career. I'm the luckiest man alive. All my dreams came true. It's not a sacrifice for me to retire from hockey. It's closing one chapter of my life because it's time to move on to the next one. I furrow my brow, realizing she's talking to me.

"Brody," she shakes her head. "I can't do this."

My heart stops beating. "You can't do what, Aubrey?" My voice catches, and I hear the emotion in my words. I hope she's not saying what I think she is.

"I can't let you do this," she whispers. "I'm not worth it."

"Aubrey—" I start to speak, but she holds up her hand, and I close my mouth.

"I can't let you give up everything you've worked toward for me. I don't want you to wake up in thirty years and regret this."

"That's not going to happen."

"How do you know that? Brody, I'm moving, and that's it." She turns on her heel and strides toward the guest room.

"Aubrey," I call after her.

She doesn't respond. Maybe she needs some time alone to gather herself. So instead of marching down the hallway to the bedroom, I collect our dishes and start loading the dishwasher.

A few minutes later, the sound of footsteps and suitcase wheels echoes in the hallway, and my heart drops. I shut off the water, grab the towel, and rush to the front door where she's standing waiting for me, her overnight bag tossed over one arm, her suitcase behind her.

"Don't go," I plead. How is she doing this? My heart feels like it's breaking in two.

"Thank you for going with me to Clara's wedding." She swallows, blinking a few times. "You were a great fake boyfriend, but I can't let you sacrifice your career for me. I *won't* let you. Our lives are on two different paths. You know that."

I push past her and stand in front of the door, blocking her way. It's probably a dick move. I shouldn't stop her from leaving if she wants to, but I can't let it end like this. Her gaze meets mine, and for a second, I think maybe she's going to reconsider.

"Aubrey." I heave out a breath, meeting her gaze and hoping she can see the emotion in my face when I say, "We don't have to be on two different paths. We can make this work."

"Brody," she whispers, "I can't. I can't do it. Maybe the real reason I'm still single is because I'm not cut out for a relationship. I'm sorry. I can't."

We stand there for a moment staring at each other, and finally, I jerk my head in a slight nod, shoulders falling as I step out of her way. I don't turn back to watch her leave. I can't. I hear the door open and close as she walks out, taking my heart with her.

"Brody, are you okay?"

I open my eyes and look up to see the whole crew crammed into my living room. Groaning, I run a hand down my face, mentally cursing myself for giving Caleb a key when I left for Key West. "What are you all doing here?"

"Aubrey called Madison," Caleb says, his brows furrowed together. "Said you might need us."

I shake my head, sitting up. How long have I been asleep? The sun is streaming through the windows, meaning it's probably midmorning.

After Aubrey left, I moved around my condo like a zombie, barely conscious of what I was doing. I paced back and forth starting and deleting countless text messages to her. Then I sat on the couch staring at the dark television until the sun set. I couldn't make myself get up and do anything except pour a glass of bourbon. Which sat on the coffee table untouched because alcohol wasn't going to solve my problems.

All night I sat and contemplated how to make her see that she's worth it. That she's all I want. I must have lain down at some point and fallen asleep, but I don't remember doing so.

"I appreciate it. But I'm fine," I say, glancing from Caleb to Cole to Hunter.

"Here." Wes hands me a take out cup of coffee.

"You don't look fine," Holt says.

"Brody," Cole says. "You're our family, and you need us. Whether you want to admit it or not."

"What happened?" Hunter asks.

I take a sip of coffee before setting the cup down. I roll my neck and shoulders, trying to work out the kinks that come with sleeping on the couch. You'd think I'd know by now that it's not a good idea.

I take a deep breath and tell them the whole story, including that Aubrey and I were faking our relationship. That she's moving to Hawaii, and she wants us to go back to being friends. I even tell them about all the craziness with Aubrey's mother and her weird, forced marriage to Arthur. I figure the more information they have, the more they might be able to help me figure things out.

"Well, shit. Sounds like she's your one," Wes says.

"Except she doesn't want him," Holt points out with a shake of his head.

"Gee, thanks, way to make me feel even worse," I say with a scowl in Holt's direction.

"Sorry, man, just pointing out the obvious," Holt says, his hands raised, and I nod, accepting his apology because I know he didn't really mean anything by it.

"What are you going to do?" Caleb asks, taking a seat next to me.

"I'm going to go after her. I'll spend the rest of my life proving to her that she's worth it. But first, I'm going to announce my retirement."

"Fuck," Cole whispers. "I get it. No offense guys." He glances at the others. "But if Hann was moving to chase her dreams, I'd be on the next plane with her. I'd miss playing hockey, but she's worth giving it up for."

"Same," Hunter agrees.

I'm glad they understand because I was worried they'd tell me I was crazy for following Aubrey. For giving up a fifteen-year career for her.

"You do what you have to for the woman you love," Caleb says, clapping me on the back. "Now how are you going to prove to her that she's worth it? Better yet, how are you going to prove to her that you're not making a mistake and you won't regret choosing her. Because it sounds like that's what she's really worried about."

I shrug. I hadn't thought that far when I was putting together this plan. My hope is that she was only saying what she thought she needed to so I wouldn't follow her. That if I show up at her door having already retired, she'll let me in. Let me love her like she deserves.

"What happens if it's not your time yet?" Wes asks after a few minutes of silence. He glances at everyone else in the room before his gaze lands on me. "What happens if you two need to go through this to be the right people for each other?"

"Come again?" I tilt my head, trying to figure out what he's getting at.

"Maybe she needs to go off and live her dream. See what life is like having the job of her dreams but not the man of her dreams. If she can be happy living that life. And maybe you need to play one more season of hockey. Put it all on the line. See what you've got one more time. Because we all know you've been obsessing over that missed goal since the second the game ended," Wes says.

"That's crazy," I mumble.

I meet Caleb's gaze. "What do you think?" I ask. I know he went through a lot when he and Jenna were first dating so maybe he has an opinion.

"I don't know. Wes kind of has a point."

My mouth falls open, but as I look around at the rest of the guys I can see it on their faces, they agree with him. "What the fuck, guys?" I rasp out, running a hand through my hair. "I thought you were on my side."

"We are," Cole answers. I open my mouth to argue, but he holds up his hand for me to remain quiet. So, I do, closing my mouth, crossing my arms, and sinking back into the couch, waiting to see what he has to say. "Do you know why she pushed you away?"

I think back to her words. "She said she didn't want me to sacrifice for her. She thinks I'm going to resent her later down the road."

"Any idea why? Is there some reason she would think like that? Because it kind of sounds like there is."

I raise an eyebrow at Cole. Since when did he become so philosophical? I take a deep breath, trying to sort through his questions. Through all of what Aubrey has told me. And then it hits me like a ton of bricks, and I gasp.

For fuck's sake.

Is it really that simple?

Chapter Thirty-Five

Aubrey

"Are you okay?"

I glance up from the books I'm stacking on my desk to see Summer leaning against the doorframe, her arms crossed as she watches me.

"I'm fine, Summer."

She steps into my office and drops into one of the visitor chairs opposite where I'm currently packing. "I don't buy it. Try again. What happened?"

"Nothing." I say, pulling items out of my desk drawers and placing them in the boxes at my feet. Refusing to look at her because I know if I do, she'll see right through my lie.

"Bullshit. What happened with Brody? You sounded weird on the phone last night." She pauses, studying me. "Like you'd been crying."

"Nothing happened. I'm fine," I say, focusing on my task and hoping that she believes me.

"Stop saying nothing because we both know there's something going on. You're in love with the man. That's not nothing."

I collapse into my chair, crossing my arms and finally meeting her gaze. "And? His job is here. He can't play hockey in Hawaii."

"Aubrey," Summer protests with a shake of her head.

"Leave it. Please."

There's nothing she can say that'll change my mind. I went through all the scenarios last night after I left Brody's place. There is no possible solution that would let both of us chase our dreams and be together.

Summer frowns. "Aubrey, I love you, and you're the smartest person I know. But"—she narrows her eyes—"right now, you're being an idiot. Why are you torturing yourself?"

I prop my elbows on my desk and drop my head into my hands. "He was willing to give up his career for me."

"And?"

"I can't let him do that for me. Hockey was always his dream. The Storm is his family. He was talking about leaving them. That's ridiculous. He has years left to play. And he's going to what? Give it up for me? I'm not worth that sacrifice." My voice cracks and tears run down my face. Summer must hear the emotion in my voice because she places a comforting hand on my arm. I lift my head and see her leaning over the desk, peering at me.

"Why do you get to make that decision for him? Don't you think he can make whatever choice he wants."

I reach for a tissue from the box on my desk and dab at my eyes, contemplating how to answer the question. "If he's going to retire, he should do it on a high. Not after a season like they had last year. He deserves to lift the Stanley Cup one more time. He blames himself for their elimination in the playoffs. I know he does. If he retires now, he'll spend the rest of his life regretting it and replaying the end of his last season."

Summer laughs. The bitch laughs at me.

"Do you hear yourself?" She takes her hand off my arm and sits up straight. "Are you sure you're not the one who plays professional hockey? Because you sure are acting like you do."

I shake my head. What the hell is she talking about? "What do you mean?"

"What do I mean? For fuck's sake, Aubrey, let the man love you. What's this about, not wanting him to sacrifice for you? How would it be a sacrifice? He's played hockey for how many years? You're not asking him to go with you. He offered."

I open and close my mouth a couple of times before turning my attention back to my desk drawers and my packing. "I don't know what you mean," I finally manage to say.

"Aubrey, look at me."

I shake my head, staring down at the desk because if I do as she asks, I know I'm going to lose it. She's right. We both know it. But all I can think about is the sacrifices my siblings made for love or, in my brother's case, for the family, and I can't do it. I refuse to give up my dreams for love, and I sure as hell won't ask Brody to do that for me.

"I'm afraid that if he gives up the one thing he's always wanted, he'll regret the decision. Or he'll spend the rest of our lives constantly reminding me of the sacrifice he made for me."

"You know he's not like that, right? Why can't you take what he says at face value?" Summer says quietly. "Don't torture the man. Talk to him."

"I can't," I say, finally meeting her eyes. "We're done. It was a fun fake relationship for my sister's wedding. Now, I'm packing my bags to move thousands of miles away." Before she can answer, my laptop dings with a meeting reminder.

Saved by the bell.

Summer gets to her feet, throwing me a *we're not done with this conversation* look before she walks out of my office. I nod because what she doesn't know won't hurt her. I hope she's not too mad at me when she finds out that I'm leaving tomorrow instead of in two weeks. By the time she reads my text in the morning, I'll be on a plane heading across the ocean. I hope she forgives me for leaving without a proper goodbye, but I know if I stay any longer, she'll convince me to talk to Brody. To figure things out with him.

And I can't.

I need to go do this.

Go live my life and let him live his.

We were never going to work. I don't know why I thought we might.

I survey my messy living room, boxes piled everywhere. How did I think I was going to pack up my whole life in one night? Even if I stay up all night, there's no way I can get everything done. It seems more and more like the one trip back here that I'd planned to make isn't going to be enough either.

My plan had been to box up as much as I could—hopefully everything—tonight. Then next month come back and finish packing, hire professional cleaners, and list my home as a furnished rental on the university website. There's always visiting professors who need a place to stay, so I figured that was the easiest and fastest way to get a tenant in the house.

I didn't take into consideration how much stuff I have. How much time it would really take to pack. I don't remember having all of this when I moved in five years ago. I glance at the books stacked along one wall, blu-rays piled on top of them, waiting to be boxed. The knickknacks and picture frames on the coffee table and floor, half packed. With a groan, I sit on the couch, grab my glass of wine, and take a healthy swig. I haven't even started in my bedroom. Or the kitchen.

My phone rings, interrupting my spiral.

"Hi sis," I say to Bri, trying to infuse some happiness into my voice.

"Hey, Aubrey. Clara's here too." *Oh.*

"Hi, Clara. Why aren't you on your honeymoon?"

"We're not leaving until next week. Chet had some things he had to take care of at work."

"What's going on?" Bri asks, her voice stern.

"What do you mean?" I ask before finishing my wine with one final sip. I don't like the direction this conversation is going. I weave my way around the boxes scattered around the room and head into the kitchen.

"You and Brody? You broke up," Clara states.

Oh shit. Maybe I shouldn't have told them.

"We were fake. It was always going to end after the wedding anyway." I grab the wine bottle from the fridge—probably going to need more than one glass if this is where this conversation is going.

"Maybe it started off as fake, but you're both in love with each other. Everyone could see it. Even Thad," Bri scolds.

I take a big gulp of my wine. "I got a job in Hawaii. Surprise. I'm flying there tomorrow."

"You what?" Clara says.

"Why didn't you say anything to us?" Bri asks softly, and I can hear the hurt in her voice.

"Because I didn't want to overshadow Clara and Chet's week. Besides, I wasn't supposed to start until October, but things changed, and their current director is retiring next month," I say, tucking the phone against my ear so I have both hands free. I grab the pile of brown packing paper off the floor and begin wrapping the knick knacks I took off the television stand earlier.

"That's awesome. But what does that have to do with you and Brody's relationship?" Clara asks.

"For starters, there are no hockey teams there. He was going to retire so he could come with me."

"And?" Bri asks.

"I couldn't let him do that for me. I refuse. You both may be okay with the sacrifices you made for love, but I'm not. I don't want him to wake up one day and hate me because of it." My words come out much harsher than I meant them to, but if the reason they called was to give me a hard time, I've got better things to do. Like packing up my house.

"What sacrifices do you think we made?" Bri asks quietly.

"You gave up law school. Clara didn't go abroad like she'd planned." I run a hand down my face. Why are we having this conversation? I should have ignored the call.

"I'm glad I didn't go to law school. I can't imagine what my life would be like if I was a lawyer working ten hours or more a day. If I had to leave Anabelle every morning and miss out on seeing her grow up." Bri says softly.

"Don't you have regrets?"

Bri is quiet for a few beats before she says, "No. I don't. I love my life. If I had to do it over again, I would. In a heartbeat. It might have felt like a sacrifice in the beginning, but now, looking back on it, I know it wasn't the right path. Besides, if I change my mind, I can always go when Anabelle is older or when we're done having kids. Or have a different career. I love my family and my life. I wouldn't change it."

"Oh," I mumble, unsure of what to say. "What about you, Clara?"

There's silence on the other end of the line for so long that I pull my phone away from my ear to make sure the call didn't disconnect.

Finally, Clara says, "I'm sure it would have been a great time, but I don't know if it really would have been the right thing for me. Yes, I love fashion, but *wearing the* clothes. I don't think I'd love selling them or even designing them. So, no, it wasn't really a sacrifice to give it up when Chet and I got engaged. Plus, now, I've been helping out at the law firm by doing research. I'm thinking about going back to school to become a paralegal."

I'm speechless.

Here I judged them, well, their relationships really, without knowing all the facts, and I was completely wrong.

"You're not going to turn into Mom," Bri says, breaking the silence.

"Wh-what?" I mumble, gulping down the rest of my wine. Where did that come from?

"Is that what this is really about? You're afraid you're going to turn into her, or Brody's going to turn into some form of her, if either of you makes a sacrifice for the other. Because it's not going to happen. Neither of you are her. You could never be her. She chose to marry Dad and give up her career. To follow him here. She could have still done some sort of acting. She chose not to. The same thing with marrying Arthur. She didn't have to do that. She just didn't want to lose control of the company," Bri states. "You. Are. Not. Mom. Nor will you ever be."

Is that what I'm really worried about? Maybe it is. "Since when did you become a psychologist?" I finally ask Bri. "Or a mind reader."

"It wasn't that hard once I thought about all of it," Bri says.

I sit in silence, surveying my messy living room. Shit. Have I made a grave mistake? I really do want this job, but I'm also in love with Brody. But it doesn't feel right that he retires from hockey after the season he had.

"What am I going to do? My flight leaves in the morning."

"Do you need to be there tomorrow?" Clara asks.

"No," I admit. My job doesn't start for a month. And it's not like I have to find a place to live because the position comes with a small house. I was going early so I didn't have to be here.

"I think you need to go see Brody. Talk to him. Tell him what's really going on. Have a conversation with him where you lay it all on the table and actually *listen* to what he says he wants. Relationships are about compromises. I'm sure there's a compromise the two of you can reach to both get what you want and be together," Bri says.

"I was terrible to him," I admit, taking a deep breath. "He might not want to hear me out, or he might listen to me, but will he believe me?"

"He'll believe you. He loves you," Clara pipes up.

"I need to do something to show him that I'm all in, no matter what he says. That I'm committed to him."

"What are you thinking?" Bri asks.

"I don't know . . ." I say, but suddenly a light bulb goes off. I sit up straighter. I know what I have to do. As much as it'll probably hurt and might backfire if he doesn't forgive me or still want me, I know it's the best way to prove to him that I'm all in. That I'm his no matter what. "I've got an idea. I've got to go."

I say goodbye to my sisters and make quick work of changing my flight back to my original departure date. I nearly have a heart attack at the fees I'm paying yet again, but I know it's worth it, he's worth it.

As I'm packing my bag, my phone rings. I answer it without checking to see who it is. "Hello."

"Aubrey Elizabeth." Mother's voice rings out over the phone. Shit. Fuck. Always check who's calling.

"Mother."

"I was calling about—-" she starts to say, but I'm done. I've had it with her, so I do something I've never done before.

I interrupt her.

"Unless you're calling to apologize, I don't want to hear it. The way you acted to me, to Clara, to everyone, was absolutely uncalled for. You left on Clara's wedding day. Why? Because you didn't get your way? Did you apologize to her?"

She huffs out a breath. "Aubrey Elizabeth. That is no way to speak to your mother."

I scoff. "What am I, five? I'm an adult. But you never treat me that way. You never show me any respect, so why should I show you any? And you didn't answer my question. Did you apologize to Clara?"

"There's nothing to apologize for."

I roll my eyes so hard I'm surprised they don't get stuck. Sucking in a deep breath, I say, "I'm done. I'm done letting you treat me like this. I refuse to put up with it. So until you can apologize to me and the rest of the family and speak to me with respect, I don't want to talk to you."

"Aubrey—" she starts to say, but I don't want to hear it. I pull the phone away from my ear and hang up, my hands shaking. I take a few deep breaths. Shit, I can't believe I did that. But also, holy hell that felt good.

I shoot off a quick text to my siblings, giving them the Reader's Digest version of what just happened. Clara and Bri both respond quickly, saying they're behind me one hundred percent and that they plan to tell Mother the same thing. Thad responds with a thumbs up. I take that as he's agreeing with us, too, but I don't know. He's in a different situation since he has to talk to her because of the business.

That done, I put my phone on silent and finish packing so I can get ready for bed.

I hope I can sleep tonight after all of that because tomorrow is going to be a long day. I plan to get up bright and early. I have things I need to take care of before I catch a midafternoon flight to Orlando.

I hope it's not too late to make things right with Brody.

To tell him that I love him.

Here's to hoping he answers the door.

Chapter Thirty-Six

Brody

"Did you get a hold of her?" Caleb asks.

"No. The university told me that yesterday was her last day."

"I'm sorry, man. And you tried calling her?"

"Yeah." I run a hand through my hair, leaning my head against the wall behind the couch and cradling the phone between my shoulder and chin. "She didn't pick up."

I've called Aubrey at least a dozen times this morning. I want, no, I *need*, to talk to her before she leaves for Hawaii. I was hoping she'd pick up the phone so I could ask her if we could talk in person. I even searched for flights last night, and there's one this afternoon that I can make.

Before Caleb can answer, there's a knock at my front door. I frown, pulling my phone away from my ear to see if I have any missed calls from the front desk. There are only a few people, mostly my teammates, who are approved to come up without the doorman calling me first. And since the front desk hasn't called, it means someone who's on my approved list is here. "You're not knocking on my door, are you?" I ask, getting to my feet.

"Nope. I can come over later if you want, though."

"Give me a minute," I say into the phone as I pull the door open.

I blink a few times at the woman standing in front of me, my mouth opening and closing, before finding my voice.

"I gotta call you back," I say, hanging up before Caleb can respond. "Aubrey?" My voice is barely above a whisper.

"Hi. Can we talk?"

I hold the door open and gesture for her to come in. Silently, we take seats on opposite ends of the couch. Aubrey turns to face me, her back against the armrest and her feet tucked up under her.

"What are you doing here?"

"I'm sorry, Brody. I was—am, an idiot. I got scared and ran. Instead of staying and having a conversation with you." She drops her head into her hands. "I'm such an idiot. I don't know why I wanted to throw away what we had."

I stay silent.

Holding my breath.

Waiting for more.

Hoping for more.

She finally lifts her head, looking up at me. "I love you, Brody. And that scared me."

I swallow down the emotions threatening to overflow. "Why?" I croak out.

"Because I thought the only way I could love you was if one of us sacrificed who we were, what we wanted, for the other. It's what I saw happen with my sisters. Or what I thought happened. And my mother. I thought I'd end up like her." My heart cracks at that admission. Fucking hell. Before I can say anything, she continues, "I understand if you never forgive me, but you're it for me. You're the only one I will ever want, and if you don't want me anymore because of everything, I understand. But I need to show you something."

I nod, and she pushes up the sleeve of her shirt, and it's then that it registers she's wearing a long-sleeve Orlando Storm shirt. In the middle of summer. Before I can ask why, she's pulling off the Saran Wrap from around her right wrist.

My breath hitches in my throat.

Inked on her wrist is a hockey puck with the number ninety inside of it. Her skin is still red. This is new. Maybe as new as today. She got a tattoo.

For me.

The woman who hates needles and has a low pain tolerance. Who's admired my tattoos over the years but staunchly proclaimed that she'd never get one.

Got one.

For me.

She got it before she came here to talk to me. Before she knew whether we'd be alright. She permanently marked her body for me. In the back of my mind, I know she could get it removed, but this is definitely a statement.

A declaration.

That no matter what happens here between us, she's all in.

And I realize that I'm all in too.

Do I wish she'd handled things differently? Yes.

Do I wish she'd talked to me? Yes, of course.

But I feel like I understand now where she's coming from. And I love her more than anything in the world, even hockey.

"Aubrey, what's this?" I ask when I finally find my voice. I need to hear her say it. Tell me why she got it.

She peeks up at me. "I couldn't think of any other way to show you that I love you. To show you what you mean to me. That you're it for me." She pulls her arm back and starts to wrap it back up. "It was probably a stupid idea. I—"

"No." I reach over and tug on her arm, pulling her toward me. "It wasn't stupid. I can't believe you did that. For me." My voice cracks, and I clear my throat, willing the wetness in the corners of my eyes to go away.

She tilts her head up, meeting my gaze. "It was worth it for you. I love you, Brody. I was an idiot to walk away from you. To say those things to you. Of course you mean something to me. That is, if you still want me."

"Want you? Of course I want you. I love you. I'll never stop wanting you." I take a deep breath. "I wish you'd talked to me."

"I know. And I'm so, so sorry."

"What made you come to this realization?"

"Bri and Clara called last night. We talked about a lot of things. I'd always thought they'd sacrificed their goals and dreams for their relationships, and gave up parts of themselves because they had no choice. But it turns out, they're both happier for the compromises they made. They called me out on everything. Why I really pushed you away. Honestly, I hadn't even realized the real reason until Bri said it."

I'm silent for a few minutes before I finally say the words that I hope don't break us, but that I know need to be said.

"I need to stay here," I mumble into her hair. "Play another season. One that hopefully doesn't end the way the last one did. But I don't want this to come between us. If you need me to go to Hawaii with you, I'll announce my retirement. I need you more than I need another season."

Aubrey pulls back so she can look up at me and rests her hand against my cheek. I close my eyes, savoring her touch. "I'll support whatever you need to do. Plus, it's only a year. Less, really. Then we'll have the rest of our lives to spend together."

"Can we do this?" I meet her gaze. "Can we really do this? Not just the distance, but the time changes too, and all the travel." I heave out a breath. "You know what it's like trying to see or talk to each other during the season when we're in the same state, now we'll be thousands of miles apart."

"Brody, I love you. I know it won't be easy, but it'll be worth it."

"I love you too, Aubrey." It's so freeing to finally be able to say those words out loud to her. It feels so right to finally be able to say them.

It'll be tough, but I'll do anything for a year if it means she's my reward at the end. But, fuck, it's only been a couple of days, and I'm aching to touch her, feel her around me. Kiss her. Taste her.

As if she can hear my thoughts, Aubrey whispers, "Kiss me, Brod. Please. Touch me. I need you."

"Say it again," I demand, my lips hovering inches from hers, my fingers ghosting along the hem of shorts.

"I love you," she whispers.

I crash my lips to hers and yank down her shorts, needing to make love to her.

Chapter Thirty-Seven

Brody

November

Grunting, I lean down and lace up first my left skate and then my right skate, ready for morning skate. As the season has progressed, it's clear that the years are catching up to me even though this is proving to be my best season yet. We're not even halfway through, and I've already racked up forty-five points and twenty goals. Which easily puts me on track for over a hundred points this season. I'm currently sitting as the league leader in points and goals. No big deal, right?

Unfortunately, the aches and pains are more consistent. I swear I bruise easier now. I spend more time in the ice bath after games and practices than I used to. Some days I feel like my body is giving up on me. I don't care what Aubrey or anyone else says. This is my last season regardless of whether we win the Cup or not.

"You okay?" Hunter asks, pulling on his practice jersey.

"Yeah. Just tired."

He studies me silently for a few seconds before getting to his feet, and we make our way onto the Los Angeles Knights's practice ice. Tonight's game is our second of a five-game, eleven-day road trip. We got here around three a.m. east coast time from Colorado. Luckily, tomorrow is an off day, so we won't fly out until the morning. I should be used to these late nights, and usually I am, but right now, I'm exhausted and ready for a break.

"What are we doing for your birthday?" Caleb asks as he skates over to where Hunter and I are stretching on the ice.

"Your birthday is soon?" Hunter asks, whipping his head up to look at me. "Why didn't you tell me?"

"I don't like celebrating," I mumble, focusing on stretching my hamstrings. It's the truth. Aubrey was the one who I usually celebrated with, and since she's in Hawaii, I won't do anything. Although, with the sly grin Caleb is giving me, I have a feeling he's got something up his sleeve. "What?" I ask.

"Oh, nothing." Caleb smirks.

I roll my eyes at him. Whatever he's planning, the answer is going to be no. He means well, they all do, and for the most part, I've stopped pretending I don't want to be friends with them. I've gone to dinner most nights with them and out for drinks a couple of times. I've even done some of the touristy stuff Caleb organized for the team. Normally, I'd hole up in my hotel room and either sleep or watch game tapes.

This season, I'm making an effort. Might as well take advantage of getting to visit all these places one last time. I'd never admit it, but it's been fun doing something that isn't hockey all the time. Plus, it distracts me from thinking about Aubrey and missing her. Speaking of which, hopefully, I'll be able to talk to her this afternoon before the game. She's been so busy lately that we haven't talked as much as I wish we could.

Coach blows his whistle, and morning skate starts. The next two hours fly by, and before I know it, we're heading back to the locker room.

"A little birdie told me your birthday is coming," Wes says, coming up to where Hunter and I are changing.

"For fuck's sake," I mumble, shooting a glare in Caleb's direction. Unfortunately, his back is to me, so he doesn't see it.

Wes chuckles before going back to his locker. Fucker only came over here to fuck with me. With a shake of my head, I go back to changing so I can catch the bus to the hotel and call Aubrey.

With a sigh, I sit down on the bench and take off my dress shoes.

"You okay?" Hunter asks, yanking his tie off. "You've been sighing a lot since we got on the bus."

"Yeah." I pause, glancing at my friend. "No, actually, I'm not. I tried to call Aubrey earlier, and she didn't answer. She texted me to say something came up," I admit.

"Sorry, man," Hunter says. "I know how hard it is not to see Madison when we're on the road. I can't imagine what it must be like for you."

"Thanks." I flash him a thin smile before unbuttoning my shirt.

He nods and goes back to getting changed. I shove my earbuds in and turn on my pre-game playlist, getting lost in the music. Once I'm changed, I walk to the stationary bikes and warm up my legs and go through the rest of my pre-game routine.

"Let's do this, boys!" Caleb shouts as we stand in the tunnel that leads to the ice forty-five minutes later. "Let's get another two points tonight." Everyone shouts their agreement, and Aleksi, who is in net tonight, leads the way out.

I'm one of the last down the tunnel, exactly the way I like it, enjoying the extra few seconds of silence to get in the zone. As I step onto the ice, a weird déjà vu feeling hits me, and I glance around, trying to figure out what's going on.

That's when I see her.

I close my eyes and open them again to make sure I'm not seeing things. Aubrey's really here?

I look around for one of my teammates, needing them to confirm the sight in front of me. Caleb choses that moment to skate up to me. He claps a hand on my arm and says, "Happy Birthday."

"You did this?" I ask, turning to my friend.

"I had some help. But, yeah. And Coach gave his approval for you to fly out on Wednesday instead of tomorrow morning with us. You'll miss practice that day, but you won't miss the game."

"Seriously?" I glance between Caleb, Coach standing behind the bench, and the love of my life sitting in the stands.

"Of course. We could see how miserable you've been. Plus, it's almost your birthday," he says with a smirk.

"Well, shit," I mumble, at a loss for words.

"Let's go win this thing," Caleb says.

I nod, and we turn to skate around our side of the rink. Hunter winks at me when I meet his eyes. Wes tips his chin at me. Cole raises his stick.

How did I get so lucky to have such a great group of guys? And why the fuck did I spend so much time fighting their friendship?

Chapter Thirty-Eight

Aubrey

I will never forget the look on Brody's face when he spotted me in the crowd. When Caleb called me a few weeks ago to ask if I could swing a trip to California while the team was here, I jumped at the opportunity. I wish I'd thought of it, but work has been such a whirlwind that some days I don't even remember to eat lunch.

It's been an adjustment going from teaching to being out in the field doing research and handling all the paperwork that comes in from other researchers requesting time on the telescope. There are a couple of staff members, but a lot of the work falls on my shoulders.

But now, I'm here in LA for the next two days, and I refuse to check my work phone or email.

The game gets underway, and from the first whistle, it's a constant battle between us and the Knights. I'm on my feet the entire game cheering and yelling. To no one's surprise, Brody scores not one, not two, but three goals. Yep, he managed to get a natural hat trick, the fourth of his career and the first one I got to see in person. He also gets assists on two of the three other goals the Storm score. When the final buzzer sounds, the Storm win six to three.

Caleb told me to wait in my seat when the game was over. That someone would come find me, so I sit and watch as the arena clears out.

"Hey." Brody's voice comes from my left twenty minutes after the game ends, and I jolt out of my thoughts.

"Hi," I say, jumping to my feet and launching myself at him.

With a laugh, he catches me, crashing his mouth against mine, and I get lost in his lips and his touch for what feels like forever. He finally breaks our kiss, and I let out a groan.

"I know, but if we don't stop now, I might not be able to," he says, taking my hand. "Let's get out of here."

"Brod," I giggle as I take him in. "Maybe fix your shirt." I gesture to his shirt that's sticking to his chest and not buttoned properly. And where is his tie? "Did you even dry your hair?" I ask, running a hand through his hair that is soaking wet.

He grumbles something incoherent, dropping my hand before rebuttoning his shirt. "I ordered us a car," he says as we make our way down the stairs and toward the players' entrance. "I can't believe you're here, Aubs."

"Me neither."

The ride to the hotel is surprisingly fast, and before I know it, he's ushering me into the elevator.

"Caleb told me he got our assistant equipment manager to move my luggage for me." He shakes his head before muttering, "What'd I do to deserve these guys?"

"They're family," I say, resting a hand on his chest and going up on tiptoe to kiss his cheek. "You know they'd do anything for you. Just like you'd do anything for them."

"Yeah," he agrees hoarsely.

The elevator dings on the tenth floor, and Brody whisks me out and down the hall. His pace quickens, and I can't help but laugh. "Slow down."

"Hurry up, woman. I've got a present to unwrap." He peeks at me over his shoulder, his eyes sweeping down my body. I shiver. He means me, doesn't he?

"Fucking finally," Brody says, coming to a stop at the last door along the hallway. "Couldn't have picked a room closer to the elevator," he mutters as I pull out the room key from my purse, unlock the door, and push it open so we can walk in.

"They got us a—" I start to say, but my words are cut off by Brody's mouth as he cages me against the wall next to the door and kisses me. I sink my hands into his still soaking wet hair as he grips my hips, pulling me closer.

"Brody." I pull away from him and turn the deadbolt on the door. "Let's go to bed."

"Yeah," he says, yanking his suit jacket off. "Too many clothes. Take them off." He steps back and starts unbuttoning his shirt. He pulls it off, and my mouth waters at my best friend turned lover standing in front of me shirtless, his hard cock pressing against his trousers.

"Aubrey. Clothes."

"Yeah, okay," I say, snapping out of my Brody-induced haze to take off my sweatshirt. I reach for the hem of my Storm jersey, but before I can take it off, Brody's batting my hand away.

"Leave it on. But everything else needs to go."

I let out a bark of laughter, doing as he asks, even reaching under it to take off my bra, which I let fall to the floor.

"Come on," I say, turning and walking to the bed.

"Fuck, that's hot, you wearing my number," Brody says from behind me. I peek over my shoulder and see him fisting his cock as he watches me. I've had this jersey for years, but this is the first time I've gone to a game as his girlfriend.

"How do you want me?"

"I can't decide if I want to watch you ride me with my name across your back or if I want to bend you over the bed and take you that way. Fucking hell, Aubrey. I never understood it when the guys talked about seeing their women in their numbers. Now, I understand one hundred percent." While he's speaking, he slips a hand between my legs and strokes my aching center.

I groan when his finger makes contact with my clit. I've been so keyed up watching him play hockey, him telling me how hot it is to see me wearing his name and number is winding me up even more. "Fuck me, Brody. Now," I demand, leaning down so I'm bent over the bed, my ass peeking out from the edge of my shirt.

"Okay, but you're riding me later wearing that."

Before I can respond, Brody lines up his cock and slides inside me. "I don't know if I can be gentle. Between all the adrenaline from the game and seeing you in my jersey. I'm dying, Aubrey."

"Fuck me, Brody. Give it all to me. I can take it."

The words are barely out of my mouth before Brody pulls out and slams back into me. My eyes roll to the back of my head at the feel of him pistoning in and out. He reaches a hand around me and finds my clit, and far too quickly, I'm yelling his name as an orgasm rockets through me. He's not far behind. I giggle as the endorphins leave my body, and he slumps over me, spent.

"I got you something for your birthday," I say thirty minutes later from where I'm lying on his chest.

We got cleaned up, then pulled back the blankets, got into bed, and cuddled. I thought he'd want to go another round right away, but I think we're both tired from today.

"You got me something? You didn't have to do that. You being here was enough."

I go over to my suitcase that's sitting next to the closet door, unzipping it and pulling out his present. I saunter back to the bed, noting how Brody's gaze heats as he watches me. He sits up, leaning against the headboard, the blanket slipping down so his bare chest is exposed, and my eyes rake down his body. My gaze dips lower, and I grin at the tent that's forming between his legs, my mouth watering for another taste of him. Clearing my throat, I hand him the small, wrapped box.

"Can we do this later? I see something else I'd like first," he rasps out, staring at my naked body. I took off my jersey when we laid down but promised I'd put it back on for our next round of sex. I make a mental note to buy another one since he seems to love it so much when I wear it.

"This first," I say, climbing back into bed and handing him the box.

Chuckling, he rips off the wrapping and opens the box. Clearly, the man is in a hurry, and I can't say I blame him.

"What's this?" he asks, pulling the pair of briefs with constellations and telescopes all over them out of the box.

"I heard it was tradition."

"Tradition?" Brody asks, pinching his lips together clearly trying to stifle a laugh. He knows exactly what I mean.

"Well, Madison told me about the pair she got for Hunter their first Christmas, so I figured it was a fitting present for you."

"Are you marking your territory?" Brody asks, putting the briefs down, a smirk on his face. "Making sure the guys know I'm taken."

I laugh. "Wanted to make sure they knew you and I were together."

Brody cracks up, reaching for me and pulling me to him. "The guys would have to be blind not to know. And I love your gift. As ridiculous as the boxers are. Every time I wear them, I'll think of you."

"You don't have to wear them. I'll just—" I lose my train of thought when Brody's cock nudges against my entrance. "Yes please."

"I love you. Always and forever. Thank you for coming for my birthday," Brody says, leaning down to capture my lips.

"Yes, that. Coming. I like that idea. More of that."

Brody chuckles against my lips, and we get lost in each other again.

We spend most of the forty-eight hours we have together in bed, only getting up to shower, go to the bathroom, and answer the door for room service. Far too quickly, we're riding in a car to the airport to go our separate ways.

Chapter Thirty-Nine

Brody

June

The second half of the season has been one for the books. I ended it as the league leader in points, winning the Art Ross Trophy for the first time in my career. There are whispers that I'll win the Hart Memorial Trophy as well, but since that's voted on, it's not a given. But I've also been skating with a minor ankle sprain and a sprained pinky the last few games, which luckily hasn't impacted my performance but is painful as hell. I'm ready for this season to be over.

It was also hard on a personal front. Aubrey and I weren't able to see each other again in person after she surprised me in Los Angeles. Video calls were few and far between because of the time change and the demands of my schedule. We talked every chance we could get. While she was getting ready for the day and I was driving to the arena for practice. When I was making dinner and she was eating lunch. Five hours is no joke, plus add in two equally busy schedules, and it's even harder.

We'd made plans to see each other for the All-Star break until the team voted me as our representative for the All-Stars, so I didn't get a break. And while it normally would be a great honor to get chosen, I was kind of annoyed that I wouldn't be able to fly out to Hawaii to see Aubrey.

But here we are—tied with five minutes to go in the third period of the sixth game of the Stanley Cup finals. If we win tonight, we'll take home the Stanley Cup. And the season and my career will be over. But if the Sea Hawks win, they'll force a game seven. Either way, the end of my career is getting closer and closer.

I don't have much time to contemplate it as the third line comes to the bench and Hunter, Caleb, and I hop over the wall and out onto the ice as the seconds tick down. The three of us have been playing together most of the season. I was shocked when Coach put us on the same line, but it worked. We've become quite the force to be reckoned with. Our line has scored the most points in regulation time this season. I couldn't be happier playing on the same line as two of my closest friends.

Wes passes the puck to Hunter, and we rush toward the Sea Hawk's goal. Hunter completes some tricky play with Wes and Caleb before getting the puck back and shooting it into the net. The goal bell rings, and the entire arena erupts.

Holy shit.

I glance over at the bench, expecting to see the signal for a line change, but Coach waves us off, and we stay on. Caleb takes the face off at center ice. The announcer says it's the last minute of the game. My heart rate picks up. If we can keep the Sea Hawks away from our goal for another sixty seconds, we'll win. This feels like the longest minute of my life.

There's a battle along the boards between Caleb and a couple of their forwards. I skate over, hoping to help. Pushing and shoving ensues, but we keep the puck pinned against the boards.

The noise in the stadium gets even louder. How is that even possible? And why? The scoreboard shows that the game is seconds away from ending. I catch Caleb's gaze over the back of a Sea Hawk's player, and he grins, tipping his chin toward the scoreboard as we both watch the final second tick down.

The buzzer sounds.

That's it.

We won the Stanley Cup.

Holy shit. We won.

I forget how to breathe. How to skate. I'm standing, stunned, staring at Caleb, unblinking, for what feels like forever. He pulls his gloves off, and suddenly we're hugging.

Gloves and sticks fly through the air as everyone starts celebrating.

The bench clears as the rest of the team makes their way onto the ice.

I skate toward our goal. Incoherent things are being shouted by my teammates, by the crowd, even by the coaches. I don't even try to figure out what's being said. No, I'm searching the crowd. Looking for her. My face lights up when I spot Aubrey on her feet, cheering and yelling. Before I can do more than raise a hand to wave at her, I'm engulfed in sweaty bodies as the team converges behind the net.

The next twenty minutes pass in a blur, but finally, all the official things are done except the team picture with the Cup. Caleb is skating around the ice with it. I know he plans to give it to Hunter next since he scored the game-winning goal, so I have time before it's my turn. Aubrey is waiting for me at the edge of the ice next to the tunnel for our locker room.

"Hi." I reach for her and scoop her up into my arms. I skate out of the way so the rest of the team can greet their families.

"Brod, you won," she says, laughing as I stand with her in my arms on the ice.

"We did."

My fourth Cup.

My *last* Cup.

I glance around the ice at the fans still packed into the arena. Waving, shouting, and cheering.

"I knew you would."

I'm at a loss for words, so I simply set her down gently on the ice. She takes my hand, and I lead her back to my teammates. I still can't believe this is happening. And I would have missed it if I'd retired last summer like I wanted to.

Someone hands me a hat that says Stanley Cup Champions, and I put it on my head. I grin watching my teammates and their families embracing. Our coaching staff and all the front of house staff that were in attendance today chatting. Reporters walking around interviewing people.

"Hey." Winston, our other alternate captain, skates up to me with the Cup. "It's your turn."

"Thanks." I take it from him and lift it above my head, reflecting on this moment. Though I've had the pleasure of hefting the Cup three other times, this time feels different. It's because it's the end of an era for me. The end of something I've worked my whole life for.

"Wait. Let me take a picture," Aubrey says, pulling out her phone.

I smile as she snaps a few photos before taking my lap around the ice. The Cup hefted high above my head. But I'm not paying attention to the cheering fans or the cameras that are sure to be trained on me. No, I'm watching my team, my family, celebrating with one another. The looks of pure joy and happiness on their faces.

Hunter and Madison are embracing. I knew she'd say yes to his marriage proposal. She's head over heels in love with him just like he is with her.

I am happy that we won the Cup, but I'm even happier that the season is over. That I can close this chapter of my life and move on to the next one—a life with Aubrey.

I finish my lap and hand the Cup to Holt. He deserves it. He stepped up in a big way this postseason when Aleksi got injured during the first round and net minding fell to him.

I head back over to Aubrey and pull her into my arms. "I'm sorry I'm a sweaty mess, beautiful," I mumble into her hair. I hope she doesn't care because all I want to do is hold her.

"I don't mind."

"It's going to be a while until I can leave. Do you want to go on without me to wait with the rest of the families in the team lounge? They probably have food and drinks set up already."

"I'm fine waiting," she says, smiling up at me.

"I love you, Aubs."

"I love you too, Brody. Always and forever."

"Always and forever," I answer back, leaning down to kiss her.

It's kind of become our thing over the past ten months to say that to each other. We've always been each other's forever, it just took us a while to get here.

But now that we're here, there's no place I'd rather be.

Epilogue

Sixteen Months Later

"Come on boys. Clear it."

It's weird being on this side of the glass. I glance over at the woman beside me and know I made the right decision. I squeeze her hand, and she squeezes mine back, shooting me a smile. We spent the last year in Hawaii, and while it was weird not to be on the ice, I found other things to occupy my time. Including starting a youth hockey league.

We only had two teams, but it's a start. I've discovered that I love coaching almost as much as I love skating. At least coaching kids, that is. Not sure how I'd feel doing it at the professional level. Although the missed call from Coach Weaver last night makes me wonder if I should change my mind about that. Maybe I'm not entirely done with hockey.

Aubrey turned down a third year at the Eclipse Observatory. She said two years was long enough and it was time to come back to Florida and our family. We packed up our house in Hilo and flew in two nights ago. Just in time for the Storm's first game of the preseason against the Miami Mockingbirds.

"That's Hunter's brother, right?" Aubrey asks, pointing to number twenty-two.

"Yeah." Elias was an unrestricted free agent the summer after we won the Cup. The Storm scooped him up to replace me on the team. This is the second season he's played with them, and from what I've heard, he's fit in well. I watch him and Hunter buzz down the ice together with a player I don't recognize.

"Are you going to teach our kid to skate?"

My heart catches in my throat. Did I hear right? Is she asking a hypothetical or real question? Having kids was one of the things we talked about during one of our long calls the year we spent apart. We both agreed that we'd like kids, but we also would be okay if that wasn't in the cards for us.

"Yeah of course," I answer, turning to look at my fiancée next to me. We got engaged last year on the anniversary of when we started fake dating. We haven't set a wedding date—Aubrey wanted to wait until we were back in Florida and could work with the guys' schedule.

"Good."

"What's going on Aubrey?" I ask, turning to her the game forgotten.

Her hand lands on her stomach, and the rest of the world stops existing when she says, "You're gonna be a dad, Brod."

Holy shit.

Holy shit.

I stare at her, unblinking, for so long that her smile begins to fall and that's all I need to snap out of my daze.

"Seriously, Aubs?" I reach out a hand and place it over hers, wondering if it's too soon to feel movement. "How far along?"

"Not very. I took a pregnancy test, multiple actually, this morning when you were at the gym. My period is a week late, but I wasn't sure if it was because I'm older now and my cycle was changing. It wasn't. I'll call the doctor's office in the morning."

"We're gonna be parents."

"Shhhh," Aubrey says, glancing around, but everyone else is too focused on the game. "It's early yet. Plus, we still need the doctor to confirm it."

I'm suddenly very aware of how close we are to the ice. We should move because sometimes pucks come flying over the glass.

"Are you warm enough?" I ask. She's wearing jeans and a long-sleeve Storm shirt with my last name and number on the back. I'm sure there's a sweatshirt in the car, maybe I should go grab it for her. Or grab one for her at the arena store.

"I'm fine, Brody," Aubrey says, laying a hand on my arm. I nod as the game moves our way, and players slam into the boards.

"I think we should move," I say, getting to my feet.

"Brod," Aubrey says, tugging on my arm. "Sit down. We're fine."

I heave out a breath and stare down at her for a second before retaking my seat. "I—"

"Brody, relax. I know that look. You are not going to confine me to our house for this whole pregnancy. There's no need to go all caveman protective of me."

I open my mouth to protest. Of course there's a need for me to protect her and our baby. This is a crazy world we live in. Anything could happen. And if anything happens to either one of them, I won't survive. I thought it was hard enough worrying about her when she was in Hawaii and I was here. This is going to be even worse. I scrub a hand over my face, another idea forming in my head.

"Brod," Aubrey warns. "Don't even think about it. I love you, and I know you love me and our baby. But I do not need you to follow me around for the next nine months. Please. You need to trust me on this."

I stare at her, at my best friend. The woman who is wearing my ring. The mother of my child. "I want to get married soon. Let's stop trying to find the perfect day. How about we pick a date when the team is off and in town and get married. We could have it at our house in the backyard, on the lake."

We decided that we wanted to move back to Orlando. It's where our family is. Aubrey took a teaching job at the university part-time. It gives her time to work on the book she's writing. We bought a house in the same neighborhood as Caleb. Which worked out perfectly since he and Jenna decided to stay here after he retired. Now our kids can grow up together. Cole and Hannah don't live that far away either. And Hunter and Madison are looking to buy a home nearby too.

"Okay," she says, smiling at me. "I like the sound of that."

I wrap my arm around her and turn back to the ice in time to see the Mockingbirds score a goal.

"Sucks, man," I say to Winston as he exits the locker room after the game. The Storm got shut out by the Mockingbirds five to zero. Not that this game really matters since it's a preseason game, and they're still working on the dynamics with all the new players. Unsurprisingly, the penalty minutes were more than the minutes played. But that's the way it always is when the Storm and Mockingbirds face off.

"Yeah. Good to see you guys," he says as he walks by.

I lean against the wall, tucking Aubrey into my chest as we wait for the rest of the guys to come out. Eventually, they start streaming out of the locker room.

Holt comes out next, staring at his phone, his face pale.

"You okay?" I ask.

He finally tears his gaze away from his phone, glancing around the empty hallway before saying, "Yeah. Just my sister. I'm worried about her."

"Who are you worried about?" Hunter asks as he walks over.

"Hadley," Holt says, scrubbing a hand down his face. Before he can say anything else Wes walks up.

"Dinner's at my place tonight," Wes says. "Hey, Brody. Aubrey. Want to join us? Caleb, Jenna, Cole, and Hannah are going to swing by too. It's a whole party, so you're more than welcome."

Aubrey smiles. "Sounds great."

"I gotta get home to Kat, but you all have fun," Holt says with a wave as he makes his way toward the exit.

"I'll wait for Elias. We drove together," Hunter says. We say goodbye to him and make our way out of the arena.

I lean closer to Aubrey as we walk toward my Land Rover. "You okay?"

"Of course," Aubrey says, smiling up at me. "I thought you were going to talk to Coach Weaver after the game. See what he wanted."

"Not tonight. We've got to tell the family there's going to be a wedding," I answer as I help her into the SUV. "They're going to be ecstatic. I wish everyone was here to hear the news at once," I admit once I've climbed into the driver's seat and started the car.

"We can wait," she says, laying a hand on my thigh. I glance down at it and see the diamond ring that's a declaration of my love sparkling on her finger. I know what she's saying, but I don't want to wait anymore. If there's one thing I've learned, it's that waiting too long can mean you almost miss out.

Waiting too long to tell her how I felt meant that we almost missed out on our chance together. And while I'd love to have everyone in one place for our announcement, I don't want to wait any longer to start planning our wedding.

Planning our future together.

"Nah, let's tell them tonight. I love you," I say, placing my hand on top of hers. "Always and forever."

"I love you too, Brod. Always and forever."

Thank you so much for reading Brody and Aubrey's story. If you enjoyed it, please consider leaving a rating/review on Amazon and/or Goodreads or Storygraph.

Want more of Brody and Aubrey? Click here or scan the QR code below for a link to the Bonus Epilogue.

Curious about Caleb and Jenna's story? They have a prequel novella (Scoring Chance) that you can get here.

Want more of the Storm? Golden Goal (Orlando Storm Book 3), Holt and Rebecca's story is available here. Turn the page to read chapter one.

Golden Goal: Chapter One

Holt

"Dinner tonight?" Wes, one of my best friends, asks as he pulls off his practice jersey.

"Can't." I shake my head as I plop down onto the bench next to him.

"Kat?"

He leans down and pulls off first one skate and then the other.

I grunt, leaning down to untie my own skates.

Wes blows out a breath. "Yeah. No problem, man."

I look up just in time to see the hurt flicker in his eyes. I'm such a fucking liar. A terrible friend. I should come clean. Tell him Kat broke up with me months ago. I know I should. I just can't make myself admit to my friends that I failed that relationship.

Add being a shitty friend to the long list of things I'm excelling at right now, like being a useless goalie. Might as well.

Hunter, one of our alternate captains and another of my best friends, walks over, his half brother, Elias, trailing behind him.

"Everything okay?" Hunter asks, glancing between Wes and me as he tugs his jersey off and sits next to me.

What a loaded question.

In more ways than one.

No, everything is not okay.

Not with me.

Not with the team.

It's a few weeks into the season, and we've lost more games than we've won. Thanks to my lackluster performance in the net. I know it. Coach knows it. The guys know it. My mind isn't in the game. And that's a big problem for the guy who is the starting goalie for the Orlando Storm. It shocks the shit out of me every game that Coach puts me back in. I keep waiting for the day he tells me they're shipping me to Upstate New York to our AHL team, the Mustangs.

Before either of us can answer, the door to our locker room opens, and Dr. Walt, our team physician, sticks his head in. "Are you boys decent? I want to introduce you to our new team physical therapist. She's excited to meet you."

The guys nod and call out that they're dressed.

He pushes the door open and ushers a woman in ahead of him. She's at least a head shorter than me, dressed in navy scrubs, her dark hair piled on the top of her head. She glances around the locker room. Taking it all in, I guess, or she's trying to figure out who needs PT. Dr. Montgomery, our previous physical therapist, could always tell who was in pain and needed PT just by looking at us.

I wonder what this new doctor thinks of us. If she's worked for another professional team before or if this is her first time working with athletes.

I run a hand through my hair.

Why do I care?

"Gentleman," Dr. Walt says, and everyone walks over to where they're standing. "Meet Dr. Rebecca Jansen. Dr. Jansen, the floor is yours."

She tucks a strand of hair that's fallen out of her bun behind her ear, a flash of something—nerves maybe—crossing her face before she schools her features, stands up straighter, and says, "Hello Team."

She waves awkwardly. The old Holt would have been amused by her greeting, but the current me stays silent, crossing my arms over my chest. Some guys mutter a greeting in response, so at least it isn't too uncomfortable.

"Nice to meet you all. I'm sure we'll get along swimmingly. I'm excited to be here and help you all stay in shape this season." She pauses, shifting on her feet, her gaze dancing around the room before she meets my eyes, and I'm lost in a sea of chocolate brown. Something akin to electricity crackles between us.

Nope.

None of that.

I'm broken.

Even the good doctor can't fix what's wrong with me.

I force myself to break eye contact with her.

"Well, go Storm. I'll let you get back to your after-practice routines." She chuckles before spinning on her heel and heading toward the door.

"Be nice to her," Dr. Walt says, giving us all a pointed look before turning and following her out of the room.

"She's pretty," Sebastian, one of the defenders we acquired over the summer, says, leaning closer to us. "Don't you think, Abbott?" he asks in his thick British accent.

I grunt and turn back to my locker to finish undressing. I take an extra-long shower, mostly so I can avoid the chit chat and so my friends don't try to guilt-trip me into agreeing to hang out or do something with them. When I finally get out of the shower, the only one left in the locker room is our backup goalie, and he's as talkative as I am. I wish the other guys understood what he does—I don't want to talk.

Twenty minutes later, I'm letting myself into my apartment, tossing my keys onto the kitchen counter, and heading over to the fridge to grab something to drink.

I take my glass of water into the living room and sink down onto my worn dark-brown leather couch, the one Kat hated and tried to get rid of countless times. The one piece of furniture I fought her on changing. A fight I luckily won. Propping my feet up on the coffee table in front of me, I survey the room. I really need to get rid of the boxes stacked in the corner filled with all the shit Kat bought for my apartment because she said it was "boring" and needed some character. I make a mental note to put them in my truck and take them somewhere to donate so I don't have to see them anymore.

"Character my ass," I mutter as I turn the television on and resume the James Bond movie I was watching last night.

The locker room is silent. Frustration radiates off everyone, myself included, at how badly we played tonight against the Ravens. No one is talking and joking the way they normally do. A few grumbles and sighs are all that's audible. I'm sitting on the bench, pulling off my gear, when Coach Weaver walks in.

"What the fuck happened out there tonight?" he barks, looking around the room. "You weren't playing like a fucking team. You were playing like a bunch of guys who'd never spent a day on the ice together."

I heave out a breath and stare at the ground. He's right. Last season was rough after Brody, our top scoring forward, and Aleksi, our starting goalie, retired, but we did alright. We picked up Elias from the Nashville Fury to fill Brody's spot, and I stepped up as the starting goalie. We didn't make it to the finals, but we at least made it to the second round of the playoffs.

This past off-season, Caleb, our captain and another star forward, retired, and our team just isn't the same.

Last week our other alternate captain got injured and is out for the season.

Shots that would normally be easy for me to block, aren't. I've let in so many stupid goals, like the two in the last five minutes of the second period of the game we just played. It's as if my brain and body aren't in sync anymore.

Things are falling to shit.

We're on a five-game losing streak, and we're sitting dead last in our division. We've got plenty of time to turn the sinking ship around since it's only October, but still. If we can't figure things out soon, we'll keep falling further and further behind.

No one speaks, and Coach says, "get some rest tonight. I'll see you at morning skate." He turns and stalks out of the locker room to do press.

The room is even more silent after he leaves, if that's even possible. Guys quickly undress.

"What are we going to do?" Hunter finally asks.

I lift a shoulder in a half shrug. *How the hell should I know what to do?* I've got my own problems to contend with. It's not like I'm much help right now.

"Having no captain isn't helping," Elias says from the other side of Hunter.

"Yeah," Hunter agrees, pulling off his jersey and pads. "I don't understand why they haven't named one. It would definitely help at least with team morale."

"We may not have anyone wearing the C on their sweater, but we need someone to step up and lead." Elias stares pointedly at his brother.

"Why are you looking at me like that?" Hunter asks, turning to Elias. "It was your idea. You were an alternate captain for the Fury. All you, E." He tips his chin at him.

Elias shakes his head. "It's your team, Hunt. The guys know and respect you more than me. Right, Wes? Right, Holt?"

Hunter focuses his attention on Wes for a second before turning to me.

I study my friend, noting the fear in his eyes, but I know that deep down he wants this. He might never say it out loud, but I know Hunter. I know it would mean the world to him to be the next captain of the Storm. He doesn't think they'll ever give it to him—he still sees himself as the rookie who isn't sure if he belongs in the NHL. Even with a Stanley Cup under his belt. But I see it. I peek over at Elias, and based on the face he's making, I think he sees it too.

Before I can answer the question, Wes pipes up. "I agree with E. We need a leader. Caleb was the glue of this team, and without him, we're falling apart."

Hunter huffs out a breath. "Don't you think it'll seem like favoritism if they give it to me?"

"So what if you're married to Coach's daughter? Everyone here knows you. If anyone deserves the captain's C, it's you. They made you an alternate captain for a reason," Wes says.

I nod my agreement.

"Hey, listen up." Elias gets to his feet. The locker room goes silent as everyone turns toward us. "All yours," he whispers to Hunter.

"Fucker," Hunter mutters before clearing his throat and addressing the room. "Listen, I know we're off to a rocky start, and we've had a lot of, err . . . changes this season, including our captain retiring. And we're not doing so hot. Actually, we're playing like shit." He pauses, and laughter breaks out. "But we're the Storm. We can do anything. There's still a lot of the season left, and we're not giving up until the last game. Let's get some rest tonight and turn this around. Let's break this losing streak." Hunter surveys the room.

Guys mutter their agreement.

"Great speech, Cap," Wes says, smacking him on the back when he sits down.

Elias was right. Hunter's our next captain. And if Coach and the rest of the front office don't see it, then there's something wrong with them.

"Not the captain," Hunter mutters with a shake of his head.

"Yet," Wes says with a smug grin.

I simply give him a tight-lipped smile. Maybe not yet, but I agree with Wes and Elias.

Soon.

Silence descends on the locker room as we all finish getting dressed.

Golden Goal is available here.

Acknowledgements

To my husband: I love you. Thank you for continuing to support me on this journey and for encouraging me when I was ready to give up. I could not have done this without you.

Emily: Thank you for being the first person to read Brody and Aubrey's story and helping me make this book even better. Thank you for being my sounding board as I worked through plot changes. I'm so grateful for our friendship.

Jordan: I'm so glad we met and became friends. Thank you for creating an amazing cover. Once again you took some vague ideas and created a gorgeous cover that I absolutely love.

Ashley: I feel like I've known you for more than just a couple of months. Thank you for listening to me ramble and for all of your encouraging messages. I look forward to our daily chats and talking to you about hockey, writing, and all kinds of random things. So glad for your friendship.

Leslie: My oldest friend, thank you for your support and friendship over the years. For supporting me on this journey and for cheering me on.

To my Beta readers: Thank you being part of my team. I am so appreciate your suggestions and feedback. This book wouldn't be what it is without each and every one of you.

Laura, my editor and Trinity, my proofreader: Thank you for giving this book a fresh set of eyes. I appreciate each of you helping me make this book the best it can be.

And to my readers: Thank you for taking a chance on me once again. For being excited for this book, for telling your friends about it. For your messages, reviews, comments, and posts on social media. I still can't believe there are people reading my books and loving them.

Also by Marissa James

About the Author

Marissa James grew up reading books and dreaming of being an author. She finally decided to pursue her dream of being a published author in 2022. She loves to write happily ever afters with a perfect blend of emotion and steamy romance. When she's not writing, she can be found working her day job, reading romance novels, watching hockey, or hanging out with her husband.

Website: www.marissajamesauthor.com

9 798869 284099